D1605999

Pam
The Women of Valley View

SHARON SROCK

THE WOMEN OF VALLEY VIEW SERIES

Callie
Terri
Pam
Samantha
Kate (coming fall 2015)
Karla (coming 2016)

DEDICATION

To my husband, Larry. You believed in the dream, but most of all, you believed in me. I love you!!

ACKNOWLEDGMENTS

When I started this journey, I never expected to write any acknowledgments for the first book, much less the third. It wasn't God's promise I doubted, but my ability. I'm so thankful that we don't function on our own ability. So first, thank you, Father, for loving me, directing my path, and for giving me the people I needed, just when I needed them.
Mark Foster, professional counselor, longtime friend, and now counselor to my imaginary friends. Mark gave me much needed insight on Pam's issues. His advice added the touch of realism I was missing.
Robin Patchen, my friend and long suffering critique partner. She knows my characters almost as well as I do by now. More importantly she loves them almost as much as I do. I value her input more with each book. My editor, Barbara Early, thanks for giving a rookie a chance.
God has blessed me with the best circle of friends and readers. My women. Kaye Whiteman, Emily Whiteman, Anne Lee, Teresa Talbott, Barbara Ellis, Wanda Peters, Sandy Patten, Lynn Beck, Carol Vansickle. Ladies, there are no thanks I can offer you as valuable as the encouragement you've given me.
And to this circle I welcome Jeff Salter, USAF Col, retired. Jeff, I hope you don't mind being named an honorary Woman of Valley View. Thanks for reading and offering input from a male perspective.
Finally the talented writers of Oklahoma Christian Fiction Writers. For your encouraging words of wisdom, propping me up when the waiting that is writing got me down, and for prayers when I needed them the most.

PROLOGUE

The bite of Alan's betrayal was lethal. The venom spread through Pam's system as poisonous as a rattlesnake coiled in the Oklahoma dust.

She sat cross-legged in the middle of her queen-sized bed, a bottle of prescription sleeping pills in her lap, memories in the form of photo albums and loose pictures scattered around her on the hunter green comforter. With shaking hands, she tucked her hair behind her ears and fanned a stack of photos out before her. One snapshot in particular caught her eye. Pam picked it up by a corner, not afraid of damaging the picture, but bracing herself for the damage the picture would do to her.

High school, sophomore year. Her long dark hair was pulled back in a ponytail, braces glinting in the light of the camera flash. Alan stood next to her, his arm tossed negligently across her shoulders, his muddy football uniform a sharp contrast to her white cheerleader sweater. Their first picture together, the beginning of their life with each other.

Pam stroked the picture and the present melted into the past. Her gaze narrowed to Alan's face, his high cheekbones, cleft chin, and the wild mop of his sandy hair. Even then she could see the future she wanted for herself in his brown eyes. Alan Archer, her first and only love.

She swallowed two of the pills and chased them with a gulp of bottled water. *Just two at a time, I can always change my mind.*

Pam steeled herself against the ache in her heart and sorted through more pictures. Homecomings and proms. His and hers. Outdated hairstyles, long satin gowns decorated with lace, sequins, and bows. Rented tuxedos, his ties and cummerbunds coordinated to match her dress. Flowers for her, wing tipped collars for him. High school graduations. His from college. She scrambled over to the window, open to catch the early summer breeze, and tilted the picture in the midday sunlight. If she squinted she could just make out the gold of her new engagement ring. She forced her eyes down to her left hand. *No gold there anymore.* Just the pathetic imprint of what used to be. That's all her heart held this morning, a sad, hollow image of the past.

Two more pills joined the toxic mixture brewing in her stomach. She closed her eyes. *Let it be quick.* A prayer? She shrugged away the thought.

Returning to the bed, she pulled a large white album into her lap. Tears dotted the closed cover as she hugged the book to her chest. The promise of their wedding day. A future waiting to be written. Cake and friends and vows to love each other forever. *How could it be forever already?* She swallowed two more pills.

Pam closed her eyes against a wave of dizziness. She really did want to pray, but nothing came from her soul except overwhelming guilt and failure. *Oh God. I did everything I knew to do. How could You take my life way from me like this? What did I do? Where did I go wrong?* A million times asked, a million times unanswered.

More pictures and albums. She traced her finger across Alan's features. His image laughed up at her.

He seemed happy. Where had that gone?

She held her fisted hands to her ears in an effort to block out the insults she'd lived with for the last year. *Stupid, fat, worthless, frigid slob.* The haunting, hurtful words ran together, mixing with Alan's laughter as she walked into his office and saw...

She moved her hands from her ears to her eyes. Pam rubbed, trying to erase the image of Alan and his secretary lying together on the sofa in his office. She failed. The echoed words from that moment still made her flinch.

"What...?"

"Don't be stupid, Pam. When are you going to understand that you were never woman enough for me?"

Oh, she understood. She emptied the rest of the pills into her hand, popped them into her mouth, and swallowed them before she lost her nerve.

She blinked rapidly, her system fighting the sleep and relief the pills promised. With time running out, Pam gathered up images of holidays and family vacations. This was her life, her world. All she'd ever wanted remained forever frozen in these little slices of time. Moments of love and happiness reduced to the devastation of failure with one phrase. Five little words she could barely bring herself to think, much less speak aloud.

My divorce is final today.

Her lawyer, Harrison Lake, had been a pillar of strength throughout the whole process. He kept trying to convince her that this was not the end, but a fresh beginning. He'd held her hand while she cried. He'd gone to battle with Alan in her stead. His phone call last night assured her that it would be over today.

Pam took one last look at the pictures displayed around the room. A hundred pieces of her broken heart fractured into a thousand more. She wanted to burn them all, but Jeremy and Megan would want them later. Jeremy and Megan. *My babies.* The knowledge that she'd failed at motherhood as certainly as she'd failed at marriage stole the last bit of her resistance. They were safely tucked away for the summer in Wyoming with her parents and better off without her.

A fresh wave of drug-induced vertigo. She laid her head on the pillow and closed her eyes. The empty bottle of sleeping pills slipped from her limp fingers. Harrison was right. It would be over today.

Hot. Pam shifted her legs under the sheets, looking for a cool spot to relieve the uncomfortable warmth surrounding her. The next sensation to penetrate the fog of sleep was thirst. She swallowed and released a sharp groan of pain. Why was her throat so sore?

"Pam?"

Pam turned toward the voice and struggled to open her eyes. *Harrison...what is he...?* Memory flooded back like a returning tide. She gave up trying to get her eyes open. Instead, she turned her back to him and surrendered, again, to the weeping that had plagued her for days. Failure. Her life was nothing but a failure. She felt a hand on her shoulder and shrugged it away. "Leave me alone." Her request came out as little more than a croak.

Harrison's answer came in a single clipped word. "No."

Pam heard his footsteps as he circled the bed. The mattress shifted under his weight when he sat beside her. He took her hand.

She jerked it out of his grasp. "Go away."

"What were you thinking?"

"You're a lawyer." Bitterness tinged her words. "Figure it out."

"Pam, why? The worst is over. After today you could've begun rebuilding your life."

Pam flipped onto her back and covered her eyes with her arm. "What life? My life ended when I walked into Alan's office and saw—"

"That's not true."

She held her tongue. If she refused to acknowledge him, maybe he'd go away.

"Do you really want me to leave?"

"Yes."

"Then tell me who to call."

Pam lowered her arm. "No one. I want to be alone."

Harrison shook his head. "Not possible."

She glared at him.

"You're on suicide watch. When I leave, they'll take you up to the psych ward and put you into a private room with a large observation window and video cameras. You won't be alone for the next forty-eight hours." Harrison pulled a small notebook from his jacket pocket. "You're allowed two visitors at a time. I need to know who to call. Parents, friends, your pastor, someone who can keep an eye on you once I leave."

Pam stared at him. Her restless hand smoothed the worn thermal weave of the hospital blanket. Her fingers picked at the lint balls left behind by repeated washings. What she'd just tried to do would destroy her mom and dad. Her friends, Callie, Terri, Karla, even Pastor Gordon. How could she make them understand? She couldn't tell anyone about this, not today, not ever. Pam realized the corner she'd painted herself into. "There's no one to call." The words were a whisper, forced around her constricted throat. Tears rolled from the corners of her eyes and ran down her cheeks.

Harrison put the notebook away and pulled out a clean handkerchief. "I have an alternate option, if you're willing to listen." Pam nodded and accepted the square of linen he pressed into her hand. "I made some calls before you woke up. There's a counseling center I've heard good things about. It's run by Christian counselors. They're very discreet." He took an index card from his pocket and laid it on the bedside table. "I talked to them and to your doctor. They're willing to take you as a patient, and your doctor has agreed to release you into my custody for transportation. I can drive you down tonight, if that's what you want." His tapping finger drew her eyes to the card. "They're waiting to hear from you."

Pam bit her lip and held out her hand. She blinked moisture from her eyes and tried to focus on the words. "Brookside?"

Harrison nodded. "That or the psych ward."

Pam closed her eyes and covered her face with her hands. *Suicide...* "Oh, dear Jesus. What have I done?"

CHAPTER ONE

Four years later

A fall storm system hovered over Garfield, Oklahoma. Rain fell in sheets. A vicious wind whipped acorns from the trees and skipped them across the roof with the sound of rapid gunfire. Pam Lake paced her shadowed living room. The tempest in her spirit rivaled the one outside. *If Alan Archer thinks I'll take this lying down...*

The Old Testament prescribed death by stoning for individuals caught in adultery. That was a punishment Pam could stand behind. God must have known that if cheating ex-spouses were dead, they couldn't resurface four years later to rip your soul out a second time and threaten your newfound happiness.

The rational part of her brain shifted her troubled thoughts into neutral. *You need to stop. You're giving him too much control over your life. What would Dr. Sylvester say?* Pam stopped her pacing. Her counselor had warned her about this four years ago.

Pam could still see Dr. Sylvester, hands clasped on her desk blotter as she leaned forward. "Pam, there are a whole bunch of fancy words I could use for the scars and trauma caused by the emotional abuse you've suffered. If you don't start learning how to deal with it, it's going to eat you from the inside out."

"I am dealing with it. I know Alan's behavior wasn't my fault. I've accepted that our marriage is over."

"You aren't eating, you aren't sleeping, and you're skipping the daily Bible studies. Your physical and spiritual well-being do not speak of improvement. You're dealing with classic post-traumatic stress disorder. You can lie to yourself; you can convince me that you're ready to go home, but the deeper you bury the hurt, the uglier it's going to be when it surfaces. If you take nothing home with you from your time here at Brookside, remember this. Any time you bury an emotion, you bury it alive. The only way to kill it is to face it."

Pam's snort echoed off the walls. Psychobabble garbage. There were no emotions left alive in her heart where Alan was concerned. She'd buried them deep and suffocated them under layers of indifference and a better life. God had moved her beyond the hurt of betrayal. He'd forgiven her for the attempted suicide. Four years after her month-long stay at Brookside, she was happy. She had Harrison and the kids. They'd made a family out of the pieces Alan had left behind. There was no need to face anything. All she needed to continue on with her life was for Alan Archer to stay in Kansas City!

Her son's casual remark rang in her ears. "You don't need to pick us up. Dad and Kate are moving into their new house today."

Alan Archer was moving back to Garfield. How could she not know this until now?

Stupid, fat, worthless, frigid slob. Her throat went dry, and her heart pounded against her ribcage. The taste of fear coated her tongue, and she layered anger over it, desperate to conquer the panic. I won't live with those words ever again. She looked up, eyes blurred with tears. "Why now, God? My insides are in knots, and I don't understand it. Alan means nothing to me anymore. You gave me Harrison, and I love him."

As if conjured from her thoughts, a car door slammed in the driveway. She blinked away the tears and allowed the warmth of Harrison's faithful love to sooth the newly exposed ache in her heart. He came. I called, and he dropped what he was doing to be with me. Always my knight.

While she watched, her husband of almost three years sprinted for the house, briefcase clutched to his chest with one arm, fighting a useless umbrella with the other. His feet gained the steps a second before a sharp gust turned his umbrella inside out. Pam sank into the window seat, the corners of her mouth twitching in a melancholy smile. He'll never know how much I love him. Leave it to Alan Archer... The mere thought of her ex-husband's name sent bile churning in her stomach.

Pam drew up her knees and propped her chin on her crossed arms as fresh tears tracked the path of the old ones. She jerked at the loud crack of thunder that followed the next burst of lightning. Her head came up when she heard her husband in the doorway.

Harrison set down his briefcase, brushed some of

the rain from the shoulders of his jacket, and crossed the room to sit beside her. He gathered her into his arms.

She relaxed against him, soaking up the comfort he offered.

He kissed the top of her head. "Sweetheart, you're blowing this all out of proportion."

"How can you say that?" Her voice was hoarse from her recent tears. "He destroyed me." She pulled out of her husband's embrace and rose to pace in front of him. "He purposely reduced me to nothing. The divorce, the embarrassment of being openly cheated on. The depression and the pills. How am I supposed to handle those memories when I run into him at the bank or the store?" Her hands shook as she raked hair away from her face, her voice a panicked whisper when she continued. "The pills. Harrison, no one knows. What if the kids, or my parents, or my friends find out? They can never understand how I felt then, much less how I feel now, 'cause they can never know the truth." She lifted her eyes to her husband. "I'm so scared."

Harrison drew a ragged breath of his own. "You're scared? I was there, remember?" He reached out and pulled her icy hands into his, trying to rub some warmth into them. "If I'd been fifteen minutes later...But you beat him, darlin'. You aren't the cowed, lost woman he left behind. He can't hurt you anymore. Everything he said to you, everything he tried to make you believe, was a lie. Doesn't our happiness put some perspective on that?"

Pam jerked her hands from his grasp and paced the length of the room. Renewed anger colored her words. "I had plenty of perspective as long as he lived on his planet and I lived on mine." Her entire body shook with nervous energy. "What is he thinking?" She turned, hands fisted on her hips, and answered her own question. "Oh, I forgot. This is Alan 'No-Brain' Archer we're talking about. He doesn't think. He just plows ahead with whatever piece of stupidity that feels good to him at the moment."

"Pam—"

"Moving back here, dragging all this back to the surface, rubbing my face in his infidelities."

"Kate isn't one of his infidelities. They've been married for almost a year now. You liked her fine when we met her a couple of months ago." Harrison held out his hand, dropping it when she ignored it. "I understand how you feel, but that doesn't change the truth. Alan has the right to live anywhere he wants, including Garfield."

Pam's temper flashed along with the lightening outside. "Whose side are you on?" She swept out of the room, her angry question left to hang in the air between them.

Pam retreated to the solitude of the bedroom. Unable to find any solace there, she continued to pace. Her arguments grew more vehement with every step she took. She wasn't sure who she was arguing with, herself or God, but the muttered one-sided conversation was a heated one regardless.

"I can't do this. He can't do this. I'm so far beyond angry right now, I don't have words to define it. How is it possible to have this kind of hatred for someone I loved so much? I wouldn't even have called it hate before today. I would have called my feelings grace-induced indifference. I truly don't care what Alan does, or whom he does it with so long as he does it somewhere other than Garfield." Her thoughts came full circle. "He cannot do this."

A light knock on the door interrupted her tirade. She glanced at the clock beside the bed. Had the kids come home early? Pam swiped at her face with a damp tissue and pasted on a smile before she opened the door. The sight of Karla Black standing in the hall crumbled the fragile seawall surrounding her churning emotions.

Pam stumbled into her friend's outstretched arms. "Oh, Karla."

"I know, honey," Karla soothed, stepping into the room and closing the door. "The kids were sharing their news at the party. I can only imagine how upset you must be. What can I do to help?"

"Do you know a good hit man?"

"Pam—"

"I'm serious, Karla." Pam pushed away from her friend. "Right now, all I want to do is wring his neck. I'm almost certain there's a clause in our divorce settlement prohibiting him from living in the same town as me. Violation punishable by death."

"That's a pretty strong statement. It's been four years since your divorce. How can you be so angry after all this time?"

Pam's frustration bubbled over. "What difference does time make? Have you all forgotten what he did to me? Fifteen years of marriage and I caught the man, in the act, with his secretary. That's not a memory..." Memories far worse than adultery clogged her throat. She swallowed what she could never share. "That's not a memory I want to look in the eye every day. Why is everyone taking his side?"

"Pam, we all know how hurt—"

"What?" Pam whirled on her friend. Fermented pain burst from her heart like a cork released from a champagne bottle. "What do you guys think you know?" She threw her hands up in frustration. "He staged it, Karla, and then laughed in my face."

"What?"

"Never knew that, did you? I called him. He knew I was stopping by the office that afternoon. When I walked in and found them..." Pam's voice broke, and she pressed her lips together in an effort to stem the tears. "He laughed at me, Karla, and told me how stupid I was. The abuse wasn't enough for him—"

Karla's mouth formed a shocked O as red crept up her neck. "He hit you?"

Pam shuddered and made another effort to control her runaway emotions. Be careful, you're going to share too much. "Not all abuse is physical." *Stupid, fat, worthless, frigid slob.* Pam slammed the lid down on the voices still alive in the dark corners of her heart. "None of you has any idea what it's like to be hurt the way Alan hurt me."

Pam hugged her arms around her chest and met Karla's concerned green eyes with a frown. "You and Mitch have the happily-ever-after marriage most people only dream of. Callie's got Benton, quite possibly the most perfect man in the world since he got saved, and Terri and Steve are still basking in some"— she waved a hand for lack of words—"some newlywed glow that a one-year-old and another pregnancy can't dull."

Karla sat on the edge of the bed, crossed her arms,

and looked at Pam over her glasses.

"You three are all snug and cozy in your perfect little worlds. Someday one of you needs to take a step down from that pedestal you're living on and join the rest of us here in the real world." Pam's hand flew to her mouth. "I'm sorry...I'm sorry. Karla, please tell me you know I didn't mean a single word of that."

Karla tilted her head and patted the mattress next to her. "Come sit."

Pam sat beside her friend, head bowed over her clenched fist. *I wish I could tell them, I wish I could make them understand what he did to me.* "Oh, Karla, I'm so sorry."

Karla put an arm around Pam's shoulders. "We all knew something was desperately wrong that last year of your marriage, but you never mentioned abuse. Can you talk about it?"

"I..." Pam shook her head. "I can't." Her breath shuddered as she filled her lungs. "I'm sorry I blew up at you. It just seems like everyone is taking Alan's side."

Karla gave her a little shake. "You know that isn't true. We love you. If it ever comes down to taking sides, you know where we'll fall. Alan hurt you, but you've got to let the anger go. You've moved on. You have Harrison and two terrific kids. Focus on the here and now."

Pam nodded. *It would be so easy if the anger was all I have to deal with.* She closed her eyes. The specter hanging over her head and living in her heart went so much deeper than anger. The urge to bare her soul to this woman shook Pam to the core. She forced it aside and repeated what was fast becoming her mantra. *No one can ever know the truth.*

"Megan and Jeremy are obviously excited that Alan will be closer."

Pam slumped into Karla's embrace. "I'm sure they're thrilled. Alan never had a problem being a good father. As much as the kids love Harrison, they're obviously happy about the opportunity to see their dad more often. He's picking them up after the party and taking them to lunch." Pam's voice lowered to a whisper. "Karla, I don't know if I can put a happy face on this, even for them. I've done my best to keep the negative remarks and feelings to a minimum over the years. Megan and Jeremy were both old enough to understand what Alan did, but I've worked hard not to rub their faces in it. That was so much easier to do when I was just putting them on a plane three or four times a year. I haven't been face-to-face with Alan Archer since the divorce. I liked it that way."

"Alan remarried a few months ago, didn't he?"

Pam nodded. "Kate."

"Have you met her?"

"Yes. Alan was sick or something when the kids were there for their summer visit." The word sick dripped with sarcasm. "Instead of going through the hassle of trying to change their airline tickets, she just drove the kids home for him. They dragged her into the house for introductions."

Karla didn't say anything for several seconds.

"I know what you're thinking," Pam finally said. "I was polite when they introduced her."

"What's she like?"

"Nice enough, I guess. The kids both like her. I know she's managed to get Alan back in church, but Kate isn't the problem here." Pam leaned her head on

Karla's shoulder. "I don't know what I'm going to do. I can't think straight. I'm taking pot shots at you. I snapped at Harrison earlier. I've been trying to pray, but all my prayers keep turning into arguments."

"Do you want me to pray with you?"

"Would you?"

"How do you want to pray?"

"I don't even know. I just know I need more strength than I have on my own right now."

Karla put both arms around Pam. "Jesus, thank You for loving us. Your word promised that You would never leave us alone, that we would never have to face the hard times by ourselves. Please help Pam find comfort in those promises. Help her find the wisdom to lean on You and the courage to go where You're taking her right now. Her heart is hurting. Help her find the healing she needs in You."

Pam swiped at her nose with a crumpled tissue. "Thanks, Karla."

"Will you be all right now?"

Pam's response was both honest and melancholy. "I don't know. I'm calmer though. That's an improvement."

"Good." Karla stood up and straightened to her full five-foot-two. "Now, go downstairs, find that man of yours, and give him a hug. He's worried about you and feeling a little helpless right now. I'll see you both at church tomorrow."

Pam stopped Karla at the door. "Karla, one more thing. Would you call Callie and Terri for me?"

"They know, hon. We're all three praying for you."

"You guys are the best friends in the world. I'll walk down with you."

17

"I know the way out. You stay up here and fix your face."

Pam nodded. "Thanks for coming by. I'm sorry—"

"Hush," Karla told her. "We all love you, and we're all here for you if you need us."

The door snapped shut behind the older woman, and Pam realized she did feel better. Karla was such a good friend.

Pam closed her eyes and slumped back on the bed. Where had those horrible things she'd said come from? Her friends had plenty of old hurts in their lives. But nothing like... Pam pushed the little voice aside and embraced the knowledge that her three best friends were praying about the situation. Maybe she'd been overreacting. Alan had that effect on her. Garfield wasn't a metropolis, but it wasn't a Podunk either. Surely there wouldn't be that many opportunities for her to run into her ex-husband.

Alan Archer turned his car into the parking lot of Valley View Church. He shut off the ignition and sat while the engine ticked and pinged in its cool-down phase. The storm continued to rage, making rivers out of drainage ditches and turning shallow places into puddles. It was a miserable day to be outside, but he was anxious to put this conversation behind him. He looked at the only other car in the lot. When he'd asked for this meeting, he'd been adamant about seeking the privacy of the pastor's office. Pastor Gordon granted his request. Might as well get it over with. He held the door tight against the swirling gusts of wind, slammed it closed, and sprinted for the overhanging roof of the church. A fit of coughing almost doubled him over as he reached the double glass doors. He stopped under the dripping eve, closed his eyes, and concentrated on a few normal breaths. The tightness in his chest loosened. When would he learn?

He took a deep breath to satisfy himself that he could and pulled open the door. One step inside the familiar hallway transported him back in time. The building was quiet and empty now, but his ears remembered the noise of boisterous kids heading off to various Sunday school classes. His nose recalled the scents of numerous potluck dinners enjoyed in the fellowship hall at the end of the corridor. Light spilled from an open office on his right and caused his heart to stumble over his most recent memories of this place. A dozen counseling sessions and Pam's tears of confusion during each of them. He did his best to shake it off as he continued to the open door. *Jesus, I'm sorry. I know You've forgiven me. Help me complete what You've sent me to do.* Alan peeked around the framework of the office door. "Pastor?"

Pastor Gordon stood and gripped Alan's extended hand in a firm handshake. "Alan, come in." He motioned to a chair. "It's good to see you. I've made fresh coffee, if you're interested. I'm afraid this late in the afternoon, its decaf, but the new blends aren't so bad. I'll fix you a cup if you like."

Alan brushed at the front of his soaked shirt, grateful that he wouldn't have to offer a decaf only explanation. "It's a monsoon out there. Hot coffee would be great."

The preacher poured two cups of the steaming liquid. "I made it in just ahead of the downpour." He nodded to the basket of creamer, sugar, and sweetener.

"Name your poison."

"Black works. Thanks."

The elderly preacher passed a brimming cup across his desk and returned to his seat. The silence stretched as the men sipped their drinks. Alan studied his former pastor with open interest. He found more age, less hair, new glasses, and deeper lines carved around the elder man's eyes. Alan squirmed a bit with the realization that he was being scrutinized just as intently.

The pastor set his cup aside, clasped his hands together on the desk, and leaned forward. "You're looking good Alan, but I must confess to some curiosity about what brings you back to Garfield—and my office—after all these years."

Alan nodded, overcome with a sudden need to stall. He looked around the room. Bookcases filled with well-worn books lined one wall. An old-fashioned monitor blinked the date and time on the corner of the desk. Alan took a breath and caught the familiar scent of roses wafting from a small bowl of potpourri. Sister Gordon's contribution to her husband's office. Little had changed since his last visit. The tension in his shoulders relaxed a bit. "This was always a peaceful port in a storm, Pastor, even during those last few months when life was everything but. It's nice to see it hasn't changed."

"I'm a man of habit. I've found my congregation appreciates continuity as well. Coming to the pastor's office can be a little like visiting the principal's office. It's a little less intimidating if the surroundings are familiar." He sat back in his chair and reclaimed his cup. "You wanted to talk. The floor is yours."

Alan bowed his head and stared at the floor for a

few seconds. *Get on with it.* He looked up and jumped in with both feet. "I've moved back to Garfield." His statement hung in the air for a few seconds. "I know I made some serious mistakes a few years ago. I understand my decision to come back won't be greeted with much enthusiasm. I've remarried, and I've re-dedicated my life to Christ. I'd like to put some of those mistakes behind me, if possible."

He met Pastor Gordon's eyes. "Kate and I decided that we wanted to live closer to my children. I'm missing too much of their lives living in Kansas City. Garfield is home." He took a deep breath. "We'd like your permission to attend church here, at Valley View."

A frown gathered between the preacher's brows. The only sounds in the room were the squeak of his leather chair and the echo of the thunder outside. "Alan, I appreciate the courtesy you've extended by coming to discuss this with me. You don't need my permission to attend service here. It's a public place. But since you've asked, I'll be honest with you. I don't think—"

"I'm dying."

The old pastor blinked. "What did you say?"

"I'm dying, Pastor. I'm sorry for blurting it out like that, but it's not an easy thing for me to say." Alan stirred his coffee. His insides twisted despite the times he'd rehearsed this conversation. "Before you tell me how healthy I look, let me assure that, in this case, those looks are deceiving. I've been diagnosed with hypertrophic cardiomyopathy. I'm in the end-stages of the disease. I came back here to spend the time I have left with my children."

"Ahh...Alan." The preacher closed his eyes, pushed

his glasses up to his forehead, while he rubbed at the bridge of his nose. "I'm a pastor, not a doctor. What, exactly, is hyper...tro...phic cardio...what?"

"Hypertrophic cardiomyopathy. The disease isn't particularly uncommon, but my doctor's diagnosis puts me in the unlucky three percent. I could bury you in medical jargon, but what it boils down to is a gradual thickening of my heart muscle. One of the oddities of the disease is looking good, right to the end. That also makes it hard to diagnose." Alan laid his cup on the edge of the pastor's desk.

"There's no way to tell how long I've had it," he continued. "Some of the milder symptoms have become so commonplace, I stopped paying attention to them a long time ago. Shortness of breath, tiredness, even palpitations and being lightheaded. I wrote them all off as occasional over-exertion or stress. When I passed out in my office a few months ago, I was fortunate enough to get a doctor in the ER who'd had an uncle with the same symptoms." Alan scraped a hand through his hair before he continued. "I've been in and out of the hospital several times for testing. My doctor tells me I'm currently in the remodeling stage of the disease. The thickened heart muscle is finally beginning to break down." His shrug was resigned. "The end result will be heart failure."

Pastor Gordon pursed his lips. "How long?"

Alan looked away to prevent the discerning pastor from seeing the lie in his eyes. *Is wishful thinking a lie?* "Six weeks, six months." *You know it's weeks, not months.* "Not long enough. The good news is, I'll make a handsome corpse."

"Alan—"

"Sorry," he apologized. "I'm working on acceptance. I'm told morbid humor is a common defense mechanism."

Alan took a sip of the cooling liquid before he continued. "Brother Gordon, there's no excuse for the way I behaved four years ago. I can't explain it to you because I still can't explain it to myself. I know I hurt a lot of people. I sat in this office and lied to your face." He swallowed back the irony of then and now. "Trust is going to be a major issue for you and everyone else. God's forgiven me. Can you?"

"Here and now, Alan. Consider yourself forgiven, but there's—"

"I know this is just the first step in a long process, but I have to start somewhere. Do I have your permission to attend services?"

"Under the circumstances, of course. I'll go with you to talk to Pam."

"No."

Pastor Gordon tilted his head in obvious confusion. "Excuse me."

"No. I don't want Pam or my kids to know about this. My wife and stepson know, and now you know, but that's as far as this information goes."

"But—"

"No," Alan repeated the third time. "Consider yourself sworn to secrecy. I've made my peace with God, but I have other things I need to make right and a limited amount of time to get it done. I don't want anyone's pity, and I don't want those things made right out of a feeling of obligation. I certainly don't want Jeremy and Megan to know about this yet. I won't have them spending the little time we have left with each other sitting on the edge of their seats waiting for me to take my last breath."

"Alan, this is a bad idea, at least share your illness with Pam. She can help you prepare the children without giving them all the details."

Alan shook his head. "I'll tell them when the time is right. Do I have your word?"

Pastor Gordon sat back in his seat with a heavy breath and closed eyes. Finally he nodded. "Of course. Would you be uncomfortable if I shared this with my wife? There aren't many secrets between us. She can add her prayers to mine. She's a powerful prayer warrior. God might grant us a miracle."

Alan raised his hands. "I know I'm placing you in a difficult position. Believe me, I wish things were different. You have my permission to tell your wife, if you're positive she can keep it from Pam and her friends. As far as miracles go, you two won't be praying any harder than I am." He stood and offered his hand across the desk. Pastor Gordon shook it, grasping it in both of his.

"Thanks for your time and your understanding, Pastor. Kate and I are both looking forward to being in service with you in the morning."

CHAPTER TWO

The storm blew itself out overnight. The sun rose in a cloudless, crystal-blue sky on Sunday morning, gracing Garfield, Oklahoma, with the contradiction of the bright colors of fall married to the warm temperatures of Indian summer. Pam got out of bed ahead of her normal schedule in order to surprise her family with breakfast.

She arranged bacon in a hot skillet, poured herself a cup of coffee, and looked around the kitchen. Everything in place. She worked hard to keep it that way, Alan...*Harrison,* Pam corrected herself, Harrison worked even harder. She didn't ever want *Harrison* to think that she took him for granted. Alan had always complained.... Pam shook herself clear of the thought. *I need to stop!* The part of her life where she felt obligated to be perfect was over. Breakfast this morning was a treat for her family, not a necessity born of anyone's implied neglect. She turned back to the stove, picked up her cup, and almost dropped it when hands circled her waist from behind. After the initial start, Pam grinned and leaned back into the comfort of her husband's arms. "What are you doing?"

"Hugging my wife." Harrison sniffed the air. "My wonderful wife who's taking time from her busy Sunday morning schedule to fry bacon. What's the occasion?"

A need to prove to you how much you mean to me. Pam let the thought evaporate. She had nothing to prove in this relationship. "An apology, a thank you, a promise to be less of a drama queen." His arms tightened around her when she shrugged. "This hit me pretty hard, but none of it is your fault. You don't deserve to have it taken out on you."

Harrison rested his chin on her shoulder. "Pam, I know you lived through a nightmare during that last year with Alan, but we have our own life now. We're happy, aren't we?"

Pam nodded. "Absolutely."

"There's nothing he can do to take that away from you...from us."

She turned in his arms and pulled him down for a lingering good morning kiss. "I love you, Harrison. You've made me happier than I ever thought I could be."

Harrison wiggled his eyebrows at her. "I love you too, but if you keep kissing me like that, we're gonna be late for church."

Pam shoved him away with a smile. "Lech. Go make sure the kids are up. Breakfast in fifteen minutes."

"Hey," Harrison complained, "you started it."

When she narrowed her eyes at him, he tossed her a lazy salute. "Yes, ma'am. Going to check on the children, as ordered."

She turned back to the stove and squealed when he grabbed her again and nibbled his way up the back of her neck. His overnight whisker stubble scraped her tender skin enticingly. His voice sounded husky when his mouth reached her ear. "I'll bet if you called Karla, she'd teach your class this morning."

Pam raised her spatula. "Don't make me use this."

Harrison released her and took a step back. "Going, really...if you're sure."

She fisted her hands on her hips and started to turn. Her husband was gone before she completed the move.

Pam came back to the kitchen dressed for service. She pulled hot plates of food out of the oven and placed them on the table while her children harassed each other.

"She's only thirteen," Megan said.

"Sorry, fourteen," Jeremy countered.

"She's a baby."

"Hello, small female sibling, you're fourteen."

Megan tossed her long dark hair. "I'm mature for my age."

"Yeah, well that's debatable. Besides, she likes older men."

Megan's eyebrows rose beneath her bangs. "There's a man involved in this conversation?" She made a show of looking around the kitchen.

Jeremy stroked the newly sprouted fuzz on his fifteen-year-old chin. Thick enough to be felt, too light to be seen. "That would be me."

"Please," Megan scoffed. "My cat has more whiskers than you do, and she's a girl."

Pam stared wordlessly at her son until he lowered the hand poised to punch his sister in the arm. Forced to call this round of sibling rivalry a draw, Jeremy focused on his orange juice with a sullen expression.

Another day at the funny farm. Jeremy and Megan were eleven months apart and in constant conflict these days. Pam hadn't decided which stage of motherhood had been the most challenging, having two toddlers in diapers at the same time, or having two fresh-mouthed teenagers at the same time. At least during their toddler years, she'd been able to confine them to cribs, in separate rooms, with the doors closed. Yeah, those were the days.

"What are you two bickering about now?"

"Jeremy is in *love* with April Caswell." Megan lingered over the word *love*, her news oozing with sisterly sarcasm.

Jeremy sent his sister a daggered look. "I never said love." But a hot blush bloomed beneath his freckles even as he issued his disclaimer.

"I saw them holding hands at the Fall Festival the other night. Their hands were under the table. They didn't think anyone saw them, but I did."

Jeremy put is head in his hands and groaned.

"He probably even kissed her good night." Megan nodded sagely.

"I did not!"

"Megan, hush and eat your breakfast." Pam put an arm around her son's shoulders and kissed the top of his head. Her heart went tender at the thought of her baby having his first serious crush. *So soon, God?* "It's perfectly OK for Jeremy to have a girlfriend, and hand-holding is fine." She tilted his chin up so that their eyes met. "But let's keep the kissing—"

"I didn't."

"I'm just saying, let's keep the kissing on hold for the time being."

Harrison walked in. "Kissing? Did someone mention kissing? That's one of my best things." He pulled Pam into his arms and proceeded to demonstrate his technique.

"Geez, you guys," Jeremy muttered.

"Jeremy's in love with April Caswell." Megan was quick to catch her stepfather up on the morning's gossip.

Harrison released Pam and took his place at the table. "That's my boy." He held out his hand. "Give me five, son. You have impeccable taste in women. She's a cutie with a capital C!"

"H!" Megan protested, using the single letter nickname both kids had adopted for their stepfather.

"Hey, good taste must be acknowledged." He leaned forward, chin in hand. "What's your favorite thing about the lovely Miss April?"

"She has the greatest smile," Jeremy began, "and..." His voice trailed off at his sister's dubious stare. "We'll talk about it later," he mumbled, eyes going back to his plate.

Harrison ruffled Jeremy's hair. "That we will, but in the meantime, I feel compelled to second your mother's good advice. Hand-holding is dandy, lip locking is a no-no."

"I got it, H. I got it." Jeremy looked up. "Mom, you and Dad met when you were our age, didn't you?"

"Yes, I was fifteen when I met your father." Pam hoped her son wouldn't notice the strain behind her smile. "We dated all through high school and got married right after he finished college."

Megan's eyes were dreamy with the inherent romanticism of girls her age. "Was it love at first sight?"

Pam's answer was cryptic. "I always thought so."

Jeremy forked up a bite of egg. "I can't believe he and Kate decided to move back here. Rick's even coming in later tonight."

"Rick?"

"Kate's son. I can't wait for you to meet him." Jeremy wiped his mouth. "Anyway, it's going to be great having Dad closer. He's coming to the school on Tuesday to take me to lunch."

"Yeah," Megan chimed in. "He promised me a trip out to the mall just as soon as they get settled. We haven't been shopping together in, like, forever."

Pam shoved food around on her plate. What was the man up to? Dinner out with the kids yesterday. Now, lunch and shopping dates. *I mean, I don't have issues with him being a father, but this seems a little overboard.*

Jeremy interrupted her thoughts, his expression troubled as he studied her. "You're OK with him moving back, right? I mean, you're not still mad at each other, are you?"

Harrison rested his hand on her knee. Grateful for the silent support her husband offered, she answered her son. "I'm glad you and your sister are going to have a chance to spend more time with your father. I know he loves you very much, and I know you've missed having him close the last few years." Not really an answer to his question. Maybe he wouldn't notice. She cringed a little when he persisted.

"You haven't seen Dad since he moved away. I just didn't want you upset when you do."

"Noticed that, did you? When did you grow up on me?"

"I haven't been a baby for a long time, Mom."

"Yeah," Megan piped in. "He's got a girlfriend and a beard and everything."

Pam glared at her.

"Eating my breakfast," Megan muttered.

Pam shrugged off his concern. Jeremy had always been more sensitive to her moods than Megan. "Don't worry about me. Your father is coming back here to be closer to you and your sister. I'll admit that I had a few unsettling moments over the thought of seeing him again, but he and I no longer move in the same circles. I don't really anticipate it becoming a problem."

Alan pulled Kate's hand through the bend of his arm and took his first step through the front door of Valley View Church. He took a bulletin from an usher he didn't recognize and stepped into a vestibule that was all too familiar. Memories made his steps falter.

Kate looked up at him. "You OK?"

He patted her hand as they moved towards the auditorium, motioning her ahead of him into the last pew as the prayer over the morning offering ended. They continued to stand with the congregation. "I'm fine. This is a little weirder than I expected." He fished in his jacket pocket for a piece of hard candy. An ever present tool used to battle the dry mouth caused by the medication he took daily. He offered one to Kate, returning his attention to the front of the building as the ushers began to make their way down the aisle with the offering plates.

Alan's eyes locked with those of the bearded man on his side of the aisle. Surprise and pleasure bloomed with recognition. Benton Stillman. Alan smiled. *God finally got you out of your seat, did He?* He watched as Benton paused next to a petite blonde in the fifth pew and whispered a few words into her ear before continuing.

The blonde turned his way, her brows climbing over her rounded eyes. The ice-blue stare he received froze the blood in his veins. *Oh yeah, I remember that look.* Alan had long ago accepted the fact that when it came to Pam and her three friends, an insult to one was an insult to all.

Callie Stillman swept her gaze up and down his length. Her gaze left him, and he tracked her line of sight straight to the silver head of Karla Black. Karla turned and Alan watched as the two women engaged in an entire conversation with just their eyes, reminding him anew of the bond that existed among the four women. Nods, headshakes, and a shoulder jerked in his direction. Alan knew the instant Karla Black became aware of his presence. The look she sent his way was hot enough to melt the ice Callie's appraisal had left behind. No more or less than he deserved. He had much to atone for and very little time to get it done.

Alan swallowed around the peppermint and offered up a silent prayer. *Jesus, You sent me here to clean up the mess I left behind. I need Your help.*

Karla nudged the man standing by her side. A quick exchange and Alan met Mitchell's eyes. Mitch and Benton had been his best friends four years ago. From the four looks he'd just received, Alan knew he'd just been weighed and found more than wanting.

Pam settled in the pew next to Harrison as Pastor Gordon approached the pulpit.

He looked out over the Sunday morning congregation. "It's a joy to have everyone with us in service today."

He removed his glasses and polished them with a handkerchief. "We've been taking a journey through the book of Mark. We'll continue today with the next sermon in the series, starting with Mark 11:25,26.

"And when ye stand praying, forgive, if ye have ought against any: that your Father also which is in heaven may forgive you your trespasses. But if ye do not forgive, neither will your Father which is in heaven forgive your trespasses."

He looked up, and Pam frowned as his eyes seemed to linger on her for a second. "The Bible didn't say to wait until someone asks you for forgiveness. It just says to forgive. I believe the reason Jesus spelled it out this way is so we could avoid the oppression that comes when we allow un-forgiveness to fester in our lives. God wants to lift that burden out of our hearts so we can focus our attention and energy on our relationship with Him."

Pam opened her Bible, pulled out an ink pen, and made a few notes in the margins as the preacher worked through the verses. These sermons from the gospel of Mark had given her a much deeper look than she'd ever managed in her own study time.

The second the amen of the dismissal prayer was spoken, Pam was surprised to find herself surround by her friends.

Callie gripped Pam's shoulders, turned her towards the altar, and forced her back into the padded pew. "How are you feeling today?"

"Fine. What are you guys doing?"

Terri Evans took the seat next to Pam and put her arm around her shoulders. "Just checking on you. We know it's been a rough couple of days. We wanted to make sure you're OK."

Pam patted Terri's hand. "I'm fine, really." She moved her hand to Terri's belly and patted that as well. "How are you two doing?"

"Couldn't be better," Terri assured her. "I've been cleaning out closets and drawers. I took all of Seth's baby clothes out of storage and laundered them. I wanted to scrub the kitchen floor yesterday, but Steve hid my mop. I'm just trying to make sure that everything's ready before the big day gets here."

"It's called nesting," Callie told her, "and you need to be careful, or the big day will get here sooner than you think."

Karla laughed in agreement. "When I was pregnant with Lucas, I got down on my hands and knees to scrub the floor and couldn't get up. I had to crawl to a chair."

An excited Megan wiggled between Pam's friends and interrupted Karla's story. "Mom, Dad wants to know if Jeremy and I can go to lunch with him."

Pam laughed. "Tell Harrison to hold his horses. I'll be ready to go in just a few minutes."

"Not H," Megan corrected her. "Dad. He and Kate are about to leave. They want Jeremy and me to come see their new house. They'll bring us back to church with them tonight."

Pam stared at her daughter. A clammy sweat prickled her skin. She embraced anger over the fear. "Alan? Your father is here? In this church?"

"So much for plan A." Callie's words were a groan. She placed her hand on Pam's shoulder and smiled at Megan. "Why don't you go ask Harrison, sweetheart?"

Megan shrugged and hurried away. Callie's grip was iron tight, keeping Pam in her seat when she started to stand. "Sit down."

"Oh, he's got a nerve." Pam's voice shook as she shrugged off the restraint and struggled to gain her feet. "If he thinks he can move back to town and just pick up his life where he left off, he needs to think again."

Terri placed her hand on Pam's other shoulder. "This isn't the place."

Pam's temper heated to a quick boil. "This is the perfect place. He can pray before I kill him." She looked at her friends, tears pressing against the backs of her eyes. "He can't do this to me. I will *not* allow him to do this to me. You guys need to let me up so we can get this straight, once and for all."

Karla leaned over from the pew in front of Pam. "Sweetheart, you need to take a couple of deep breaths and think this through. I know his being here hurts, especially after what you told me yesterday, but this is God's house. Everyone is welcome here."

"Not him." Her voice broke as fear won the emotional tug of war. *Stupid, fat, worthless, frigid slob.* Pam cringed away from the internal voice that whispered old insults and ripped the bandage off her still tender heart. "Not him, not here." She bowed her head, tears finally spilling onto her cheeks. "You guys don't understand."

The men finally came to join their wives. "He's

gone," Benton told them.

Callie made room for Harrison next to Pam.

"Let's get you home." Harrison pulled Pam to her feet.

Pam turned into his chest. "Harrison, I can't."

"Darlin', I know. We'll fix it." He led her out the side door.

CHAPTER THREE

Alan sat at the kitchen table with his Monday morning coffee. An open newspaper littered the space in front of him. His eyes skimmed the pages, but the content failed to register. A hand settled on his shoulder, and he raised his face to receive Kate's good-morning kiss.

"You're brooding," Kate scolded gently.

He reached up to pat her hand. "Maybe, just a little."

Kate fixed her own cup and joined him at the table. "You knew this wasn't going to be easy."

Alan pinched the bridge of his nose. "You're right. But they all missed service last night. I didn't expect to run the whole family out of church."

Kate studied him through the cloud of steam rising from her cup. "You hurt her."

He closed his eyes, shamed by the memories that flooded his mind. "Things got pretty ugly that last year."

"Maybe you should just tell her—"

"No."

"Alan—"

"No, Kate. We've had this discussion." Alan reached across the table for her hand. "I need to do this in a way that clears the air between Pam and me without pity or obligation on her part. I don't want her forgiveness because I played the guilt card. I want to lay all the old, painful memories aside, so when I'm gone she can share the good times with our children without old bitterness coloring her words. Neither of the kids has ever asked me about what happened between Pam and me. But I know they know, at least the basic details. I can't undo any of that, but I want to give Jeremy and Megan some positive memories of their mother and me at least being civil to each other."

Alan rubbed the dull ache in his chest. "I don't even know if that's possible, but I have to try. I feel like God has laid two things on my heart. Making peace with Pam and being a Christian father to Jeremy and Megan in the time I have left." He pulled Kate's hand up, turned it over, and pressed a kiss into her palm, hoping to take the sting out of his words. "Not what you signed up for, huh?"

Kate pulled her hand free and cupped her husband's face. "I'm here with you, aren't I?"

"Have I thanked you lately?"

"For?"

"For being here. For understanding how much I need to do this. I don't think there are a lot of women who'd uproot their lives in support of their husband's need to reestablish a relationship with an ex-wife."

"Hey, God talks to me, too. I understand how important this is to you, to the kids. All I want is to spend as much time with you as I can." Kate's voice broke. "*Where* we live isn't as important to me as the living."

The hiccup of emotion in Kate's voice stung his heart. "Sweetheart."

Kate held up a hand and took another sip of her coffee. Her voice was steadier when she continued. "You do what you have to do, and I'll pray." She took her cup to the sink. "Right now I have to go to the grocery store and get something in here besides coffee and sandwich stuff. I need to run by the bank and open a new checking account. Once the lawyers are finished haggling over the sale of your third of the business, your buyout check will need a place to go." She dug in her purse for her car keys, eventually finding them on the hook by the back door. "Any special requests from the store?"

"Apples and grapes?"

"Already on the list. What are you going to do while I'm gone?"

"Call Harrison's office, try to make an appointment to see him. If I can convince him that I come in peace, maybe he can persuade Pam to talk to me." He looked around their cluttered house. "Some of these boxes need to be unpacked."

"Don't overdo," Kate warned. "You make Patrick get up and help you."

"I will. It was so late when he got in last night, I don't want to bother him too early."

"Well, you tell him his mother threatened to box his ears if he sleeps all day. He may be twenty-two, but I can still take him."

Alan waved her on her way. "I promise I'll get him

up in plenty of time to help."

"Don't let him forget that he needs to go out to the university and enroll this afternoon."

Alan laughed at her. "Woman, would you just go run your errands? We men can take care of ourselves." The door shut behind his wife, and he closed his eyes when he heard her car start.

"Father, I know I haven't thanked You yet today, but thanks. Thank You for bringing Kate into my life when I needed her the most. I know this isn't what she expected when we got married, but she's sticking. I can't thank You, or her, enough for that.

"Thank you for the chance to spend some more time with my kids. Help me be the dad I should be. I want to leave a Christian legacy for them. I want them to be able to lean on that once I'm gone. Please Father, could You soften Pam's heart just a little? I know I haven't always been a good man, especially where she's concerned, but I'm doing my best to make that right. Open a door for me. You're the only one who knows how much time I have left. I just want Your will in my life and theirs. Amen."

Pam pushed her shopping cart through the grocery store early Monday morning with a heavy heart and leaden feet. Cooking had always been more of a hobby than a chore. She loved the challenge of new recipes and the comforting routine of old ones. The opportunity to put her special touch on special foods for the special people in her life was, well...special. Not so much this morning.

The bright lights and wide, clean aisles of her favorite market did little to improve Pam's sour mood.

With an iPod clipped to her shirt and the grocery list for tonight's Bible study/baby shower refreshments in her hand, she waited for the soothing praise music coming through the earbuds to calm her nerves. She considered the fact that she was up and functioning a major victory. Part of her wanted to curl up in her bed and never move again. She knew from experience where that could lead. Pam had promised herself a long time ago that Alan Archer would never have control of another minute of her life.

She crossed items off her list, lost in thought. The anticipation she should have had for Terri's baby shower during tonight's Bible study was replaced by a feeling of dread. Her friends loved her, and they wouldn't push for more information than she was willing to share, but Pam knew they'd want to talk about what was bothering her. *I can't go there with them, not tonight, not ever.*

If it wasn't for the shower, she would have stayed home tonight where it was *safe.* Jeremy was home from school today with a stomach ache. He didn't have a fever or anything, but he loved school and never missed unless he was really sick. Under other circumstances her friends would have accepted that excuse, no questions asked.

She stopped in the baking aisle and considered food coloring options. Terri and Steve had chosen, once again, not to know the sex of their baby. That meant sticking to a gender neutral color for the cake and cookie frosting. *Green and Yellow.* Pam tossed bottles into her cart and continued her shopping and her grousing.

There had to be a way to drown out the little voice

in her head urging her to confide in her friends. Her head shook, and she turned up the music. If—or when—the time came for sharing those dark secrets, Pam would face it, but for now she really wanted to lock things back up in the dark corner of her heart where they'd been stored for so long.

Pam turned into the next aisle, functioning on autopilot, concentrating on her list and her music. An unexpected tap on her shoulder made her jump. She rolled her eyes. *Which one of them found me?* Brushing the earbuds aside, she turned. The smile she'd forced to her face transformed to stone.

Kate Archer looked fresh and chipper in a navy linen pantsuit and matching pumps. Pam crossed her arms over her shabby pink sweatshirt and wished she'd spent five minutes primping. Kate obviously had. Her shoulder length blonde hair hung in artfully tousled waves around her face, perfectly highlighted by the sun. The hairdo should have looked messy or childish; it didn't. Pam decided she didn't care for the color, though. That streaky blonde surely came from a salon and didn't suit the other woman's features any more than the color choices she'd made with her morning makeup. Kate was taller than Pam, thinner than Pam, but surely that sun-kissed tan beneath those unfortunate freckles was *store bought.* No one in Pam's circle of friends still had their summer tan this late into the fall. The little voice in Pam's head continued to whisper. *Catty, unfair, petty,* and *foolish* managed to penetrate before she slapped a mental hand over the imaginary mouth of reason.

Kate's clear green eyes crinkled at the corners in a friendly but hesitant smile. "I thought that was you. I'm sorry if I startled you." She motioned to the earbuds dangling around Pam's neck. "I called your name. I guess you didn't hear me."

Pam continued to stare in stony silence.

"Can we go someplace to talk?" Kate nodded at Pam's loaded cart. "It looks like you have a busy day planned, but I'd love to buy you a cup of coffee if you have time."

The air chilled ten degrees. "I don't think that's a good idea." Pam turned her back and prepared to continue her shopping.

Kate walked beside her. The woman couldn't take a hint. "Pam, please. I know we don't really know each other, but I'd hoped we could be friends. Not best friends, but friends. I wanted to tell you how much I'm enjoying being a part of Jeremy's and Megan's lives. They're such terrific kids. I know how strange this must be for you having to share them with a stepmother." Kate paused. "Having us suddenly show up on your doorstep. But I want you to know how much I already love them."

Pam took a deep breath and turned back to Kate with a frosty stare.

"I know Alan hurt you." Kate's voice had dropped to a whisper. "He... If you could just give him a chance, he'd like to make amends for some of that. "

Pam read sympathy in the other woman's face. *How dare she feel sorry for me?* It pushed her temper over the edge. "I don't need another friend, and I don't want your sympathy. As for what Alan wants or needs, please take a message back to him. He can quit trying, 'cause there's no way he can fix what he did to our family. If the ground opened up and swallowed Alan

Archer whole this afternoon, I would dance on his grave."

Kate took a step back, eyes wide, a hand fisted at her throat. The color blanched from her tan. "Pam, you don't mean that." Her response was a strangled whisper.

"Every single word."

"I know—"

"You don't know anything. You don't know because he doesn't know what he cost me." She stopped, too close to her own secrets, and willed her heartbeat and breathing back to normal. "Look, you seem like a nice person, but you really don't have any part in this one way or the other. I just need to be left *alone*." Pam wheeled her cart away.

Patrick Wheeler turned over in his bed and cracked open an eye to test the light in the room. He pulled a pillow over his head and let out a quiet groan. Daylight, but *way* too early in his twenty-two-year-old, I-got–to-bed-late opinion.

He snuggled back under the covers, took a deep breath, and tried to convince his body to go back to sleep. His eyes popped open under the pillow despite his best efforts. Now that he was awake, curiosity about his new surroundings battled with the dread that came from knowing the truth about their move. Trying to ignore that truth only made it linger longer in his thoughts. They'd moved to Garfield so Dad could make peace with his old family and friends before he died.

The thought made him more sad than angry these days. Patrick had known about his father's illness long enough to be past the futility of anger and the ineffectiveness of denial. All he and his mom had left was the bitter truth. The bitter truth that the only man he'd ever loved enough to call *Father* would be gone from his life almost before he was there.

When Mom and Alan began to date two years ago, he'd been happy for his mother. Once he'd gone away to college, Patrick had come to understand some of the sacrifices his mom had made for him over the years.

Patrick didn't remember his real dad. Chad Wheeler died in Iraq during Desert Shield, before Patrick's first birthday. Mom raised him on her own, never dating, always available, unselfishly devoting all of her time to the various endeavors of a growing boy. *Dad* had been a picture on the mantel, a nebulous entity his mom mentioned on occasion. He hadn't considered the arrangement odd at the time.

Patrick stuffed a couple of pillows behind his back and crossed his arms behind his head. He'd never forget the image of his long-legged mother, blonde hair scraped back and stuffed through the opening of a ball cap, hands fisted on her hips, toe-to-toe with an umpire, referee, or coach who'd had the nerve to make a bad call involving her son. The memory made him chuckle.

Mom liked sports. She pitched a mean fastball, none of that sissy underhanded stuff. She understood the most intricate play on a football field. And basketball? Patrick had been thirteen and over his first growth spurt before he'd been able to beat her in layups in the driveway. His mom never argued for him when he was wrong, and she *never* let him win.

Patrick had reciprocated by learning how to change

the oil in the car, mastering the use of simple tools, performing household repairs, and maintaining the yard. They'd been a team—hadn't needed anyone else.

Along came Alan Archer and the word *father* had taken on a brand-new meaning. Alan hadn't just wooed Patrick's mother. He'd made a point to include a twenty-year-old, fatherless young man in the equation. Phone calls to see how Patrick was doing at school, a weekly *guy* night during the summer, not to mention the soft glow of love on his mother's face.

Patrick began to look forward to making up for some things he'd never missed. Now, he wouldn't get that chance. Alan's death would affect Patrick in ways he really could have lived without. Maybe that sounded selfish, but—

"Patrick. Are you awake?"

"Yeah, come on in."

Alan eased the door open, carrying a mug of steaming coffee. "Morning. I have orders from your mother not to let you sleep the day away."

Patrick accepted the mug. "Thanks, Dad. What time is it? I didn't unpack my alarm clock, yet."

Alan propped a shoulder against the wall. "Just after ten. Your mother will be home from her errands soon, and if some of those boxes aren't unpacked, she'll rough us both up."

Patrick snorted. "Give me twenty minutes to find clean clothes and my toothbrush. We'll try to make a dent before she gets back."

Alan straightened. "Sounds like a plan."

Patrick watched the door close behind his *father*. He took a sip of his coffee, smiling at the creamy, sweet taste he preferred. Dad had fixed it just as Patrick liked.

Dad. A sarcastic snort filled the empty room. Mom did her best to hide the ache in her heart behind layers of smiles and faith, but he saw through the fluff, straight to the truth. Their family was on borrowed time. He'd switched schools midterm, left his friends behind, and moved to this tiny spot in the road. He'd play the game because when the final whistle sounded, Mom and·he were a team, and she was going to need him in her corner.

CHAPTER FOUR

The short drive home from the market did nothing to improve Kate's mood. The empty driveway bore witness to the fact that Alan and Patrick had departed for their separate errands. A few minutes alone suited her just fine. Kate let herself into the house and slammed the door. The satisfying noise reverberated around her. She avoided the strong temptation to give in to the urge to open it and slam it again.

The nerve of that woman! Dance on Alan's grave, would she? *She'll have to come through me, first.* Kate made an effort to get her anger under control. She looked around the front room of their new home. Boxes to unpack, bare walls to decorate, a home to make for Alan and Patrick...a funeral on the horizon.

"Well this just bites. Here I stand in a strange house, in a strange town. I quit my job, uprooted my life...for what? To be treated like a pariah?" Kate threw herself into an overstuffed wing chair. Tears had never been her style. Her emotions tended to be more physical.

She was momentarily grateful that most of the breakables were still snuggly packed away.

She leaned her head against the cushions and continued to vent her frustrations to the empty room. "Church yesterday was a joke. I enjoyed the sermon, one that Miss Dance-on-his-grave should take to heart, but they hustled us out of there when service was over like we had the plague or something. I never expected to be bosom buddies with Pam or any of her friends, but I did expect some civility." Kate threaded her fingers through her hair. "I told Alan I was prepared for this. Did I lie?"

Kate leaned forward and put her head in her hands. "Jesus, did I lie? I never meant to. Alan was honest with me. I know he hurt Pam in almost unforgivable ways." The memory of the talk Alan had insisted upon having before their marriage flooded Kate's mind. He'd been brutally honest with her about his treatment of Pam. No one deserved the torment Alan had subjected his first wife to. *I really do understand how hard this is for Pam to accept, even if I can't picture Alan in that role.* "Father, please soften her heart. Alan has to do this in his own way and in his own time. I'll stand behind him because I've never doubted that You've dictated this path for him, for us. I need wisdom, and he needs direction. Most of all, we both need time. Jesus, please give us more time with each other."

Harrison Lake's law office was small but well-appointed. A comfortable striped sofa flanked by a couple of matching chairs. Heavy wooden chairs and accent tables along the wall matched the desk in the corner. A pretty secretary sat behind the desk. Alan fidgeted in the hard wooden chair he'd chosen, sucked on the ever-present peppermint, and flipped through a second magazine. *Why can't I ever think to bring a book?* A book might have distracted him from the conversation to come. *Will he listen? He was Pam's lawyer. He's probably the only other person alive who understands exactly what I need forgiveness for.* He tossed the magazine aside. A quick glance at the clock showed him that it was exactly three minutes since the last time he looked.

The telephone on the desk rang. The pretty blonde smiled at Alan as she picked it up. She listened, nodded, and mumbled a quick, "Yes, sir." She returned the phone to the cradle. "Mr. Wheeler, I'm so sorry for your wait. Mr. Lake will see you now."

He scrambled to his feet and looked at the plaque on the desk. "Thanks, Stephanie."

She gave him a brilliant smile and nodded down the hall. "First door there, on the left."

Alan nodded, strode down the short hall, and pushed the door open. Harrison was standing behind his desk, a smile of welcome on his face, hand stretched out to greet his two o'clock appointment. The smile and the hand both froze in place when Alan walked through the door.

"Patrick Wheeler? Is this your idea of a joke?"

"I borrowed my stepson's name," Alan admitted. "I figured I wouldn't get an appointment with you otherwise, and we need to talk."

"Oh, we really do." Harrison stepped from behind his desk, crossed the office, and closed the door with a firm click. Returning to his cluttered desk, he pushed the intercom button and spoke to his secretary. "Steph, please hold my calls for the next ten minutes." He settled in his chair—king of his own domain and comfortable on his own turf—and left Alan standing. "You've got ten minutes. You need to start by giving me one good reason why I shouldn't toss you out of here on your slimy backside ."

"I'm not here to cause any trouble, but—"

"You're off to a miserable start."

"I need to talk to Pam."

"Wrong answer." Harrison's response was firm and to the point.

"It's important."

"She's got nothing to say to you."

"Look, I know how much of a jerk I was." He paused at the choked sound Harrison made at his choice of words. "Jerk is the strongest word I'm comfortable using right now.

"I know what I did was unforgivable, but I'm here to ask forgiveness anyway. I'm not the same person I was four years ago. I came back to Garfield to spend some quality time with my kids and to try to make amends for some of the garbage I dumped on Pam." He raised his hands in a universal gesture of truce and appeal. "I just want the chance to talk to her. One hour of her time, one Christian adult to another, to try and lay aside some of the past, for the sake of our kids."

Harrison leaned back in his chair, elbows on the arm rests, steepled fingers tapping his lips.

Alan squirmed under his stare, an undesirable lab specimen under a microscope.

"Let me clarify the situation for you. I speak for my wife and, in this case, my client. Stay away from her."

In an effort to keep his hands from shaking, Alan braced his hands on the back of the chair he hadn't been invited to sit in. *Be patient, appeal to his Christianity.* "Harrison, I hoped that, by coming here first, you'd see I was sincere in my desire to do this the right way."

Harrison's smirk defeated Alan's internal plea.

"Your help would be appreciated, but I don't need your permission to see the mother of my children."

"Wrong again." Harrison's chair rocked forward. "I'm a lawyer, Alan. I can—and will—use every legal avenue available to keep you from upsetting the balance Pam's managed to restore to her life. I cleaned up the mess you left behind four years ago. Since that worked out to my advantage, I'll say thanks. But you don't get any second chances." Harrison stood and walked across the plush beige carpet of his office. "This conversation is over. If you persist in trying to see Pam, I'll file harassment or stalking charges against you. I might not be able to make them stick, but I can make your life difficult in the short term."

Alan straightened and turned to the door, determination squared his jaw and his shoulders. "You can't keep me away from her forever. Kate and I are here to stay." He jammed his hands into his pockets, jiggling keys and change, and faced Harrison across the threshold. "We've bought a house, and we intend to continue worshiping at Valley View. I will get my chance to talk to Pam, eventually."

"Good luck with that." Harrison closed the door in Alan's face.

After making a negligible dent in the boxes stacked around the house, Patrick spent his afternoon checking out his new school and getting enrolled. His previous contact had been conducted through phone and

Internet. He was anxious to see the campus for himself.

Mom had argued with him about the move. He was in the middle of his senior year. Next year, when it would be necessary to change schools to accommodate his transition to a good law school, was soon enough to make a change. But with Dad sick, *dying*—he closed his eyes against the reminder his brain insisted in tacking onto his thoughts—Patrick wanted to stay close. The university in the neighboring town had a solid legal department, and once he'd explained the circumstances, they were very helpful in getting things set up for his transfer. He took an hour or so to walk around the grounds. Green lawns stretched wide, decorated with plots of fall flowers, shaded by tall old trees in the process of shedding their leaves. With classes over for the day, young people hung out in clumps. Resident students prepared for dinner and homework. Commuters trickled out to the parking lots for their drive home. Patrick was pleased by what he saw. At least this part of the move would be painless.

Patrick shunned the interstate and took the old two-lane highway back to Garfield, deciding to invest some time in exploring the single street downtown. He smirked. A church on almost every corner, a gas station on the ones left over. Main Street consisted of a dry cleaner, a hardware store, City Hall and the library, a jewelry store, a rundown coin laundry, and two banks. Barber shops and beauty salons took up the rest of the space. A couple of hole-in-the-wall restaurants rounded out the mix. *What have I gotten myself into?*

Exploration finished in five minutes, he turned a corner and found a fairly new carwash with a Sonic on the other side of the street. *Civilization.* He patted the dash of his faithful blue Chevy Silverado. "Time for a bath, girl."

Five dollars and thirty minutes later, he finished drying his truck and considered the Sonic Drive-In across the street. The weather was just warm enough to make the thought of a root beer float appealing. He navigated the parking lot. The place was packed with late afternoon snack-seekers, but there was one spot open on the far side. *It must be my lucky day.* The car next to the open spot contained a black Mustang convertible. The car's top was down, and Patrick smiled as he got a good look at the occupants. Two, count 'em two, dark-haired beauties. Garfield's possibilities were looking up.

He followed the drive around the building and the assessment of his luck changed. The Mustang was leaving. Patrick halted his freshly washed blue truck to allow the convertible ample room to back out of the narrow stall. The car inched closer and closer. It looked like the two girls were arguing, the driver paying more attention to her passenger than her surroundings. *Hey, you can stop now.* He beeped his horn just a second too late, cringing at the sound of bumper meeting bumper.

Patrick lowered his head to the steering wheel. *Perfect.* He shifted the truck into park and climbed out to check the damage.

The driver of the Mustang met him at the intersection of their vehicles, apologies mixed with concern. "Oh my gosh. I'm *so* sorry. I can't believe I just backed right into you. Are you hurt? Is your truck hurt?"

"I'm fine," Patrick assured her. "Let's take a quick look." He squatted down between the vehicles, looking first at his truck. His hand brushed gently over the point of impact. "Mine looks fine." His attention turned to the Mustang to repeat the inspection. He released a soft whistle when he encountered a small series of deep scratches. "Well, I think I came out of this better than you did." He stood up, making room between the vehicles for the girls to conduct their own examination. "Nothing much hurts these old fashioned chrome bumpers, but yours is fiberglass. The paint is scratched pretty good. It wouldn't surprise me if there were cracks to match the scratches."

The older of the two girls knelt down and ran her hand over the damage.

"Dad's going to kill you," the younger one told her.

Sisters? He looked between them and noted the resemblance. The older one would not get away before he had some contact information. And it had nothing to do with the accident. She was gorgeous.

The driver of the car fingered the scuffs in the black paint. "If he does, it'll be my own fault for not paying attention." She stood, combing long dark hair back from her face to reveal sapphire blue eyes framed in thick black lashes. "We're really late for our mom's baby shower, but Iris just had to have a soda." She took a deep breath. "And you could care less about my rambling." Her straight dark hair fell forward again as she bent her head and rummaged through her purse. She found a note pad and wrote her name and phone number on it. "Take this. Have your truck looked at. If there's damage we've missed, call me, and please accept my apologies."

Patrick grinned as he took the note. "No harm, no foul on my end." The folded paper disappeared into his shirt pocket. "But I'll keep this handy just in case." He held out his hand. "I'm Patrick, by the way. Patrick Wheeler."

"Samantha Evans. Sam to my friends. This is my sister Iris."

He sent Iris a wink while refusing to surrender Samantha's hand. "You live around here?"

"Yes." She gently tugged her hand free.

"I'm new in town." Patrick walked Samantha to the door of her car and opened it with a flourish. "Can I call you, even if it isn't about the truck?"

Samantha blushed under his scrutiny. "I hit you and you're returning the favor?"

He patted his pocket where her phone number resided. "This could be fate. It'd be a shame to waste it."

"I—" The sound of a car horn interrupted Samantha's response, drawing their attention to the line of cars stacking up behind their little accident. "We're blocking traffic." She climbed back into her seat and started the engine.

Patrick closed the door and leaned forward on the door frame, eyebrows raised in question.

"Yes." She laughed. "Call me. I'll show you where to find the best pizza in town." Samantha put the car in gear and drove away.

Patrick climbed into his truck, his smile firmly in place. Mom always told him to make lemonade from lemons. Samantha might just be the sweetener needed to brighten this whole sour situation.

CHAPTER FIVE

Pam found refuge from her chaotic thoughts in the bustle of Callie's kitchen. A little voice in her head urged her towards guilt over her earlier treatment of Kate Archer, but she buried it under the simple joy of making the evening special for Terri. Even the part of Pam's heart that counseled her to confide in her friends lowered its volume as she unpacked containers of baked goods and cold finger foods.

Karla and Callie were occupied in the other room, putting the finishing touches on the decorations. All Pam saw of them were blurs in her peripheral vision as they rushed back and forth. She piped decorative borders onto cookies, a chore she'd intentionally saved for now, in case she needed an excuse to be *busy*. Her deep breath of relief filled the room and the tears, present behind her eyes for most of the day, receded a little further. She picked up a plate of cookies and started for the dining room. Maybe the night would pass with smiles and laughter after all.

Agreement had been made to keep this evening's shower casual. This was Terri's second pregnancy in two years, so they didn't need to go all out. Callie and Karla seemed to have forgotten that arrangement.

Callie's dining room was an explosion of yellow and green, echoing Pam's offhanded choice at the market. Sometimes it seemed like they could read each other's minds. The tray of cookies in her hand thudded onto the table as Pam pushed the fanciful thought aside. *Coincidence.* She didn't want anyone in her troubled head.

The doorbell rang, and Terri's stepdaughters, Samantha and Iris, rushed into the living room with their gifts.

"Sorry we're late," Sam said. "Iris insisted we stop at the Sonic, and we had a little accident."

"Little accident?" Iris grinned. "Sam ran over the most gorgeous guy in Garfield. Tall, blond, blue-eyed hunk. He was totally hitting on her in the parking lot. One of us should be in love."

The women gathered around the girls. "Are you two all right?" Callie asked.

"Iris, you're such a brat." Sam filled in the blanks of Iris's story. "We're fine; he's fine."

"He certainly was," Iris agreed.

Sam shook her head at the interruption. "My car will be fine. He was a cutie, but the damage was so minor, I don't think I'll hear from him."

Karla laughed as she took their packages and added them to the growing stack in the corner of the room. "If you two weren't getting into trouble, you wouldn't know how to act."

Iris held up her cup. "When Dad sees the car, Sam

will be the one in trouble. I just wanted a soda." The fourteen-year-old snagged a cookie and looked around the room. "Rats, I was hoping for a clue."

Callie put her arm around the youngster. "You knew better than that."

"Callieee," Iris pleaded.

"I'm going to tell you the same thing I told you last year. Just because I have access to Terri's medical records doesn't mean I can share that info. *I* know the sex of your future sibling. *You* will just have to wait a couple more months."

Iris sulked. "That is *so* not fair"

"You're right," Karla agreed. "It's not fair for her to know and not share. It goes against the code."

Callie put her hands on her hips and faced her silver headed friend. "What code?"

"The girlfriend code of ethics," Karla responded. "When have we ever kept secrets from each other?"

Karla's words slammed into Pam's soul with the force of a jackhammer. *She's kidding.* That self-assurance couldn't stem the tears.

"Karla," Callie hissed.

"Oops," Karla moaned. "Pam..."

Pam fled to the kitchen with Karla on her heels. She leaned over the sink, her breath coming in noisy gulps as she tried to stop the tears.

Karla pulled her into a hug. "Pam, I'm sorry."

Callie pushed through the swinging door and put her hands on her hips. "I thought you came in here to fix things."

Karla looked up. "I will, just as soon as she stops crying."

Pam glanced at Callie and burst into a new wave of

tears.

Callie shook her head, crossed the room, and rubbed Pam's arm. "Sweetheart, you've got to stop this."

Karla took a step back. "Pam, I'm sorry. I wasn't thinking of you when I said that. I obviously wasn't thinking at all when I said it. We all know my sense of humor needs help sometimes."

Pam drew in a shaky breath and grabbed a paper towel from the rack above the sink. She blotted her eyes and blew her nose. "I know. It's not your fault."

Callie pushed Pam towards one of the bar stools on the other side of her kitchen island. "Sit down for a few seconds and take some deep breaths. Think party."

Pam leaned on the bar, her face in her hands. "I know," she repeated. "I told myself earlier today that this was Terri's night, and I was going to focus on her. I'm trying so hard to get what I'm feeling buried back where it belongs. I'm obviously not doing a very good job."

Callie put an arm around her friend's shoulders. "Pam, maybe that's part of the problem. Maybe it's time to un-bury those things. Whatever's bothering you, whatever you're so hurt over...maybe you need to drag it out into the light of day and deal with it, not bury it deeper."

Pam closed her eyes and hugged her arms around herself. *She sounds just like Dr. Sylvester.*

Karla leaned on the counter. "You know you can talk to us."

"I do know that. I know you love me, and I know you're praying for me." Pam's voice caught on a fresh sob. She stopped and took the deep breaths Callie had recommended. When she continued her voice was a whisper. "I know you guys don't understand. I spent part of the day looking for ways to avoid this conversation. I can't go there right now. I may *never* be able to go there. Not because I don't trust you, not because you might not understand, just because it hurts too much." Pam's gaze traveled from Callie's face to Karla's. The love she saw reflected in their eyes caused her breath to hitch again. "Can you accept that?"

"If acceptance is what you need most from us right now, that's what you'll get," Karla assured her.

"With one provision," Callie added. "When you need more, you'll remember that we're here for you."

Sam stuck her head through the doorway. "Everything OK in here? Terri's on her way up the walk."

Callie nodded her acknowledgement. "We'll be out in sec." She turned Pam towards the bathroom in the back hall and gave her a little nudge. "Go fix your face. We have a baby shower to give."

The Bible study group trickled out one by one 'til only Pam, her three friends, and the two girls remained. Their study topic had been sacrificed this week in favor of celebration. There was a verse somewhere, maybe in Proverbs, that said something about laughter or merriment being good for the soul. Pam agreed. As the party progressed, baby stories were shared, gifts were opened, and she'd regained her calm.

Terri sat back in her chair, her dessert plate propped on her ample belly. "This cake is terrific, Pam. You'll have to give me the recipe. In a couple of months, when I feel like moving again and I've lost some of this baby fat, I'll make it for Steve and the girls."

"When you feel like moving again?" Pam questioned. "If I remember right, you were trying to scrub the floor two days ago." The plate and fork on her friend's stomach rattled as it received a healthy kick from the belly's occupant. Pam leaned forward to catch the dish as it slid towards the floor.

Terri laughed and rubbed her stomach. "That was then; this is now. I've had *no* energy today, my back is killing me, and my ankles are swollen. I don't remember feeling this way when I carried Seth. I don't know if I can make it another two months." She stilled her hands and looked longingly down at her belly. "Come out!" she demanded.

Iris sidled up to Terri's side. "It might help if we had something solid to look forward to. If we knew what the baby was..."

Sam groaned. "Give it up, Iris."

"But..."

"Ohhh." Terri sucked in a breath. Her hand went to the small of her back.

"What?" five voices asked in unison.

Terri waved her hand in a dismissive gesture. "Back spasms. I told you guys it's been hurting today, but that was an extra hard twinge."

Callie narrowed her blue eyes at her pregnant friend. "Hard twinge? How often are you having these *hard twinges?*"

"Off and on all day. Why?" Terri laughed when Callie continued to stare at her. "Relax, it's a backache not labor pains." Her disclaimer ended in a frown.

"Another one?"

Terri expelled a deep breath and nodded.

Callie motioned to Karla. "Call the guys and tell

them dinner is over. Yellow alert."

"What...wait," Terri insisted. "Backache."

Callie shook her head. "Two words...back labor."

"Do you think?" Pam asked.

Terri stood up, sat back down, and stood up again.

"Labor? Callie, I have eight more weeks."

Callie made an effort to reassure her friend. "And it may very well be muscle spasms, but there's only one way to be sure, especially if this has been going on most of the day. You're going to the hospital."

Iris crowed with glee, obviously excited at the prospect of an early end to the suspense.

Karla closed her phone. "The guys are on their way. They all rode with Mitch. I told them to hurry. Somehow I don't think they'll have a problem convincing Steve to cut their evening short."

"Wait a minute. I need to go home," Terri began, "Megan's sitting with Bobbie and Seth. She's got school tomorrow. I need my bag. The bassinette isn't made up. I haven't..."

Pam placed her hand on Terri's shoulder. "I'll call Megan. If this turns out to be the real thing, she can miss a day of school. What you need to do is calm down, stretch out on the sofa, and wait for Steve."

Terri allowed Sam to lead her to the sofa. She lay back on the cushions, pulling in a sharp breath on the way.

Callie looked at the clock. "Those twinges are pretty frequent, but they're erratic. Any other symptoms we should know about? Bleeding, anything that felt like an actual contraction?"

Terri shook her head. The door opened, and Steve rushed into the room ahead of the other men. His collar-length black hair was askew, his blue eyes sharp with concern.

He took the hand Terri extended to him and dropped to his knees next to the couch. He kissed her knuckles and rested his other hand on her stomach. "Labor?"

Terri shrugged her shoulders and flinched at the same time, her only answer a hiss. "Ouch..."

"All righty then." Steve stood, bending down to scoop Terri off the couch. "I guess we'll go find out."

"Steve, I can walk."

"Yeah, but why bother?"

"I need my purse and my jacket." Terri sucked in a breath and buried her head in her husband's shoulder.

Steve paused in mid-stride and hefted her closer. "I think we'll hurry."

Pam hung Terri's purse from Steve's shoulder, pressed the keys to his wife's car into his hand, and shooed them towards the door. "Go. We'll pack up the rest of your stuff and be right behind you."

Pam hated hospitals. The smell, the impersonal décor. She rubbed her arms through her light jacket and added the constant chilly temperatures to her list of complaints. She avoided this place like the plague, never quite able to put that horrible night, four years ago, out of her mind. Even here in a maternity ward filled with the hope of new life and the laughter of those waiting to welcome it, her mistakes and Alan's cruelty dogged her.

She sipped a cup of really bad coffee while the guys paced, Karla and Callie reminisced about having their own babies, and the girls talked excitedly about a new brother or sister.

"It's got to be a girl this time." Iris sent a pointed look at Callie. "Dad really wants a girl."

Callie's carefully neutral expression pulled Pam out of her broodiness. "Oh, Callie, I'm glad it's you keeping this secret. Her grilling is brutal."

Callie shrugged and twisted an imaginary key between her lips. "She'll get nothing out of me."

Iris threw her hands up and looked at the ceiling. "Come on," she begged. "One clue. Me and you, we'll go outside. No one will ever know you told me."

Pam had to laugh when Callie winked at the impatient fourteen-year-old over her cup and mouthed a single word. "No."

Defeated, Iris crossed her arms and slumped back into the hard plastic chair.

Steve stepped through the large swinging doors and everyone stood in anticipation. The father-to-be gestured them back to their seats. "They're still checking."

"Can we go see her?" Sam asked.

Steve smiled at his oldest daughter. "If they decide this is the real deal, she can have two visitors at a time but not just yet. She wanted me to come out and give you guys an update." Steve glanced at the doors with a worried expression. "We're seven weeks early. If her doctor decides this is true labor, he's going to give her some meds to try and stop it. It could turn out to be a long night. I need to get back in there, but I'll let you know what's happening just as soon as we know."

Pam smiled as Steve hurried back to Terri's side. *He reminds me of Alan when our babies were born...*She drew in one calming breath and tapped her empty cup. "If we're going to be here for long, I'm going to need more coffee."

"Me too," Karla and Callie echoed.

Harrison stood and stretched. "I need to stretch my legs. I'll go."

Callie smiled gratefully at her friend's husband. "Thanks. But could you go downstairs to get the coffee?" She frowned into her empty cup. "This was pretty bad, but there's a table just outside the ER. It gets more traffic, and there's actually a coffee station with a real coffee pot, not this vending machine sludge."

Harrison held a hand out to his wife. "Walk with me?"

Pam nodded and allowed herself to be pulled to her feet, grateful for the distraction. She looked at Sam and Iris. "You girls need anything?"

"Soda, please," Sam answered.

"And a candy bar." Iris dug in her bag and held out a dollar bill.

Harrison shook his head. "I think I can handle that for you." Hand-in-hand, he and Pam moved to the bank of elevators. "We'll be back in a few. Call us if anything important happens."

Alan held Kate's hand as Dr. Richards frowned at the pink and white EKG printout. The black tracings meant nothing to Alan. If the doctor's expression could be taken at face value, he was equally confused.

Dr. Richards shook his head. "I've never seen an advanced case of hypertrophic cardiomyopathy, but I called your heart specialist in Kansas City. He says these readings are pretty normal for this stage of your disease. He—"

Alan coughed, intentionally interrupting the doctor. He squeezed his wife's hand. "Sweetheart, my throat and mouth are so dry. Could you go out to the nurse's station and see if they can get me a cup of ice water or something?"

Kate nodded and hurried to do his bidding. Both men remained silent until the heavy wooden door swung closed behind her.

The doctor stared at Alan. "My degree is in emergency medicine, not psychology, but even I can see through that. Why are you hiding the progression of your disease from your wife?"

Alan closed his eyes and leaned his head back on the pillows, suddenly weary of the uphill battles in what was left of his life. "I'm not hiding anything, not really. But there are so many things I need to do. If Kate knew just how far this thing had gone, she'd never let me out of her sight." He massaged the heel of his hand across the flesh and bone covering his traitorous heart. "What did you and Dr. McBride decide?"

Dr. Richards clasped his hands behind his back and studied his patient. "You've been on the monitors for a couple of hours. Things are as stable as they are likely to get. I don't like it, but I'm going to send you home. There's a new heart hospital an hour west of here. Dr. McBride arranged for your records and care to be transferred to that facility. The doctor there, Dr. Hamlin, wants to see you in his office at ten in the morning."

"I was supposed to have lunch with my son tomorrow."

The doctor's face hardened into a no nonsense

mask. "Make it dinner." He tapped the sheaf of EKG papers with his index finger. "I'm no more a heart doctor than I am a psychologist, but I don't like these readings at all. You promise me you'll keep that appointment, or I'll find a reason to admit you overnight. It won't be a difficult search."

Kate pushed the door open, holding the requested glass of water. She froze in the doorway. "You're admitting him?"

Alan spoke before the doctor could. "No, sweetheart. He was just saying that he could if I didn't feel like going home. Isn't that right, Dr. Richards?"

The doctor narrowed his eyes in Alan's direction. He reached for the chart at the foot of the bed, signed his name, and ripped the sheet free. "Take him home, Mrs. Archer."

Provisioned with six cups of coffee, two sodas, and a candy bar, Pam and Harrison turned from the counter.

The door to the ER swooshed opened, and Alan and Kate stepped through. Heads bent, hands clasped, their conversation whispered between them.

Pam stopped short, knees weak, heartbeat pounding in her ears. Her hands began to tremble, sloshing hot coffee over her fingers. Yesterday morning, she'd been ready to do battle, but now, face- to-face with her own private monster... *stupid, fat, worthless, frigid slob...* her courage fled. It was all she could do to stand on her two feet and breathe.

Harrison set the drink carrier on the counter and grabbed a handful of napkins from the dispenser. He took the cups from Pam and pressed the napkins into her shaking hands before turning to confront Alan.

"You just don't give up, do you? What are you doing here?"

Alan looked up. "What?"

"Here," Harrison repeated. "Here, where Pam is. How did you even know where to find us at this time of night? Have you been following us?"

"Excuse me?" Alan looked around. "Public place."

"Yeah," Harrison agreed. "It's a public place, just like church. I thought I made myself clear in my office earlier today. You need to leave Pam alone. That includes using *public places* as an avenue to try and see her."

"Oh, don't be stupid," Alan protested.

"You're one step away from a lawsuit, bud. You need to pay attention. Stay away from my wife."

Kate took a half step between the two men. "Stop it," she whispered. "Alan was having some chest pains earlier. We came to have him checked out." She raised his hand in hers and held it up where they could all see the hospital ID bracelet still encircling his wrist. "He's fine. Thanks for asking," she said with a tight smile. "We're going home now." Kate pulled Alan down the hallway, and the two disappeared around the corner.

Pam struggled to pull air into her lungs. *Stupid...stupid...stupid.* She sank into one of the seats that lined the hallway and bent over double.

Don't be stupid...

Time and place melted away, leaving her trapped in the moment of Alan's betrayal. "I need to go home."

"But, Terri—"

Pam shook her head. "Take me home."

Harrison didn't argue. He pulled out his phone. It

rang before he had the chance to enter a single number. He looked at the screen. "It's Benton."

"Yeah?" He took a couple of steps away while he listened. "No, we'll leave from here. We ran into Alan. Pam is pretty upset." He shook his head to a question only he could hear. "No, that's OK. If you'll ask Sam to bring Megan home, we'll be good to go. I'll talk to you later." Harrison closed the phone. "False labor..."

Her husband's words faded, lost in the pain of a wound ripped wide open. Pam huddled in the chair, her body wracked by silent sobs.

CHAPTER SIX

The aroma of her favorite chocolate raspberry coffee tickled Pam's nose and teased her eyes open. She stretched beneath the blankets and turned to look at the clock on the nightstand. *Eight thirty?* Her lazy stretch shifted into adrenaline-fueled overdrive. She'd overslept and would bet money that Megan and Jeremy were still in bed, too. She tossed back the covers, shoved her feet into slippers, and flew across the hall. Pam pulled up short in the doorway of Jeremy's room. The room was neat by her son's standards. The bed was made and bore no evidence of a hurried departure. The large glass terrarium, home to her son's four foot iguana, Spot, had fresh lettuce in the bowl. Whatever stomach issues he'd suffered yesterday seemed to be better now.

She peeked into Megan's room. Same story. Bed made, no lizard, but a large orange and white cat snoozed on the comforter in a shaft of sunlight. Reddy opened one eye then stretched her spine before turning over to ignore Pam and resume her nap.

Pam leaned against the wall as the adrenaline faded. Harrison must have gotten them all out the door without her help. Another day started in the negative column thanks to Alan Archer. The burden of the last few days settled across her shoulders like a heavy cloak. She got another whiff of raspberry and chocolate and straightened. The corners of her mouth lifted.

Smelled like he'd made her favorite coffee as well. *I so don't deserve that man.*

That man appeared at the bottom of the stairs and waved a mug in her direction.

Pam descended and accepted the steaming cup. "Why are you still home? It's after eight, and you have court at nine."

Harrison didn't answer. He kissed her forehead, put his arm around her shoulders, and steered her to the breakfast nook. Buttered English muffins waited on the table, served on her best china, flanked by the apricot preserves she preferred.

"Coffee and breakfast?" She slid onto the bench. "Did they cancel court this morning?"

Harrison slid in across from her and spread his muffin with his favorite boysenberry jelly. His voice was calm and measured when he answered. "I called the clerk and asked her to speak to the judge for me. He granted me an hour's continuance."

Pam laid her muffin aside and leaned against the high back of the bench. "You shouldn't have done that. Miles and his family are depending on you this week."

Two years ago, Miles Roberts had taken his car to the local branch of a nationwide chain of brake stores to have his car serviced. Coming home that night, his brakes failed. The resulting accident left Miles paralyzed from the neck down.

"Miles and his family will be fine." Her husband reached across the table and took her hand in his. "Some things are more important than work. You are at the top of that list for me." He rubbed his thumb across her knuckles. "Pam, I need you to help me understand what's happening. I thought we were happy."

Tears stung her eyes at his words. "You know we are."

"I don't know anything right now." She looked up and found herself eye to eye with his best the-truth-and-nothing-but lawyer's face.

"Do you still have feelings for Alan?"

Pam stared at her husband, cut to the quick by his question. *Is that what he thinks?* "How can you even ask a question like that?"

"Think about it, Pam. You fly into a rage every time you hear his name. One minute you're ready to wring his neck, the next you can barely function. When you saw him last night you melted into an emotional puddle at his feet. I'm a lawyer. I see clients sitting across from my desk every day who are dealing with that fine line between love and hate." He raised her hand and brushed a kiss across her knuckles. "I know what he did to you. I know what his betrayal cost you." He shook his head. "But I thought you'd moved past it. I need you to help me understand what's going on."

Pam focused on their hands clasped in the middle of the table. "Harrison, if my life depended on my ability to tell you how much I love you, they'd have to kill me. I love you more than I can say." Shaking free of his hand, she slid out of the seat and paced next to the table. "I just need some time to deal with everything right now. I obviously have no say in any of this. He can come back to Garfield to live, plant himself on a pew in the sanctuary at Valley View, and I'm just supposed to suck it up, put on a happy face, and go about my life. I'm really trying to pull my act together, but I've gotta tell you, my happy face is just about worn thin, and he hasn't been back in town a whole week." She picked up her cup and drank deep of the cooling coffee. The liquid in the cup rippled in concert with the tremors in her hands.

"I'm terrified and angry and confused." She looked up, praying he could see the love on her face above the rest. "You were my lifeline four years ago. I need you to be that again."

Harrison nodded at her empty seat. When she sat, he pushed his untouched breakfast aside and gathered both of her hands in his. "I love you, Pam. Have since the first moment you came into my office. I'd fix this for you if I could, but you're going to have to work through this on your own." His gaze went to his watch. "I've got to get to the courthouse. I want to pray with you before I leave."

Pam's eyes flooded again at the sheer sweetness of this man. She pressed her lips together and bowed her head. "Jesus," he began, "we need You in our home today. Help us find our peace and balance once more. Restore calm to Pam's heart and grant her the wisdom she needs to deal with the past. Father, I'm asking for Your will in court this week. Guide our words and our work for Your glory."

He squeezed her hands as he prepared to stand. "I

want you to stay home today and get some rest. This is an important week for our clients. They need you in the game tomorrow and so do I."

Alan buttoned his shirt and leaned back on the exam table on fisted hands. The phone in his pocket vibrated. He ignored it. He didn't care for the expression on Dr. Hamlin's face. The doctor's grim countenance told Alan that he was equally unimpressed with the test results he studied through narrowed eyes.

"Your echocardiogram shows a sharp increase in the deterioration of the heart muscle since the last one you had done eight weeks ago." He stopped and folded his arms across his chest. "After my phone consultation with Dr. McBride, I'm not surprised by that. What surprises me is the fact that you're not confined to bed by this point. You look good, and you're here under your own power. I'm not arguing with what my eyes tell me, but I can't explain it. Can you?"

Alan shook his head. "I feel pretty good actually. There have been a couple of small incidents in addition to the larger one last night. But, for the most part, if I use my head and pay attention to what I'm doing, I'm getting along all right." He straightened. "Doc, you believe in miracles?"

Dr. Hamlin lowered his chin and looked at Alan over his glasses. "Excuse me?"

"I can't explain the way I feel. But I know God has given me a couple of tasks to complete, and I think He's the one keeping me strong right now. He wants those things done, and I have to do them." Alan shrugged. "At least I hope that's what's going on. I need more time than you're ready to give me."

The doctor harrumphed, uncrossed his arms, and flipped to a new page on his patient's chart. "Chest pains, shortness of breath, palpitations?"

"All of the above," Alan answered. "And before you ask, yes, they are increasing in frequency. But like I said, if I stop what I'm doing and rest for a bit, I generally recover pretty quickly."

The doctor scribbled a few notes and folded the chart away. "A patient with a positive attitude will always fare better than one who gives up on the life they have left. I don't want to take any of that away from you, Mr. Archer, but these things will get worse in the coming weeks. I'm going to send a copy of your medical records and some instructions to the doctor who treated you in the ER last night. Living an hour away, you need someone local to manage your day-to-day care and the episodes that are coming. I want to see you again next week, sooner if you experience a marked increase in your symptoms."

Alan scooted off the table and tucked in his shirt. "I'll see you then."

The doctor shook Alan's hand and left the room. Alan took out his phone to check on the missed call. Jeremy's number flashed on the screen. *My boy!* Probably just verifying their dinner plans. Living closer already had its benefits. He thumbed over to his voice mail.

"Dad, um...I'm...sorta sick. Can we do dinner later?"

Alan stared at the phone. *Sorta sick?* He looked at his watch. Too early for the kids to be out of class, but he pressed the redial button anyway. His call went straight to voice mail. His shoulders slumped in disappointment. But it was still early. Maybe he could get Megan to take her brother's place.

Alan leaned a hip against the glass case of the department store cosmetic case.

Megan studied the selection of makeup.

"Anything I want, really?"

Alan nodded. "With the understanding that Mom has the final say. I'm not much of a fashionista."

Megan giggled.

"But I'll add to your collection of war paint if you promise not to pitch a fit if she says no."

His daughter pursed her lips and walked the length of the counter, her fingers trailing lightly along the glass. "She let me start with lipstick and mascara when I turned thirteen. I got blush and powder on my fourteenth birthday. It's really not that long 'til I'm fifteen."

Fifteen? He knew that. What he didn't know was where the time had gone. He'd been in Kansas City for four years. During that time, he'd taken advantage of every opportunity to fly the kids north to spend a week with him and a whole month in the summer. He studied the young woman his daughter had become when he wasn't looking. *I'm going to miss so much of your life. Who's going to intimidate your boyfriends? Who's going to hold your hand and walk you down the aisle on your wedding day? Who's...?*

"Dad?"

Alan shook his head and brought his thoughts back to the here and now. "Sorry, did you decide?"

"You all right?"

He hung an arm around her shoulders. "I'm fine, just overcome by your beauty. Now, what can we buy—that you really don't need—to make you even more beautiful?"

Megan snorted at his teasing. "Yeah, right." She pulled away slightly, her gaze intent on his face. "You know I'm not a baby, right?"

Alan motioned to the array of cosmetics spread out before them. "I'd say that message has been clearly delivered."

His daughter shook her head. "Daddy, I'm trying to be serious. You moved back home, you aren't working, haven't even mentioned the office, and you've lost a ton of weight." The crease deepened between her eyes. "Is everything OK?"

Alan reached up to brush aside her bangs and kissed the furrowed spot between her brows. "You really have grown up on me, haven't you?" He swallowed past the ache in the back of his throat "Don't worry about me. I've been on a special diet." She didn't need to know it was one designed to give his ailing heart the most time possible. "As for work, one of the benefits of being a business owner is taking a vacation whenever I want to spend some time with my favorite girl. You got a problem with that?"

Her brow smoothed. She tugged him over to an eye makeup display, worries apparently forgotten. "Mom and I have talked about liner and shadow, so if we stay neutral, she should be good with it."

Alan took a step back and watched Megan study eye liner pencils and little squares of colored powder. It reminded him of picking out crayons and water colors when she was five and on her way to kindergarten. He forced the memories aside, reluctant for her to catch him daydreaming again.

She held up her selections. "These should work."

Alan dug out his wallet and waited for their transaction to complete. The clerk handed the bag to his daughter and the credit card to him. He passed the card on to Megan. "Go pick out a bottle of perfume, and then we better get on to the restaurant. It's a school night."

Her smile was almost enough to lighten the weight on his chest.

Pam worked to put dinner on the table and tried to ignore the little niggle of resentment at Megan's unexpected absence. She really didn't have a problem with the kids spending extra time with their father, but Alan had been a part-time father for so long, the change was an adjustment. A disgusted snort echoed in the empty room as she pulled the salad from the fridge. Her hip bumped the door closed with more force than needed. The man was rearranging her entire life, and she had zero say about it.

Harrison came into the kitchen, lifted the lid on the simmering spaghetti sauce, and breathed deep. "How much longer? Arguing a case is hungry work, and I'm starving."

"The bread is almost done. You'll be eating in five minutes." She drained the pasta into a colander propped in the sink and then dumped the tangled mess back in the heavy pan to keep it warm. "How did it go today?"

Her husband picked a couple of cherry tomatoes out of the salad and popped them into his mouth. "I rested our portion of the case. The defense will start tomorrow morning. I don't expect them to surprise me, but just in case they have a curveball hidden in their briefcase, I'm going to need you at your computer in the morning."

She bristled at the reminder. "I know. I'll—"

Jeremy slid into the kitchen on stocking feet. "Is dinner about ready?"

Pam studied her son. "I thought your stomach was bothering you again. I was going to bring you some soup and crackers."

"Nope, all good. I'd rather have spaghetti."

She reached out to feel his forehead. He didn't feel hot. He didn't look sick. "Set another place."

The phone on the counter rang. Jeremy reached for it, but Pam batted his hands aside. "Plate," she reminded him as she plucked the phone from the charger. "Hello."

"Mom, can I spend the night with Dad and Kate?"

"What?"

"Dad and I are still shopping. We found the cutest jeans and sweater. We still have to eat, and I want to show the outfit to Kate. Please, please, pretty please? I promise they'll get me to school on time in the morning."

Pam leaned against the cabinet. "Homework?"

"They didn't assign any for tonight. Can I?"

Pam took a deep breath. Her inward *no*, transformed into an unwilling, "Yes."

"Thanks, Mom. I'll see you after school tomorrow. I can't wait to show you all the stuff we bought. Love you!"

The click of a disconnected call echoed in her ears. Pam crammed the handset back into its charger and returned to her dinner preparation. "Zero say."

"What's wrong?" Harrison asked.

"Nothing." She fought to cool the anger and slow her actions. Harrison didn't deserve to have it taken out on him. Pam put dinner on the table. "Megan's spending the night with Alan and Kate. Ya'll sit."

"Mom, are you OK?"

"I'm fine." She winced at her tone, forced a smile to her face, and prayed it reached her voice. "Let's eat while it's still hot."

Jeremy slid into the seat and bowed his head over his plate, his words barely audible. "I'm really sorry."

When Pam didn't acknowledge the boy, Harrison did. "About what, son?"

Jeremy lifted a shoulder. "I thought Dad moving back would be a good thing. Not so much, I guess."

Pam started to speak, but the words died in her throat when her eyes met Harrison's frown. He reached across the table and ruffled Jeremy's hair. "Look up here, son." He paused long enough for Jeremy to meet his gaze. "Is this what's bothering your stomach?"

Jeremy slid down in the seat. "I guess, a little." He faced Pam. "I didn't want to spend so much time with Dad if it was going to make you mad."

Harrison nodded. "That's what I thought." He held out his hand. "I'll make a deal with you. You focus on enjoying extra time with your dad. Your mom and I will work on the rest." He turned back to Pam. "Won't we?" His voice held a rare note of censure.

Pam looked from her husband to her son. *Zero Say.* She forced another smile for her son's benefit. "Absolutely."

CHAPTER SEVEN

Pam stood on the bottom step of the staircase and flinched as the front door slammed behind Harrison Wednesday morning. Angry words, his and hers, hung in the air, thick and tangible enough to be felt. The remnants of a rare argument. Well, rare until this week.

She fisted her hands on her hips and shouted at the closed door. "Yes, I know you have to be in court all day. Yes, I know you need me in the office this morning. And yes, there's research to be done for next week." Pam sat on the steps and pulled her robe around her legs. She rested her head on her knees and fisted both hands in her hair. "I do know that you love me. I love you, too." *Still worthless.* The hateful words echoed in her heart and made her cringe. "I think I'm losing my mind." Her eyes went back to the door. "How can he not understand what this is doing to me?"

Pam remembered yesterday's breakfast and her sense of fairness kicked in. *Of course he understands.* She lowered her head again. *I can't keep this up. Alan hasn't even been back in town a week, and he's wrecking my life, again.* "I knew this would happen."

No one remained in the house to hear her whispered lament. Thankfully, Jeremy had been long gone before the shouting match began and Megan...Had this morning's meltdown really been a result of her daughter's request to spend last night at Alan's? Pam pulled herself up using the polished oak banister. There wasn't an ounce of energy left in her body. She longed to pull the curtains tight and crawl back into bed.

The climb up the stairs felt like an Everest expedition. Sitting on the edge of the mattress, she watched dust motes float in the sunbeams filtering between the slats of the blinds. Sleep offered the simplest form of escape. But would another day of escape accomplish anything? Suddenly solitude lost its appeal. Too much time to think. Too much time to brood. Too much time to consider the hit man that had only been a half-hearted joke four days ago. She needed to work, needed her computer to keep her mind away from the dark memories she refused to confront.

Pam crossed the room and yanked a shirt and a pair of slacks from the closet. Going to work was an act of self-preservation. It had nothing to do with the fight. Harrison would be happy with her, and her mind would be occupied with the legal research she'd come to love. Her mind rambled off into fantasy land. *And if I happen to stumble across a good murder-for-hire site...*Well, at least they wouldn't be able to trace it back to the house.

Patrick worked the keyboard of his phone. Two

days, and he couldn't get the pretty little demolition driver out of his mind. He hoped Samantha was somewhere she could pick up her phone.

HUNGRY 4 PIZZA R U.

He hit send. The phone chimed with an answer before he could return it to his pocket.

PATRICK?

At least she remembered his name.

YEP. PIZZA?

DEPENDS.

Patrick grinned. He hadn't misjudged her. Beautiful with a quick sense of humor. He typed his response.

ON WHAT?

He laid the phone next to his computer and went back to his game. The boxes were unpacked, Mom and Dad were both out running errands, and on Monday, he'd be back in class. He planned to veg in front of a screen, computer or television, for the next four days. *Unless the fair Samantha rescues me.* The phone chimed again.

PEPPERONI OR HAMBURGER?

Patrick's reply was immediate.

WHICHEVER U LIKE?

Samantha responded just as quickly.

PERFECT ANSWER.

He signed out of the game and kicked his feet up to the corner of his desk.

CAN U TALK?

Samantha's quick answer.

CLASS OVER AT 3.

He sent a final quick message.

CALL U THEN.

Patrick laid the phone aside, and with a satisfied

smile on his face leaned back with his hands behind his head. Not too shabby. Less than a week in town, and he had a date with a fine-looking woman.

Alan scrunched down in his truck outside of the small diner thirty minutes east of Garfield. He'd been there long enough to see both Mitch and Benton arrive, but he hesitated to join them, needing some time to put his thoughts in order first.

Before he'd forced the implosion of his marriage to Pam, he'd enjoyed a comfortable relationship with many of the men in Valley View's congregation. Father-son campouts, ball games, fishing weekends, occasional hunting trips. All those things formed a solid core of casual friendships, except for Mitchell Black and Benton Stillman.

Because their wives were so close, Alan never considered it strange that the husbands should be as well. The three men found something to do together most weekends. One of them always had a project going that could be *helped* along by the loitering presence of two good friends. Pam often teased that the three men had one brain between them, split three ways. Incomplete until they joined forces. Alan lifted his shoulder in a shrug. Nothing wrong with that. They'd leaned on each other, worked with each other, depended on each other. Until the day Alan succumbed to what he could still only describe as a severe midlife crisis, when he renounced his faith, cheated on his wife, and deserted those friends.

He'd moved to a satellite office in Kansas City, six hours away from Garfield. Not so far that friendships needed to be sacrificed, but there'd been no contact between him and his friends in all the intervening years. Alan had insured that the break had been complete. Phone calls unanswered, e-mails unreturned, all offers of help ignored. Now he'd come back a changed man...a dying man. He took a deep breath as memories of those days assaulted him. *Jesus, I don't just need your help with Pam and my kids. I let so many good people down. Give me the words to start making things right.*

Alan climbed out of the truck and opened the door to the diner. Mitch and Benton had seats at a table in the back corner. They appeared to be watching the door, uncertainty wafting off of them in waves. Alan gathered his resolve and hurried forward.

Mitch stood and offered his hand. The lump of misgiving in Alan's gut melted away as years of kinsmanship bubbled to the surface. Dodging the hand, he went straight for the hug. He pulled Benton to his feet and made it a three way embrace, clapping both men on the back repeatedly.

With a hand on each of their shoulders, he took a step back. "Oh man, it's great to see you guys. I wanted to call the minute I got back to town, but I wasn't sure how you would react."

A hovering waitress curtailed further conversation. The three men took their seats and studied menus. Alan's mouth watered when Mitch and Benton ordered double cheeseburgers and fries. Kate had him on a strict low fat diet. The diet would kill him before his heart condition would. He swallowed. What Kate didn't know wouldn't hurt either of them.

He smiled up at the waitress. "Make it three."

She nodded, gum snapping, and departed for the kitchen. Her absence left an uncomfortable silence around the old, scarred table.

Alan leaned back in his seat. "Come on, you two. I know you have some tough questions for me, especially after Sunday. Fire away."

Mitch cleared his throat and took the invitation. "I think all the little questions can be rolled into one big one. What are you doing?"

Benton sat back and crossed his arms, his chair balanced precariously on two legs. "That works for me."

Alan traced absent designs into the moisture on the outside of his glass. When he looked up he hoped his expression reflected what was in his heart. "Would you believe me if I said that God told me to come back to Garfield?"

Benton rocked forward. "God told you to come home and drive Pam back over the edge?" He frowned at his old friend. "Do you have any inkling of the mess you left behind?"

"I wasn't here, but I have a pretty good idea. And before you ask, I didn't have any excuses then, and I don't have any now. I look back on what I did, and I have to be glad God forgave me, because I haven't been able to forgive myself." Alan peeled the paper off his straw.

"I've never understood how something so good could have gone so wrong. It was never about Pam or anything she did or didn't do, not really." He stopped and chewed on the end of the plastic tube. Memories of Pam's tears and his harsh, abusive words still gave him pause. "You guys have been married to the same women for half your lives. Didn't you ever...want more?"

When two stony stares met his question, Alan continued. "My business partners were both single. The business was booming. The money was good. It seemed like they were having such a great time every night while I went home to *the family*. I went out with them a couple of times. It was such a different environment. I thought it was what I wanted." Alan shrugged. "Abbreviated version. I asked Pam for a divorce, she refused, and I made it my mission to get her to agree. I wasn't real picky about the methods I used."

He propped an elbow on the table and leaned forward. "There's an old saying that cautions us to be careful about what we wish for. So true. I had what I wanted and I was miserable. All the time to party that I wanted and an empty house to come home to. My soul was even emptier, and I was pretty sure God would never forgive me, so I didn't ask. Then I met Kate. She wouldn't date me unless I attended church with her. Six months later, I rededicated my life to Christ. As soon as I got my relationship with God back on track, He began to speak to me about the unfinished business I'd left behind in Garfield, hurts that needed to be healed, and kids who needed more than a long-distance father." He stopped to take a long drink of his tea. "I didn't come back here easily. I argued with God for weeks before the decision was made."

"But to just show up, back in the life you left behind?" Mitch shook his head. "Alan, you can't come back after four years and act like you just stepped out for a soda."

Alan nodded. "I agree with you. I told God all of that, but He didn't want my excuses." Alan studied the men across from him. "You know those verses in Matthew where Jesus tells us that when we come to pray and we remember someone with a grudge against us, we need to go to that person and attempt to make it right so that God will hear our prayers?"

When both men nodded, Alan continued. "That's all I'm here to do. I know God has heard my prayer for forgiveness, but my past sins are always going to be there. God didn't say asking for forgiveness was going to be easy or even successful. He just told me to make the effort."

Alan tapped a finger on the outside of his glass. "If I never get the opportunity to talk to Pam, at least I'll get the chance to be with my kids a little while longer."

"Be with your kids a little while longer?" Mitch asked.

Alan rubbed his forehead with one hand. *Careful.* "I meant more time...quality time. I know it's hard to understand, but I really did come here with good intentions." He paused for another drink of his tea. "Either of you want to give me odds on getting close enough to Pam to have this conversation with her?"

Benton snorted. "I wish you luck with that. Based on what we've seen so far, you probably won't live that long."

Alan choked on his tea, and choked, and choked, and choked.

CHAPTER EIGHT

Patrick dialed Samantha's phone number at five minutes after three.

"Hello, Patrick."

He heard the smile in her voice.

"Samantha. I've been waiting to hear your voice all day."

"Oh, wow...correct answers to trick questions and extra points for flattery. You're good."

He laughed. "I try. So about that pizza. Friday night work for you?"

"Yes," Sam answered, "but..." Hesitation replaced the smile in her voice.

"Such a small word, such large implications."

This time it was Sam's turn to laugh. "But," silence filled his ear for a few seconds, "there's something I need to tell you, because if it's going to be a problem, we're both better off knowing from the start."

"You're a guy dressing up as a girl?"

Samantha continued to laugh. "No."

"Good, you had me worried for a second."

"Patrick, I'm trying to be serious."

"Me, too. That guy-in-a-dress thing would have been a serious turnoff for me."

Sam's deep breath echoed through the phone. "I have a little girl."

Wow. Patrick slumped in his chair. A kid? *Maybe this isn't such a great idea.* The memory of Samantha's smile forced his hand. "Is she as gorgeous as her mother?"

"Patrick..."

"How old is she?"

"Three next month."

"Does she like pizza?"

"Yeah, why?"

"Bring her along on Friday," Patrick suggested. "I'd love the chance to get to know both of you."

"Seriously?"

"Absolutely. My reputation will be forever secure when word gets around town that I had a date with two beautiful women at the same time."

"We'd like that." Samantha sounded relieved. "When I get home, I'll look up the address of the restaurant and send you a text."

"Great. Six o'clock?"

"Perfect."

"Can I call you tomorrow?"

"Even more perfect. Talk to you then."

Patrick disconnected the call and stared at the phone. *A kid?* That was an unexpected wrinkle. He mulled the thought, trying to decide if it made a difference to him or not. *Not* won. He still really wanted to get to know Samantha. If that meant two for one, then so be it. It was a pizza date. How much trouble could one little girl be?

Kate rushed through the emergency room doors. The presence of Alan's old friends registered in her peripheral vision, but she took no time to acknowledge them. She held a brief, whispered conversation with the nurse on duty and hurried through the swinging doors to the treatment rooms.

Time slowed to a crawl. Alan slept while the machinery recorded his every breath and heartbeat. Kate held his hand, prayed, and waited. *Jesus, please not yet. There's so much left undone.* The door opened and a white-coated doctor entered the small room. He held out a hand to Kate.

"Ms. Archer."

"Dr. Richards." Kate released his hand with a nod, her attention going back to Alan. "Is he going to be OK?"

"I've looked over the records from his primary physician and compared them to the test readings from the other night and an hour ago. There hasn't been any noticeable decline, but I'd like to keep him for a couple of hours to get some additional telemetry."

"Whatever you think is best."

Alan stirred and held out his hand.

Kate took it and pressed a kiss to his knuckles. "I'm here."

Her hand received a weak squeeze in return. "Sorry to scare you."

Tears threatened to fill Kate's eyes. He wasn't being truthful with her. A stray facial expression, a flash of intuition that niggled in her stomach each time he told her he was fine, a second trip to the hospital in a week.

He wanted to shield her, but there was no way he could. She pushed the tears aside. They wouldn't make the situation better for her, and they only made her husband feel worse. *I'll have plenty of time for tears later.* Kate released his hand and brushed sandy hair from his forehead. "Don't worry about me. How are you feeling?"

Alan shifted and released a groan. "Like I've been run over by a semi." He looked at the doctor. "I'm not usually sore after one of these spells. Something new to look forward to?"

The doctor folded the chart away and stuck it under his arm with a chuckle. "You don't usually have two friends standing by to administer CPR. They thought you were having a heart attack."

"I forgot all about Mitch and Benton." He frowned at the doctor. "You didn't tell them...?"

Dr. Richards shook his head. "Of course not, but they're still waiting to see how you're doing. If you want to see them, I'll authorize a short visit."

Alan nodded. "I'd like that. Thanks, Doc."

The doctor turned to go. "I'll let them know at the desk. I'll check back with you in a couple of hours."

Kate watched the door close and turned her attention back to her husband. *Too pale.* "Are you going to tell them?"

Alan coughed, and Kate helped him take a sip of water.

He put his hand over his breast bone. "I'm not sure which one of them pounded on my chest, but if I were stronger, I'd be tempted to return the favor." He looked at Kate. "Yes, I'm going to tell them. Not a lot of choice now. Would you go get them for me?"

Kate nodded, brushed a kiss across his lips, and hurried out to talk to Alan's friends. She stopped just out of sight of the men. Even from here she could read the concern on their faces. An unexpected surge of envy enveloped her. *Father, I'm so glad Alan has friends, but I could use one or two as well. A phone call to Kansas City just isn't the same as sitting down with real people for coffee and gossip. I don't think I can handle what's coming alone.* She pushed the self-pity aside. Just like her tears, there would be plenty of time for pity parties later.

The men were sitting with their heads bowed, hands clasped between their knees. They looked up at the sound of her footsteps on the tile floor. Mitch hurried to take her arm, leading her to the bank of chairs against the wall.

"How is he?" Mitch asked.

"OK for now."

"Can you tell us what's going on?" Benton asked gently.

Kate looked up at the ceiling and shook her head. "It's not my place to tell you," she answered. "He'd like to see both of you though. The doctor cleared a short visit."

Mitch tried again. "Kate...?"

Kate lifted a hand to stop him. "Please." She paused when her voice caught. "I know the three of you are old friends, and I appreciate your concern. Just go see him. If you still have questions when you're done, I'll answer the ones I can. He's in treatment room four."

Alan watched his two friends push through the door together, their steps to the bed accented by the beeps and pings of monitors recording his bodily functions.

Benton and Mitch took up positions on either side of the bed with grave expressions. *Jesus, give me words.*

Alan managed a smile. "I guess that was one too many greasy hamburgers." When his friends merely looked at him expectantly, he dropped the pretense, his explanation simple and direct. "I'm dying. I have a heart condition, hypertrophic cardiomyopathy. The game's in its final innings."

His friends shared a grim look across the bed. "This is why you came back now," Benton said. "Why didn't you just tell us?"

Alan looked around the room with a defeated chuckle. "I wanted to avoid this. All of the things I told you at lunch were true. There's just a little more urgency to the situation than I planned to share right now." *Understatement.* He pushed the thought aside.

"Well," Mitch began, "under the circumstances, I think you can expect that visit from Pam before the day is over..."

"Stop right there," Alan told him. "I brought you two in here for one reason. I want your word before you leave. My condition stays in this room."

"But..."

"No buts," Alan told them firmly. "I wanted a chance to visit with you. I've missed hanging out with the two of you, and Pam isn't the only person I came back to apologize to. I didn't intend to cough myself into a cardiac episode. I'm fine for now." He rubbed his chest. "Fine, except for some bruised ribs."

Benton raised his hands at the mention of the failed attempts at emergency aid. "Hey, I thought you were dying...I mean..."

Alan shook his head, continuing his explanation. "I

have an irregular heartbeat caused by the progressed stage of my illness. The choking spell was severe enough that it interrupted it further, but I'll be home this evening. They want a couple of hours on the monitor, but there's nothing they can do and no reason to keep me here." He read the hesitant expression on the faces of the other men. "Look, guys, I need to do this my way. The way I feel God is telling me to do it. Kate and her son Patrick, Pastor Gordon, and now you two are the only ones who know the truth about this. I have some time left." He coughed lightly to cover the lie. "I have to admit that two episodes in a week…"

"Monday night," Benton said.

"Yeah, two times this week gives me a little pause, but I need you to consider something." Alan stopped and shifted under the light blanket. He looked at Benton. "Crank this bed up a little bit, will you?" He was silent as the head of his bed raised slowly to a more comfortable position. "That's good. Thanks.

"Like I was saying, I want you both to consider something. It's not just about keeping this from my kids and my old friends. It's about giving Pam a chance to heal. I hurt her beyond anything either of you two can imagine. If she feels forced to forgive me out of a sense of guilt, there's always going to be a place in her heart hiding some bitterness. I know God brought me back here to do this. I have to trust that He's working things out in Pam's life as well as mine. If she can forgive me without knowing about my illness, it's better for everyone, even after I'm gone."

The men went silent for a few moments.

Mitch crossed his arms and stared down at his old friend. "Forgive me for being blunt, Alan, but what if you die tomorrow? How's she going to feel if she never makes it that far?"

Alan shifted under the sheet, Mitch's words just a little too close for comfort. "I've thought about that. I don't have a good answer. I have to trust that God isn't going to let that happen." He took a deep breath and battled weariness. He had to make them understand. "Can you give me two months? If I haven't managed to put things right by then, we'll revisit our arrangement."

"Two weeks," Mitch bartered.

"Six," Alan countered hopefully.

"Four, final offer." Benton's voice was firm. "One month, take it or leave it."

Alan watched the monitor that beeped with his heartbeat for a few seconds and finally nodded his head. "Four weeks then." He looked from Mitchell to Benton. "Can you keep it from Callie and Karla for that long?"

Benton drummed his fingers on the bedside rail and looked at Mitch. "If the girls ever find out about this, we'll be the ones in the hospital."

Mitch nodded his agreement. "Oh boy, you got that right."

Alan was quick to qualify his demands. "It's not that I think they'd blab to Pam. It's just that I *know* they love her too much not to tell her if the going gets tough."

"*If?*" Benton ran a hand down his beard. "Are vows of silence Biblical?"

Mitch raised an eyebrow in question.

"You know," Benton explained. "Like a forty day fast, only instead of giving up food we sacrifice talking to our wives. If it's a religious thing, they might go for it."

Alan laughed quietly and clutched his chest. "Please don't make me laugh."

Mitch shook his head with a pessimistic chuckle. "Nope, we're just going to have to be very careful and pray really hard that things work out in a hurry."

Benton looked at his watch. "Starting now. Callie will be wondering where I am, and right now, the fewer questions I have to answer, the better. I've never been so grateful for Wednesday night service in my life. Less opportunity to be grilled."

Mitch nodded. "I hear ya."

A nurse stuck her head in the room and directed a pointed look at the large clock over her patient's bed.

Alan nodded in acknowledgement. "Guys, they're gonna toss you out of here. Does this mean you'll keep my secret?"

Benton and Mitch nodded. "Fine," Benton told him. "But we need a promise from you as well. If your condition gets noticeably worse in the next four weeks, you'll tell us."

Alan nodded his agreement.

"Can we pray with you before we leave?" Mitch asked.

Alan felt tears blur his vision. He closed his eyes before they escaped. His response was barely a whisper. "I'd like that."

CHAPTER NINE

Pam resumed her pacing, desk to door and back. The office was small, and a complete circuit didn't take nearly long enough. Her work as Harrison's legal researcher was rarely stressful. It had certainly been a haven from her tumultuous thoughts today, but the wait this afternoon threatened to drive her crazy. Just as Harrison had predicted, their case had gone to the jury.

Harrison had dropped by the office at lunchtime, obviously surprised to find Pam at her desk. Cheerful despite their earlier argument, he'd been full of news from his morning in court. Testimony in the case had wrapped up more quickly than expected. The judge had promised to send the jury for deliberation right after lunch. Harrison had promised to call the minute the jury returned a verdict. Four hours was not unusual, but this should have been a slam-dunk case. This was taking too long. She went back to her desk and tried to focus on next week's research, but her heart and her mind just weren't in it. Two things vied for her attention. The situation with Alan and the resolution of this case. She chose the case out of self-defense.

Father, please. You know how important this is to Miles and his family. I can't say that all twelve people on the jury are Christians, but even if they aren't, You can still turn their hearts in the right direction. This case has become so personal for all of us.

Restless, Pam abandoned her computer a second time and got up to pace some more. She'd been working in Harrison's office as his researcher for almost three years. She couldn't remember ever being this nervous about a verdict. But then, few cases they'd dealt with were this important.

Since his paralyzing accident, Miles, a family man with five small children, could no longer support his family. They were dependent on only his wife's teaching salary to pay the bills.

The insurance company and the corporation toadies argued back and forth for months, finally arriving at the conclusion that, while unfortunate—we're so sorry for your problems—the technician followed policy and neither he nor the company was at fault.

Miles and his wife came to Harrison as a last resort, and Pam started digging. Cyberspace could be a marvelous tool or a dangerous weapon, depending on your level of honesty. Pam's computer skills had been honed by years of digging out the best for Harrison and his clients.

When Harrison rescued her from her attempted suicide after her divorce from Alan, part of his recovery plan included something new to focus her attention on. His legal researcher was leaving for greener pastures with a large firm in the state capital. Harrison offered the job to Pam. She didn't blink twice before she accepted.

She'd enrolled in some online paralegal courses to complement her existing computer skills and, with God's help and Harrison's encouragement, set about rewriting her future.

Pam loved her job almost as much as she loved her boss, and in Miles's case she'd managed to unearth enough lies and deceit in the brake company's past to fuel a healthy personal injury suit.

She continued to pray and pace. *Father, this is a Christian family. You know they need this money, You...* She turned when she heard a noise in the doorway. Harrison was leaning against the doorjamb, polishing his nails on his lapel.

"Harrison?"

Harrison stepped into her office with a broad smile. He grabbed her around the waist, giving her a twirl and a hearty kiss. "Call the kids and get them duded up. We're celebrating before church."

"You won the verdict?"

"Every single cent. It's not a fortune, but managed properly over time, Miles and his family will be comfortable for the foreseeable future."

Pam exhaled a relieved breath. "Have you shared our decision with them yet?"

Harrison leaned against Pam's desk. "Nope, I want it to be a surprise. I told them from the beginning that we'd discuss my fee after the verdict. I know they're expecting a settlement less the standard fee."

"That's one meeting I want to be present for," Pam told him. "When they sign those final papers and see you've waved your fee, it's going to seem like a lifetime of Christmases all wrapped up in one contract." She picked up her phone and punched in their home number. Her side of the conversation was brief when her daughter answered. "Megan, good clothes, thirty minutes, seafood." She hung up the phone. "That should get them moving."

Harrison grabbed Pam for another kiss. He held her eyes with his, jubilation marred by worry. "Feeling better?"

"Working on it," Pam assured him. "I've got a ways to go, but having a victory to celebrate makes it easier."

"You're going to church tonight?"

"No reason not to. I'm working in the gym."

"Pam, hiding in the gym isn't going to fix this."

Pam turned her gaze down. "I'm not hiding, Harrison. I'm working. If working keeps me on this side of sanity, that's got to be a good thing."

Harrison pulled her close. "Let's get out of here. I've got a date with my favorite girl and a basket of warm cheddar biscuits calling my name."

Relishing the security of his arms, Pam stood on her tiptoes and brushed her husband's lips with her own. "I think I hear that, too." She collected her bag and headed out the door.

A full moon lit the sidewalk from the car to the front door. A brisk fall wind swirled the dead leaves on the lawn and carried the scent of a neighbor's fireplace.

The rustling of the leaves reminded Alan that he needed to find a local lawn service before fall got too carried away. Caring for the lawn was a task he enjoyed, but he didn't see Kate allowing him the indulgence of even minor chores even if he promised her discretion.

Alan shrugged. The ups and downs of this disease kept him baffled. Weak as a kitten a few hours ago, his strength had bounced back with what he considered amazing speed. He was grateful. It gave him hope for the unfinished tasks ahead. He put his arm around Kate's waist as they walked, pulling the wood-scented air into his lungs. "Let's christen our fireplace this evening."

Kate snuggled closer. "I'd like that."

Alan stopped on the stoop and dug for his keys. "Oh, I forgot. Mitch took my keys so they could bring the truck home tomorrow."

Kate held up her key ring with a quick shake and unlocked the door.

"Where's Patrick?" Alan asked.

She dropped her keys into her purse and, just inside the door, dropped the purse on the tile floor. "He sent a text while you were sleeping. He joined a study group at the university the other day. They called to invite him to dinner. I knew we'd be late, so I told him to go." Kate stopped speaking, her brow wrinkled in a small frown.

Alan tilted her head up into the light filtering in from the kitchen. "What's wrong, babe?"

"Stress headache."

He leaned forward and kissed the furrowed spot between her eyes. "Go get ready for bed. I'll get the fire started. Shoulder massage, movie, and popcorn?"

"Just the thought makes me feel better. But are you sure you don't need to lie down? We can watch the movie in the bedroom."

"I know my limits. You've been taking care of me all

afternoon. Now it's my turn." He put a finger over her lips when she began to protest. "Scoot." Alan watched her go. Melancholy threatened to override his peace. They'd had so little time together, and she'd sacrificed so much to give him this opportunity. "I don't deserve you," he whispered to her back as the bedroom door closed.

Alan turned to the corner fireplace and began to lay the fire. Selecting appropriate logs from the recently filled basket, he stacked them just so and twisted old newspapers into thin ropes to stick between the logs. He held a lighter to the paper and watched in satisfaction as the fire caught and began to spread to the smaller pieces of wood. It wasn't long before the smell of burning wood mingled with the aroma of fresh popcorn.

Kate carried a huge bowl in from the kitchen. Alan snagged a handful as she moved to the sofa and tried not to frown at the taste of the low fat butter substitute she'd used in place of the butter he loved. He studied a selection of DVDs. "What's your pleasure?"

"Oh, I don't know. Something funny."

He held up two Tom Hanks' classics. "*The Money Pit* or *The Burbs?*"

Kate settled onto the sofa. "Burbs."

Alan fed the disk into the player and then took the bowl from his wife and set it on the side table. "Shoulder massage, remember? Assume the position."

Kate sat in the indicated space between his thighs and allowed her head to fall forward. She moaned as Alan's fingers dug into the knotted muscles of her neck.

"Too hard?"

"Oh, no. It's perfect."

Alan continued to rub. "Your neck muscles are as tight as ropes. We're gonna have to figure out a way to get you to relax more."

Kate's head slipped further forward as he kneaded. Her blonde hair was thick and luxurious against the creamy skin at the base of her head. He leaned forward to brush a kiss at the joint of her shoulder and neck, breathing in the fragrance of honey and almonds from her shampoo. The scent was uniquely hers. "I love you, Kate."

"I love you more."

He nibbled at the soft skin on her shoulder. The simple contact tightened his gut and filled him with longing. His heart condition and the medications he took prevented any real physical intimacy between them, but these moments were special.

Kate finally sat up and leaned against him. She settled their snack in her lap and fed Alan a handful of popcorn over her shoulder. "Do you think your friends will keep your secret?"

Alan rested his chin on Kate's shoulder. "I think so, at least for the four weeks we agreed on. Beyond that...hopefully there won't need to be a beyond that. Surely, God will open a door for me by then."

Kate was silent for a few moments. Her bowed head and quiet hands told Alan that she was using the time to organize her thoughts. She picked up the remote and paused the movie.

"Sweetheart, I don't want you to spend your energy fretting about this. You're trying to do the right thing. If Pam never gives you that chance, your conscience is clear."

Alan's mouth formed a thin line at her words. "I don't think my conscience can ever be clear where Pam is concerned. I've tried to be honest with you about the last year of our marriage. But for all my efforts at honesty, I don't think anyone can understand the monster I allowed myself to become." He closed his eyes against the memories his words invoked.

"There are some verses in the twelfth chapter of Matthew that describe my life during those months. I can't quote it, but it talks about a man who turns away from God's will and how the original evil in his life comes back into his heart looking for a home and finds a heart swept, clean, and *empty*. The evil moves back in and becomes seven times worse than it originally was. I allowed that, Kate. God never walked away from me. I did the walking, but my family paid the consequences."

Kate folded her arms over his. "I've never seen that side of you—"

"And you never will."

She squeezed his arms. "But you need to stop punishing yourself over something God forgave you for. And in the words of another Tom Hanks' classic, 'That's all I've got to say about that.'" Kate lifted the remote and resumed the movie. Their laughter joined and echoed through the room as Tom's fictional summer vacation unraveled on the screen.

CHAPTER TEN

Pam took the stack of papers off the printer and flipped through them. The research on the Erikson case had taken most of the morning, but the results in her hand were worth it. Harrison could present all this documentation as evidence in the case going to court next week. She tapped the pages on the edge of her desk to straighten them.

"Ouch!" She jerked her finger to her mouth, and then surveyed the narrow slice across the pad of her right index finger. Why did paper cuts always sting so badly? Blood welled from the cut as she watched. Harrison couldn't enter these documents as evidence if she bled all over them. Pam grabbed a tissue, wrapped it around the cut, and headed for the reception area. Stephanie kept a box of band aids in the top drawer of the filing cabinet next to her desk.

There were no clients in the waiting room, and Stephanie wasn't at her desk. Pam looked at the clock. Almost noon. She shrugged. Harrison must have sent her on an errand, or she'd popped out for an early lunch. She rummaged in the drawer and found the box of bandages and a small tube of antibiotic cream. Finger bandaged, she restacked the papers and headed back to Harrison's office. A muffled female giggle slid from under her husband's door and momentarily froze Pam in her tracks. *What?*

Pam continued through the door without knocking. A groan rose in her throat. The blood drained from her head and left her groping for the doorframe in a sudden wave of dizziness. The carefully ordered papers in her hand slipped to the floor at the sight of Stephanie draped over the back of Harrison's chair, her mouth hovering a breath away from her husband's ear, the image of a cruise ship blazing from the screen. Two pair of eyes looked up at her intrusion. Pam read surprise and guilt on both faces. Turning away without a word, she fled to her office.

"Pam!"

She ignored Harrison's call. Shocked adrenalin tingled through her veins. She had to get her purse, had to get out of here now. *I won't go through this a second time.* Pam grabbed her bag and turned to leave, only to find Harrison filling her door, blocking her only means of escape.

"Move," she ordered.

"I will not. What's wrong with you?"

Pam swallowed, battling back the words that gushed from four-year-old wounds laid bare by a second betrayal. *Stupid, fat, worthless, frigid slob. You're just never going to be woman enough for me.* Not again. She straightened and narrowed her eyes at her husband. "How could you?"

Confusion etched itself on Harrison's face. It was almost sincere enough to be believed. *Almost.*

"How could I what?"

Pam ignored his question. "Move," she repeated. "I'll get out of your way so you can return to your little *liaison* with Stephanie." Despite her best effort her voice broke. "Harrison..."

Harrison straightened and ran both hands through his hair, dragging them down the length of his face. "Why would you think...?"

"I don't think. I know. I know what I saw. She was practically in your lap, for mercy sake. Well, I've got the souvenir mug from that excursion, thank you very much. It's not a boat I plan to sail on twice. Now get out of my way."

"Ship."

"Whatever, now move."

Her husband shook his head and approached her slowly, backing her up with each step. When the backs of her knees bumped into her chair, Pam was forced to sit. If she hadn't been so hurt and angry, she might have taken a minute to wonder at the hurt and anger she saw on Harrison's face.

Harrison put his hands on the arm rests of her chair and leaned in. His voice was a barely controlled whisper. "Is that what you think?"

"It's what I saw."

Harrison lifted a shoulder. "What can I say? You caught us red-handed. We were looking at cruises. Planning a romantic getaway."

His words sliced Pam's heart open. There were no words left to speak. No longer bothering to control the tears she struggled to get up.

Harrison leaned in closer. "For you and me."

Pam's struggle ceased.

"For us," he repeated. "I thought you might like to get away for a few days. Now that we have the Roberts' case behind us, I can take some time. I asked Stephanie to help me look at destinations, because I wanted a woman's opinion before I booked anything." His blue eyes studied her face. Pam couldn't read what she saw there.

Her husband continued, his voice ragged. "Have I ever given you a reason to distrust me?"

Pam couldn't speak but managed a small shake of her head.

"Have I ever done anything to hurt you?"

Pam bit her lip and sniffed. "No."

Harrison stood and pulled Pam to her feet. He wrapped her in his arms, and she felt his body trembling with controlled fury. "I love you." Tender words delivered with a harsh force she'd never heard before. His mouth came to her ear. "I. Am. Not. Alan." His voice shook as he delivered each word with individual emphasis. He released her and strode from the room. The door slammed behind him, the sharp noise echoing with her husband's anger and hurt.

Pam sank back into her chair, lowered her head to her desk, and wept.

Alan opened the front door Thursday afternoon. Benton and Mitchell stood on the stoop. In a fairly decent Sean Connery impersonation, Benton mumbled a single word under his breath. "Beachcomber."

"What?"

"Every   clandestine   meeting   needs   a   good password," Benton answered. "Especially the second one in two days." He shook his head. "We're going to be in so much trouble if our wives ever get wind of this—"

Mitch elbowed his bearded friend. "How old are you?" Turning his attention back to Alan, he held up a set of keys. "We brought your truck home, safe and sound."

Alan craned his head and saw his pickup sitting in his drive. He motioned his friends into the house. "Thanks. Do you have time to sit?"

"A minute or two," Benton told him. "We told the crew we were going to lunch. We have to be back in thirty minutes or so."

"We've got plenty of sandwich stuff and chips. If I feed you, can you stay longer?"

Mitch and Benton looked at each other and shrugged. "Sure," Mitch answered.

Alan led the way to the kitchen. "Everything go all right last night? No third degrees from Karla or Callie?" He stacked lunchmeat, cheese, and bread on the table. "You guys help yourselves."

Benton selected ham and roast beef, piled slices on top of the bread, and squirted the lot with mustard. "Well, it's not like our wives are going to just guess, out of the blue, that we're spending time with the enemy. But I made it a point to fall asleep in my recliner right after church. Callie's worried about Pam. The subject is never far from her conversation."

Mitch took a bite of his own multilayered creation and nodded. He chased the sandwich with the iced tea Alan sat in front of him. "Same here," he confirmed. "It's tough, having the solution to the problem and

111

being sworn to secrecy. You need to get a move on."

Alan chuckled. "According to my calendar, I've still got twenty-seven days before our agreement reaches term."

The men across the table grunted. Mitch laid his half-eaten sandwich on a paper towel. "After Karla went to bed last night, I looked this hypertrophic cardio whatchamacallit up on the Internet. Did you know there's an association for this disease?"

Alan nodded.

"Anyway, they don't paint a pretty picture. How long do you think you've had this thing?"

"Mitch." Benton laid his own sandwich down.

"No, it's fine," Alan told them. "I don't mind talking about it. But I don't have a good answer for that question. Why?"

"Well, after I read about all the symptoms, I got to remembering some things. All the times over the years we gave you a hard time for being too *tired* to participate in some activity or another. We teased you, a lot, about being a hypochondriac. I wanted to apologize."

Benton sank down in his seat. "The ball game."

Alan searched his memory and came up empty. "What?"

"A few years ago, one of the church softball games. Your team was losing and you bowed out after the fourth inning. Claimed you were dizzy. I just thought you wanted out of the game because we were wiping the field with you. I remember offering to call you a *whambulence*." He scrubbed at his face. "Man, I'm sorry. Isn't there a Bible verse somewhere about idle words? If ever there was an argument in favor of keeping your mouth shut, this is it."

Pam spent the rest of the afternoon in her office, grateful that hers was the last one on the hall. She kept her door closed and her computer busy, only sneaking out a time or two to go to the restroom across the hall. She'd open the door to her office a crack, peer out, rush across the hall, repeat the process in reverse.

She knocked her fisted hand against her temple. *How could I have been so stupid?* The question remained unanswered after a dozen askings. The outlook for an answer didn't appear promising.

Her hands stilled on the keyboard, her humorless chuckle the only sound in the small room. A cruise? They'd talked about it. She'd been a time or two, but Harrison hadn't. Stephanie had, just recently. Her experience was what had initiated the conversation between Pam and her husband. Which only re-enforced Harrison's wisdom in asking Stephanie for advice. *How could I have been so stupid?* No answer was forthcoming.

She wanted to blame her conclusion jumping on Alan. Several hours had gone into that endeavor only to come up empty. Yes, Alan had hurt her, but Harrison never had. There were many sins she could lay at Alan's feet. This wasn't one of them.

If Stephanie quit over this, Pam would never live it down. She needed to apologize. A glance at the clock showed her that it was almost five. She bowed her head. First things first.

"Father, I'm so sorry. I've been chasing myself in circles for almost a week now. I haven't talked to You about this nearly as much as I should." Her whispered prayer died away as she gathered her thoughts. "I don't know what to do. This thing with Alan is so much bigger than I am." She stopped again, realizing she was on the verge of another *Alan tangent*. "I'm sorry for how I acted and the things I said. Please help me make this right."

She cracked open her door and listened. No sound filtered up the hall from the waiting room. From her vantage point, she could see Harrison's door, firmly shut. Pam took a deep breath and forced herself into the hallway.

Stephanie looked up at her approach. Her eyes went back to her computer, a blush stained her cheeks.

She didn't look up as Pam stopped at her desk. Pam sent another prayer heavenward. *Jesus, give me words.*

"Stephanie, I'm so very sorry."

The secretary's head remained bowed. A tear splattered on the desk. "Pam, you know I'd never...I mean, Harrison...he was only..." She finally looked up and stared at Pam through tear-glazed eyes. "He'd never do anything like that. I've never seen a guy so much in love with his wife as he is with you. He only wanted to surprise you."

Pam swallowed hard. "I know that. It's been a difficult week, and I let it get to me. Can you ever forgive me?"

Stephanie nodded. "I couldn't work here if you thought...I'd quit first."

Pam laughed through her tears. "If you quit over my stupidity, Harrison will never let me live it down." She rounded the desk and held out her arms to the younger woman. "Are we good?"

Stephanie stood to return the hug with a laugh.

"Good over what?"

Pam released her. "I just hope I can make Harrison forget as easily as you." She looked at the closed door of her husband's office. "Is he alone?" At Stephanie's nod Pam turned to that task, her feet almost dragging as she approached the door of his private space.

She entered without knocking. Crossed the space without speaking. Pam rounded his desk, scooted his wheeled chair away from his desk, and crawled into her husband's lap. Strong, welcoming arms wrapped around her. She'd rehearsed her apology for hours, but she didn't need to say the words. Harrison knew. They held each other for a time. She finally shifted to look up into his face. Their lips met in silent forgiveness. Pam snuggled against Harrison's chest, grateful for the calm he offered in her personal storm. Unfortunately, dark clouds still loomed on her horizon.

CHAPTER ELEVEN

Patrick sat in the shadowed Pizza Shack parking lot Friday night, waiting for Samantha and her daughter. They weren't late; he was early. Tonight's dinner would not be "the best pizza in town" that Samantha—*Sam*, he reminded himself—had originally suggested, but something more accessible and kid-friendly. Pizza plus two solid hours in Sam's company. *I can deal with that.* The black mustang turned into the parking lot. Sam must have spotted his truck. She waved from the driver's side window.

He slid from the truck, watching as Sam got out of her car and leaned back through the open door into the backseat. She straightened and reached a hand back into the car. A miniature replica of his date scrambled from the backseat and stood next to her mother. Samantha bent down and brushed wrinkles away from their matching dresses.

Patrick stopped a couple of feet away. He grabbed his chest with one hand and took a staggering step backwards. "Wow!"

Samantha laughed while Patrick walked around them in a wide circle and whistled in appreciation. He came to a stop in front of them and nodded. "I *am* a lucky man."

"Lucky? Have you ever shared a pizza with a three-year-old?"

"Not that I can remember. But how bad can it be?" He stooped down to the child's level. "You gonna introduce me?"

Sam swung the toddler's hand in hers. "Patrick, this is my daughter, Bobbie."

Patrick held out his hand. "Hey there, Bobbie." He looked up at Sam, a little startled when Bobbie held out a tiny hand in response to his. He shook it gently.

Sam looked down at him, her nose wrinkled in amusement. "We shake hands a lot at church."

He poked the toddler in the stomach. "Polite and beautiful. My kind of woman."

Bobbie giggled in response, shook her hand free of her mother, and held out her arms.

"She's a flirt," Sam warned him. "She got her arms around her first man when she was four months old. She's been hooked on the male of the species ever since."

Patrick straightened with Bobbie in his arms and offered his free hand to Samantha. "I can only hope her mother is as easily impressed. Let's go eat."

The host led them to a table in the corner of the crowded restaurant. Patrick watched intently as Sam secured a high chair, reclaimed her daughter, and grabbed a handful of crackers from the salad bar. She strapped Bobbie in the chair, unwrapped a couple of crackers, and handed her a cup of something red with a weird looking lid. Finally, she took her own place in the booth opposite Patrick.

"That should hold her for a while so we can visit."

Patrick gave the waitress their order and then watched Bobbie as she crushed the crackers and swiped the crumbs gleefully to the floor. She demonstrated the purpose of the odd lid on her cup when she upended the drink and shook it like a tambourine. What would have been an unfortunate deluge came out as a miserly trickle, sprinkling juice on the few crackers left on the table. The toddler mushed the soggy pieces between her fingers, completely entertained.

"I was going to ask if you were worried about the crackers ruining her dinner. I can see that's not going to be an issue."

"You really haven't spent any time around a small child, have you?"

"Practically none."

Sam reached out to save the cup from tumbling to the floor. "Lesson number one," she began sagely. "Little guys don't eat their food, they absorb it through their skin. Hands, faces, top of the head, these are all favored locations. Belly buttons will work if they can be reached. And if I didn't have her tied to the chair, she wouldn't hesitate to use her knees. Eating is not just a time for nourishment. It's an opportunity to explore the world. But, you're lucky on two fronts."

Patrick laughed at her explanation. "How's that?"

"Her table manners are improving as she gets closer to her third birthday and pizza is a personal favorite of hers. If you pay attention, you might actually see a bite or two make it to her mouth."

"All right!" Patrick held out his hand to Bobbie. "Give me five."

Bobbie grinned, slapped his hand in response, and held out a sodden piece of cracker. It was tinged pink from the contents of her cup.

"She's offering to share with you," Sam said.

He looked from the soggy cracker clutched in the little hand and back to Sam, unsure how to respond.

Sam laughed at his obvious discomfort. "Lesson two." She plucked a napkin from the table top dispenser and held it out. Bobbie dropped her offering into it. Sam enfolded the crumbs, brought the napkin to her mouth, and pretended to eat. "Mmm, that's good, baby. Thank you." She slid the napkin to the back of the table. "I have seen some mothers actually eat these offerings, but I can't bring myself to go there."

Patrick shuddered, nodding to the pizza that had just been delivered to their table. "I'll stick with this, thanks."

"Absolutely."

Patrick separated two pieces, laid them on separate plates, and slid them across the table to Sam. He brought his piece straight to his mouth, and fumbled it when Sam bowed her head to offer a blessing.

He put his slice down, struggling with a scalded mouth and stringy cheese, and mumbled, "Sorry."

When Sam looked up he repeated his apology. "Sorry. Mom and Dad always say grace at home, but I don't think about it when I'm out by myself."

"That's OK. I haven't been a Christian for very long, and sometimes I forget, too." She smiled at Bobbie. "I'm trying hard to set a good example for her."

Great. Patrick chewed a bite of his pizza, his eyes fixed on his plate. *I should have guessed...Bible belt, small town, a church girl.* He raised his eyes and watched while Sam fussed with her daughter. *A church girl.* Maybe... "Can I ask you a question?"

Samantha cut the second slice of the pizza into pieces to cool for Bobbie. "Sure."

"You really believe all that stuff?"

Sam's head cocked in a curious angle, her tone uncertain. "Stuff...?"

"All that church stuff," he clarified. "Look, I know we're just getting to know each other. This is probably a weird topic for a first date, but I'd like to hear what you have to say. No parents, teachers, or preachers around. Do you really believe what they say?"

Sam returned his intent stare. "Seriously?"

Patrick nodded.

"OK." She paused for a few seconds. "I need to remind you that I haven't been saved for all that long. I still have a lot to learn, but yes, I believe. Not just what they say, but what I've experienced for myself. Our pastor preaches wonderful sermons, but he encourages us to study the Bible for ourselves. I'm constantly amazed by the truths I find in its pages."

"So you think being *saved* makes a difference?"

Sam sat back with a frown. "I don't think I understand what you're asking?"

"The whole being saved thing." Patrick pulled a second piece of pizza from the pan, the cooling cheese trailed rubbery strings from the pan to his plate. He broke them with his fingers and leaned forward. "I'm saying this all wrong. Look, my mom took me to church every Sunday when I was a kid. I could count the services I missed on both hands and have fingers left over. I know it's wrong to lie, cheat, steal, and kill. I don't curse, or drink, or do drugs." Patrick lifted his hands. "I don't intend to start. If I had to describe myself, I'd say I'm a good guy. I don't need to go to church or read my Bible or get *saved* to continue being a good guy." He shrugged. "It's a little frustrating."

"Being a good guy?"

"Being a good guy and not getting any credit for it." He took a couple of bites of his pizza and chased it down with his soda. "Now that I'm old enough to make my own choices, Mom's always after me to go to church with her. I need to get saved. I was raised better than this." He lifted his hands in appeal. "What am I doing wrong? I'm not an atheist or anything. I believe in God. I'm just not sure I buy into the whole *God is watching over us* thing. If He's watching, He's got his hands full without worrying about someone who's doing OK."

Patrick wiped his mouth and balled up his napkin. "Preachers are always talking about how getting saved will change your life. I can't think of a single thing in my life that needs to be changed." Patrick shook his head. "Frustrating."

"What about the next life?" Sam asked him. "Sometimes I think it's not so much about living here as it is about getting ready to live there. Do you know how blessed you were to have someone take you to church? I didn't go to church much when I was growing up. I never really heard about a Jesus who cared about me 'til I moved here. But when I did hear, I realized how much He loved me. I saw that He'd been watching out for me and my sister through some really difficult times. My relationship with Him is one of the most important things in my life. I want my daughter to have that as she grows up."

"You make it sound simple."

"I think it's simple and hard at the same time." Sam raised her hands in a slight shrug. "Simple, because all you have to do is ask. What makes it hard is the fact that, until you do ask, you'll never understand how much you needed to ask."

"At the risk of proving your point, I still don't get it."

Samantha smiled. "I'll pray that you do. You could come to church with us sometime. We have a terrific youth pastor. I'd love to introduce you to him."

Patrick smirked. "We'll see." His insides slumped. He really liked this girl, and the kid was a cutie, but he didn't need another person in his life badgering him about church. But just in case... "If you really believe in all that and you're gonna pray for someone, make it my dad. He's pretty sick. He needs God's attention more than I do."

Samantha smiled. "I'll pray for both of you."

Patrick nodded and apologized again. "Sorry."

"For?"

"Venting all over you. It's a sore subject right now. Since we moved, Mom's upped her campaign to get me to visit their new church."

Sam sipped her soda. "I don't want you to feel ganged up on, but I'll repeat my invitation. I think you'd enjoy our church."

Patrick shrugged and allowed the subject to drop. He eyed the final slice of pizza. "You want to split that?"

Sam sat back and rested her hand lightly on her stomach. "Go ahead. I think we've had plenty."

He picked up the last piece and looked at Bobbie. The kid's face and arms were colored a bright orange from liberally applied pizza sauce. "You weren't joking about that absorption thing. How did she get so much sauce out of the few bites you gave her?"

"It's a gift." Sam pulled a package of wet wipes from her bag and began cleaning the worst of the smears while the conversation transitioned into more normal first-date topics.

"Did you get into trouble about the car?"

Sam shook her head. "Seriously? Dad barely looked at it. I took it to the body shop. The bumper is scratched, not cracked. We get a few days out of class at Thanksgiving. I'll get it touched up then." She grinned. "Dad's so preoccupied with my one-year-old brother and the new baby on the way, I could probably get away with wrecking *his* car this month."

"You mentioned being on the way to your mom's baby shower the other day. You already have a baby brother?"

Sam nodded.

"Wow."

"Wow?"

"It's...odd, I guess, to see a couple starting over when they're so close to freedom."

Sam nibbled her last bite of pizza in silence for a few moments, a faraway look on her face. "Our mom died a few years ago. Dad and Terri have only been married a couple of years, so this is round one for Terri, but Dad's having as much fun with the babies as she is though. It's sort of a long story. I'm just glad God gave Iris and me someone we could love as much as our real mom."

Patrick studied his date. "I know what you mean. I feel the same way about my dad." He shook off the automatic sadness and changed the subject before Sam could ask any questions. "So, what are you studying?"

"Some general business courses and required subjects for now. I haven't decided on a specific career path just yet."

"No preferences?"

"Not really. I'm good with numbers. That could evolve into lots of choices. Mom was a foster parent for a little while. That's something else I'm interested in. There are so many kids out there who need someone to take a stand for them, so social work is a definite option. I'm praying about it. God blessed me with a full four-year scholarship. I figure He had his reasons. I'm trying to find His direction."

Patrick nodded. "Sometimes it's hard to choose. How's the university as a whole? I enrolled last Monday. I know what the brochures have to say, but from someone who goes there..."

"I think you'll like it. The professors I've had so far have been pretty easy to work with. What are you taking?"

"Prelaw. Mom says I'm a natural born lawyer. Arguing is my favorite sport."

With the pizza mess cleared away, Samantha did a final cleanup on Bobbie's hands and face before they walked to the front. Patrick paid the bill, held the door for Sam and Bobbie, and followed them to the Mustang. He opened the car and stood back while Sam buckled Bobbie into her car seat.

When Sam straightened, he met her gaze. "I enjoyed tonight," he said.

"So did I."

"Can we do it again?"

Sam grinned up at him. "I'd like that."

Patrick leaned down and brushed her cheek with his lips. "I'll call you."

Bobbie waved from the backseat and blew him a kiss.

He grinned. *Oh, you are a little flirt.* He wiggled his fingers at the toddler and waited on the sidewalk while Sam started the car and backed out of the parking spot. She lifted her hand in farewell and pulled out into traffic. Patrick watched until her taillights vanished around a corner. He rocked on his toes a time or two, stuck his hands in his pockets, and whistled all the way back to his truck, wondering how soon was too soon to make that call.

CHAPTER TWELVE

Pam sat in the stillness of her sun-dappled kitchen on Saturday afternoon. Megan and Jeremy were spending the weekend with Alan, again. Harrison was taking advantage of the mild November weather for a final golf game before he retired his clubs for the year.

She leaned against the wall, legs stretched out along the length of the bench-style seat. Bare feet crossed at her ankles, a cup of fresh coffee at hand, she studied her Sunday school lesson for the next day. The topic was forgiveness and the Scriptures taken from Matthew 18:21-35.

Pam smiled. These were the kinds of lessons she enjoyed sharing with her class of fifth graders. Old familiar stories, teaching timeless lessons. The story was simple and easy to understand. The tale of a servant who was forgiven much and later refused to forgive little. She reached for her cup and her hand stilled as she read the last three verses.

"Shouldest not thou also have had compassion on thy fellow

servant, even as I had pity on thee? And his lord was wroth, and delivered him to the tormentors, till he should pay all that was due unto him. So likewise shall my heavenly Father do also unto you, if ye from your hearts forgive not everyone his brother their trespasses."

Tears welled in Pam's eyes, and she forced herself to read the verses again. She read them through a third time. She stared at the page, words blurred by tears that fell, unheeded, to dot the thin pages of her Bible.

Jesus, I'm not dumb. I know what you're trying to tell me. I know what I should do. I just don't know if I'm strong enough to do it. I don't know how to dig far enough under the hurt to find the forgiveness. How can I forgive him, face him, after everything he did? I can't. I've lived so long with indifference where Alan is concerned. I thought that came from You. A way to get past the hurt. I was happy there. I could function there. Please help me find my way back there.

Pam blinked and forced herself to read the verses a fourth time. *I can't do it, Father. I know all the reasons why I should, but I can't. Indifference is the best I can do. Forgive me...* Her request dwindled off. She waged an internal war between what she knew and what she felt. *Jesus, how can I even pretend to share this lesson with my class when I can't follow it for myself? I won't be guilty of hypocrisy as well as un-forgiveness.*

Karla was her alternate. Maybe she could teach this lesson tomorrow. Pam dialed her friend's number with fingers that trembled. *I'll tell her I'm not feeling well. That's no lie.* How much longer could she dump these emotions on her friends without offering them some sort of explanation?

"Can we do Orlando this summer?"

Alan looked at his daughter. "Where'd that come from?"

Megan shrugged. "I just thought, since you're closer now, we could do a real vacation this year."

Jeremy sprinkled pepper into his tomato soup and nodded. "For once I agree with prissy pants. Mom and H have not upheld the vacation tradition. Seems like he's always got a case in court. Now that you're back, I think we should get back to it. Rick—"

Megan frowned at her brother. "Patrick."

Jeremy shook his head at his sister. "You're prissy pants, Harrison is 'H,' and until I can come up with a more annoying nickname, he's Rick. You need to work with me on this one, PP. As the younger siblings, it's our duty to climb under his skin at every opportunity." He refocused his attention on Alan. "As I was saying, Rick could come with us. We'd have a great time."

Alan stirred his soup. *Plans for next summer. Will I have a next summer?* He accepted a grilled cheese sandwich from Kate and looked over the heads of his children and into her green eyes. The corners of her mouth lifted in a sad smile. She retreated to the stove without a word.

Jeremy continued the conversation, oblivious. "Kate, do you think Rick would come?"

Kate took a seat at the table with her own lunch. "I don't know. You'll have to talk to him about that."

"I bet he would." Megan swallowed a bite of her sandwich. "I loved our summer vacations. Mom has pictures somewhere. We snorkeled in Hawaii, parasailed in Cozumel, rode the mules down to the bottom of the Grand Canyon."

"Yeah," Jeremy added. "After you stopped crying."

He jerked his head in Megan's direction. "She took one look down from the rim of the canyon and decided she'd wait in the car."

"Did not."

"Dad?"

Alan smiled at the memory. "Sorry, sweetheart. You did. But once you got acquainted with your mount for the day, you got over it."

Jeremy snorted. "Mount? A horse is a mount. These were long-eared, long-faced, bad-tempered mules."

Megan tore off a bite of her sandwich. "Self-portrait, dork face?"

Kate sat back and laughed at the two youngsters. "Are you two ever nice to each other?"

Megan made a face. "Ewww..."

"Nope," Jeremy answered. "It goes against the sibling rules of conduct."

"So, Dad. What do you think?" Megan rested her elbow on the table and her chin on her fist. "We used to have so much fun on those trips."

Jesus, how do I answer her question? He was saved the necessity when Jeremy doubled over in his chair, arms wrapped around his middle.

"Jeremy?"

Laughter came from the hunched over teenager. "I'm fine." He sat up. "I just remembered the surfing incident."

Megan's giggles joined her brother's. "Oh, oh, tell Kate."

Alan narrowed his eyes at his son. "You don't have to."

"Oh, Dad, I really do." He looked at Kate. "We were in Hawaii. I was nine, I think. Dad decided we should learn to surf."

"Mom thought he was crazy," Megan filled in.

Jeremy shook his head. "Let's see, how did she put it? 'What are two landlocked Okies going to do with surfing lessons?'

Anyway, Dad wanted to go, so he signed the two of us up for lessons on our last day on the island." He swigged his can of soda. "The instructors fixed us up with boards and stuff. Showed us how to lie on our bellies and paddle out to the waves. Then how to stand up without losing our balance once we got out in the water. Out to the beach we marched, surfboards tucked under our arms. Mom and Megan followed us with the cameras and stretched out on beach towels while Dad and I headed for the waves. We actually did pretty well at first. We both made it to our feet on some small waves. It really is easier than it looks. Then Dad decided to start fooling around."

Alan pretended to be indignant. "I was not *fooling around*. I was polishing my style."

"Yeah." Jeremy snickered and looked at Kate. "His *style* happened to include taking on a six-foot wave and losing."

Alan grimaced at his son's story. He remembered the sick nausea that had sent him off the board. *Was I already sick?*

Jeremy continued. "Best backward flip I ever saw, right off the tail end of the board. I could see him from where I was. I knew he was all right, but Mom and PP here, they were on their feet in the sand, hollerin' and trying to get the lifeguard's attention. Dad survived the wave, but Mom almost killed him when we got back to the beach." Jeremy finished his story and pushed his half- eaten lunch to the side as his laughter faded. "That was our last vacation." His expression shifted from amusement to anger.

Alan met the belligerent stare of the fifteen-year-old. "Jeremy?"

"What happened, Dad?"

Alan sat back. "Just lost my balance, I guess."

"Not with the surfing." Jeremy crossed his arms, his expression hard. "With us. With you and Mom. Why'd you have to mess it all up?"

"Jeremy." Megan hissed.

Jeremy jerked a hand in her direction. "I need to know. You can pretend everything's cool with this whole thing if you want, but I need to know what happened." He faced his dad and waited.

Alan rubbed his hands down his face. "Son, I'm not sure how to answer that. I know I messed up. I'm trying to fix things."

Jeremy shoved back from the table with a loud snort, grabbed his can of soda, and crossed to the back door. "Ya need to try harder." The door slammed behind him.

Pam dressed for her date night with Harrison, pulling the peace of a quiet house around her, determined to apply that calm to her troubled spirit. She met her own eyes in the reflection of the bathroom mirror and grimaced. Dark shadows were smudged beneath her eyes, her nose was red and chapped from almost a week of come-and-go crying jags. She opened her cosmetic case. A little makeup magic would fix most of the obvious problems. *If only my heart could be mended as easily.*

She slammed the lid on those thoughts as she applied highlighter and lipstick and dabbed on Harrison's favorite scent. Her husband had put up with enough moodiness from her in the last six days to last a lifetime. Pam fluffed her hair and studied the results in the glass. Black skinny jeans topped with a white shirt, belted around the waist with a knotted red scarf. She undid the two top buttons of her blouse. They were still newlyweds, of sorts, their third anniversary still five weeks away. Tonight—she looked out the window at the late afternoon sunshine—this afternoon, just as soon as he got home from the golf course, she planned to capitalize on that status. *You'll never be woman enough for me.* She closed her eyes against the taunting words from her past. Harrison had never treated her like that, never would. It was an insult to his love and the life they'd built together to think of him in the same breath as Alan Archer.

Pam looked up when she heard the car in the drive and hurried to put away the bottles, tubes, and jars. She gave her reflected image a sassy wink. The midday seduction on her agenda would catch her husband completely by surprise.

Her fingers trailed the banister as she descended the stairs. She stepped through the entry to the living room to find her husband pacing the far side of the room, his back to her, cell phone to his ear. Pam leaned against the doorjamb, waiting to catch his attention. Harrison turned and stopped in his tracks. He nodded in response to something he was hearing on the phone, but his eyes traveled Pam's body from head to toe. The heat in his gaze stole her breath.

"I'll talk to you later, Stan." He tossed the cell phone

onto the coffee table and crossed to take Pam into his arms. "Hello, beautiful."

Pam reveled in the feel of Harrison's strong arms. The warmth of his hands through the fabric of her shirt as they glided across her back and rested at her waist. Goosebumps on her arms competed with the butterflies in her stomach when she felt his breath on her neck as he bent to inhale the deliberately sexy perfume.

"You smell good enough to eat." He followed his whispered proclamation with light nibbling bites along her collar bone.

Pam tilted her head to one side to give him better access, quivering at the desire that coiled at his touch. She straightened up before her knees had a chance to turn to jelly and tucked her hands into the back pockets of his jeans. "Shouldn't you be getting ready for our date?"

Undeterred by her question, Harrison's lips continued to trace lazy circles on the sensitive skin of her neck. *How did I get so lucky?*

"Umm...Harrison...dinner?" She grinned at the sigh that rumbled in her ear.

"It's only four."

"I know. But if we leave early, we can beat the weekend crowd."

"All right." He rested his head on her shoulder. "What are you hungry for this evening?"

Pam took a step away from the wall. Harrison followed her lead like a good dance partner, moving with her but never releasing his hold on her.

"Let me go, and we'll decide."

He raised his head and pulled her closer. "But this is

so nice."

Pam pinched his butt through the fabric of his jeans.

"Oww."

"Sissy."

Harrison spread his fingers across her back. "I double dog dare you to do that again."

Pam pressed against him and grinned at the desire that heated his expression. She tilted her head back and wet her lips. "Kiss me."

He bent to accommodate her request. His hands moved up her back and around to frame her face, his lips insistent against hers. He pulled back just enough to whisper against her mouth. "Come upstairs with me."

Pam stood on her tiptoes and drew him into a second kiss. The fingers still buried in his pockets delivered two more sharp pinches.

"Hey."

"Sissy."

"I'm gonna..."

"Gotta catch me first." She danced away with a mischievous laugh and sprinted for the stairs. His first grab missed her by centimeters as she gained two steps on him. He caught up with her just as she stepped through the door of their bedroom. They faced each other across the expanse of polished wood floor, both breathless from the race up the stairs. Pam's heart quickened as Harrison nudged the door closed, turned the lock, and reached for the top button of his shirt. His voice was husky when he spoke. "And here we are, right where I wanted you."

Her fingers shook as she slowly untied the scarf at her waist. "All your idea? Really?" The worries of the past week evaporated as she surrendered to Harrison's desire. She tumbled with him to the bed, the yearning to lose herself in a few precious moments of intimacy with her husband, almost a physical hunger. His lips moved from her shoulder to her ear and finally took her mouth in a possessive kiss.

The front door slammed. "Mom, I'm home."

They both stiffened as Jeremy's footsteps thundered up the stairs.

CHAPTER THIRTEEN

Whoever said women were the gentler sex hadn't met the ladies of Valley View's Monday night Bible study. They were fierce about what they believed and not the least bit shy about expressing their opinions. Pam sat in Terri's kitchen and allowed the debate to rage around her. Normally, Monday night was one of the highlights of her week, but tonight she had too much on her mind and just wanted it over with.

Saturday night's attempt at normalcy ended with Jeremy's unexpected return. His admission that he'd walked home following a disagreement with his father, coupled with his stubborn silence about the details, had put Harrison's usually mild temper on a slow simmer. Her refusal to attend church yesterday had boosted the simmer to a boil. The resulting harsh words with her husband—and the strain of a day spent avoiding each other—only reinforced her opinion that Alan Archer had to go. He would be the ruin of her happiness a second time if he persisted in his determination to live in Garfield.

So here she sat, stuffing her face with cheesecake, trying to keep a low profile, and hoping to avoid the questions she read in the eyes of her three best friends every time they looked at her. She had plenty of dessert options to choose from. In an effort to keep Terri off her feet, Pam had joined forces with Karla and Callie. Each arrived on Terri's doorstep with a different flavored cheesecake. They weren't the only ones still concerned about last week's false alarm. Terri's husband, Steve, kept watch from the living room. The husbands had recently fallen into the habit of a guy's night out while the women gathered. They were one short tonight, no amount of persuasion able to budge Steve out of the house.

The debate ended without fanfare, as if someone flipped a switch to the off position. Terri began the task of escorting her guests to the front door. She waddled back to the kitchen, her hand pressed to the small of her back, a wide grin on her face.

"What's funny?" Callie asked.

"Steve. He wanted to know if there were any bodies he needed to bury. I think he was afraid there'd be bloodshed."

"Men are such wimps." Karla forked up a bite of her peanut butter cheesecake. "You couldn't pay Mitch to stay home when it's my turn to host."

"Benton either," Callie said. "At least not in the house. If he doesn't have someplace to go, he hides in his workshop 'til everyone clears out." She sipped her coffee. "Speaking of husbands, has Mitch been acting weird the last few days?"

"Define weird. It's Mitchell."

Callie shrugged. "Just...weird. Benton is being either very quiet or way too eager to follow any thread of conversation he can grab hold of. He isn't generally interested in my recipe magazines, but we had a whole conversation about the new one over lunch yesterday. It almost felt like he was trying to keep my attention focused on something harmless."

"Oh, you know those two," Karla said. "If they're up to something, they'll let us in on it when they're good and ready."

Pam zoned out of the conversation. She searched her heart again for answers she could live with. She hated this feeling of being trapped in the middle. Between the man she loved and the man she hated. Between what her friends thought they knew and truths she could never share. Between what was wrong and what she needed to do to make it right. *Jesus, I don't know where to go next.* An unconscious sob escaped her throat. Pam felt a hand on her arm and looked up.

"Sweetheart, is there anything we can do for you?" Callie asked.

Pam closed her eyes. *Tell them the truth.* She shrugged the little voice away, her response a whisper. "Are you praying?"

Callie answered for all of them. "You know we are."

"Then keep doing that. I..."

Samantha stepped into the kitchen. "Can I talk to you guys for a minute?"

Pam breathed a silent prayer of thanks and made room at the table for Terri's stepdaughter, grateful for any interruption capable of derailing the course of the current conversation. "What's on your mind?"

Sam scooted around the table, took the indicated

chair, and helped herself to dessert. "I'm confused. I need some advice, guy advice."

Pam's thoughts on the subject were gloomy. What advice could she give to Sam in regards to men? *Run while you can?* That was unfair to ninety five percent of the male population but pretty much on target with how she felt tonight.

Terri laughed. "I was twenty-nine before I fell in love, sweetheart. Guys aren't my best subject, but I'll give it a shot. What do you want to know?"

"Well, it's sort of Christian guy advice. I thought, since you were all here, you might be able to help me figure some things out." Sam folded her hands on the table. "I had a date with a new guy on Friday night."

Terri nodded. "Patrick?"

"Patrick Wheeler. That's right."

Karla chuckled. "The guy you ran over at the Sonic?"

Sam rolled her eyes. "I didn't run over him. I bumped into his truck." She waved the teasing aside. "I'm beginning to think our accident might have been a God-thing."

A puzzled frown wrinkled Callie's face. "Why do you think that?"

Sam sighed. "He's just the sweetest guy. When he called to ask me out, I felt like I should be honest with him from the start. I told him about Bobbie. Instead of being put off, he insisted on her joining us Friday night."

"That must have won him some points," Callie said.

Sam nodded. "Serious points. I wish you could have seen them together. He was really great with her, and I have to tell you, Bobbie is in little-girl love."

"Aw..." Pam said.

"We had such a good time, and I like him a lot. I just got off the phone with him. He said he just wanted to hear my voice."

"That's good, right?" Terri asked

"Very good," Sam agreed.

"So what's got you confused?" Karla wanted to know.

Sam bowed her head, her expression tinged with the confessed confusion. "He isn't a Christian."

"Ooh, that's not a good thing," Callie sipped her coffee. "You need to be careful there."

"I know," Sam whispered. "But I think it could turn out to be a good thing."

Terri sat back in her chair, her hands circling her swollen belly. "Is this the fate, or God, or something part?"

"And the confusing part." Sam rushed ahead. "Patrick says he was raised in church, but he just doesn't get the whole *being saved* thing. He told me he isn't sure how being saved could make him a better person than he already is. He asked a lot of questions that I'm not sure I answered properly." She stopped, crossed her arms, and blew dark brown bangs out of her face. "I know I shouldn't date an unsaved guy, but how can I be a Christian example to him if I avoid him?"

Karla held up a hand and gave her head a little shake. "Whoa, you're making me dizzy. Slow down just a little. You like him?"

"More than I probably should. Just from the two meetings we've had, I can tell he's got most of the qualities I've prayed for. He takes his studies and his future seriously. He's got some deeply ingrained values, and the way he accepted Bobbie was more than I ever expected."

"But...?" Karla prompted.

"But he doesn't have any kind of relationship with Christ. He was raised in church. He doesn't drink, or smoke, or do drugs. He's basically an all-around good guy. He just doesn't understand how or why being saved makes a difference."

Pam shook herself out of her funk. She could worry about the impossible issues of her life all day or help Sam with hers. "I'm familiar with the concept. One of my best friends in high school was a preacher's kid." She leaned over and rested her arm across Sam's shoulders. "She'd been *forced,* by virtue of her father's calling, to attend church her whole life. If you looked at her, you saw a Christian young lady. She knew how to walk the walk and talk the talk. It's the only way she'd ever lived. It shocked me to find out she'd never taken that final step of self-dedication. She believed in God. She thought going to church every Sunday, living in a Christian home, saying grace over her meals, and being nice to others equaled a relationship with God. She didn't see the need for repentance because she'd always been a good kid."

"Exactly," Sam agreed. "Did you stop being her friend?"

Pam squeezed her shoulders. "Oh, honey, no. You can't live in this world without having relationships with unbelievers. I don't think that's what God intended. It's certainly not how Jesus lived His life."

"Absolutely," Terri added. "Jesus told His followers a story about two men who owed a debt, one large and one small. The person who loaned the money cancelled both debts. Jesus asked a question. Who do you think was the most grateful?"

Sam shrugged. "The one that owed the most?"

Terri nodded. "We're the same way. When you got saved, your life was a real mess, and you knew you'd been forgiven for many sins. You love Jesus accordingly. Someone like Pam's friend, like Patrick, finds it hard to accept or be grateful for forgiveness when they don't feel like they've done anything wrong."

"So, what can I do for Patrick?" Sam asked. "That's the fate or God part. I feel like he's looking for answers, whether he knows it or not. I might be able to help him find them, but I can't help him if I don't spend time with him." Her shoulders slumped. "But if I do spend time with him and I fall for him..."

Callie leaned forward and looked the younger woman in the eye. "I can answer that better than the others. You know Benton wasn't saved when we got married. I wouldn't change a minute of the time we've had together, but we were blessed, and not everyone in that situation is. Be Patrick's friend, but guard your heart. That's a lot harder than it sounds, Sam. You need to pray for him, and yourself, every day. Invite him to church. This new college group the Siskos are trying to kick off is your perfect opportunity. Most of all, make sure that in your friendship *you* lead *him*, not the other way around."

"And," Pam added, "somewhere down the road, you may need to be firm with him about advancing your relationship from friendship to romantic involvement. Patrick needs to understand that it can't happen until he makes a sincere commitment to Christ."

Sam was silent for a few moments. "That's pretty much everything I'd already told myself. I just needed to be sure I was on the right track." She smiled at the women gathered around the table. "Thanks. I guess I'll just keep praying, for both of them."

"Both of them?" Pam asked.

Sam nodded. "Yeah, he mentioned that his father is very sick."

"Bless his heart," Karla said. "Do you want us to help you pray?"

"Would you?" Sam asked. "That would be awesome."

"Do you know his father's name?" Karla asked.

Sam shook her head. "He didn't say."

"Doesn't matter. God knows who he is." Karla held out her hands, and the others followed suit, forming a circle around the table.

Pam closed her eyes as Karla led them in prayer.

"Jesus, as always, we give thanks for this special time with our friends. I ask Lord, that You would keep Your hand of protection over each of us through the rest of the week. Lord, make Sam a positive influence in Patrick's life. Open his eyes to the necessity of a relationship with You. Give Sam wisdom and direction where this friendship is concerned. Guard her heart. We ask for a special touch of healing for Patrick's father. You know his name and You know the situation. Please have Your way in his life and ours. Amen."

The meeting broke up as the women prepared to return to their homes. Pam hugged Samantha. "I'm so proud of you. I'll be praying for Patrick and his father every day."

CHAPTER FOURTEEN

Pam stacked the last dish in the dishwasher Tuesday night, wiped down the countertops, and allowed herself to take a deep breath of contentment. The kitchen was her favorite room in the house, and today had been a good day. Busy at work, things back to normal—*at least what was passing for normal these days*—with Harrison. A laughter-filled family dinner with both of her children in attendance. She turned and leaned against the sink. No one needed to tell her how blessed she was. Their little family had never endured any of the blended family nightmares she'd read about. Jeremy and Megan truly loved and respected Harrison. But Harrison wasn't Alan. Having their father close again...she had to admit that her children were happier than they'd been in a long time. Well, at least Megan was. Worry over Jeremy's recent issues pricked at her contentment.

The kids knew a little bit of what their father had done four years ago. There'd been no way to avoid that, but Pam had done her best to keep the worst of it from them, to keep the scars of that last year to herself. The majority of Alan's cruelty had occurred behind closed doors. There was no need for them to know. Keeping those scars and feelings to herself since he'd returned had been difficult, but, so far, with the exception of her initial meltdown at church that first Sunday, she'd managed to keep her children out of it.

Haven't I? Pam bowed her head. *Thank You for today, Father. I needed the space. I'm just so...* A noise drew her attention. She looked up and found Megan and Jeremy wrestling in the doorway.

She shook her head at them. "It's too early for a snack, kids. Go finish up your homework. Then we'll talk."

Megan and Jeremy looked at each other. Megan shoved through to the kitchen and left her brother frowning in the doorway. "We aren't here for a snack. We wanted to talk to you."

"*She* wants to talk to you," Jeremy corrected.

Caught off guard by their serious expressions, Pam motioned them to the café-style booth tucked into the corner of the kitchen. She slid into one side. The kids faced her from across the table. When neither child spoke for several seconds, Pam prompted them. "You called this meeting, guys. What's on your minds?"

Megan swallowed loudly and tucked a stray strand of hair behind her ear. "We," she shifted away from Jeremy's elbow jab. "All right," she hissed at him. "*I* wanted to talk to you about Daddy. Why do you still hate him so much?"

Jeremy gave his sister a disgusted look.

Megan shrugged at his silent rebuke. They both turned back to Pam. Jeremy tried to redeem his sister's bluntness.

"Mom, we know adultery is wrong." Jeremy stumbled over the word, his face flushing in obvious embarrassment. "But, it's been a really long time..."

Megan interrupted her brother a second time. "You both have new people to love."

Jeremy buried his face in his hand. "Lame, sis, real lame."

"And," Megan continued, "we wanted to find out what we could do to get you two to make up, 'cause we wanted to ask you for a favor."

Pam's breath shuddered in her chest. Her voice was a strained whisper. "A favor?"

"Jeremy said you wouldn't even listen to us, but I said you would 'cause you love us and you're a Christian and so is Dad..."

"What's the favor?" Pam was taken aback by the direction of the conversation.

"Thanksgiving," the kids said together.

"Thanksgiving?"

Megan nodded. "We wanted to ask if we could—"

"Guys," she said, "I don't have a problem if you want to spend part of Thanksgiving Day with your father. Terri and her family aren't coming 'til later in the afternoon. You can spend the whole day with your father and still be here in time for dinner that evening."

Jeremy's smile was pained. "That's great, Mom, but that's not what she has in mind."

Megan met her mother's eyes. "I wanted to know if we could have Thanksgiving together."

Pam blinked. She must've misunderstood. "What?"

"I know Terri and Steve are coming, but it's just three more people. Jeremy and I are willing to help out in the kitchen. You could meet Rick. He's very cool."

"She didn't ask them yet," Jeremy assured his mother. "I told her we needed to talk to you about it first."

"Can we please ask them?" Megan pleaded.

Pam slumped in the bench and stared at the table. She jumped when two fat tears spattered on the polished wooden finish. *Jesus, I have no defense against this.*

"Mom, we're sorry," Megan whispered. "It was just an idea."

"We didn't mean to make you cry," Jeremy whispered. "I told her it was a dumb idea. I'm sorry we brought it up."

Pam snapped out of it enough to brush the tears from her face. She held out her hands to her children. "My poor babies. There's so much you don't understand, so much I can never begin to explain to you. But I guess you're too old for pretend as well."

She stopped to take a deep breath. "I'm not sure I can ever forgive your father for some of the things he did. I know that goes against everything I've tried to teach you about being a Christian. I'm praying for God to help me."

She squeezed their hands but focused her gaze on her son. "I don't want my feelings to come between you guys and your father. I'm happy that you're getting to spend some extra time with him, I really am. But Thanksgiving? I'm going to have to say no to that plan."

Jeremy tried to tug his little sister out of the booth. "That's OK, Mom. We can just go over there for a while instead."

Megan was not as ready to give up. "Is it all right if

we pray, too? Maybe God can make things better between now and then."

Her daughter's simple request twisted the knife in Pam's heart. She put her head down on the table and wept.

Harrison cleared his throat from the darkened doorway. "You guys go on up and watch some TV or something."

Old hurts and new indecision squeezed Pam's heart. She didn't move as the kids scrambled to obey. Harrison scooted in next to her and gathered her into his arms.

"What am I going to do?"

"Shhh," he whispered into her hair as he rocked. "I'm here. Just hold onto me."

Pam lay awake, eyes tightly closed against the reality of the late morning light filtering through the bedroom blinds. Their law office had opened hours ago, and she should have been there. If her boss were anyone but Harrison, she probably wouldn't have a job at this point. She discarded that reality as well. Turning under the covers, she drew up her knees and wrapped her arms around a pillow. Even closed, her eyes felt swollen and gritty from crying herself to sleep the night before. Pam's hand trembled when she reached up to brush her hair from her face. One eye squinted open. The angle of the sun light told her it was even later than she'd imagined.

Harrison had put her to bed last night and held her while she cried. He deserved so much better than she was giving him right now. So did her babies. Her babies...Pam's breath caught when she remembered

149

their innocent questions and the answers she could never give them. She hugged the pillow tighter. *God, I'm letting them all down. I'm letting You down. I'm so sorry. I need Your help. Please show me what to do, where to find some answers...*

Pam forced herself to scoot up to a sitting position against the carved headboard. Her silent prayer dwindled away. She stared at her chest of drawers and wondered if the index card Harrison had given her was still in there after all this time. Covers thrown to the side, she padded barefoot to the chest and pulled open her sock drawer. After removing the socks from the very back corner, Pam found a small white rectangle of paper. *Brookside Retreat* were the only words written on it. A phone number was printed neatly under the words. She hurried back to the warmth of the bed and picked up the phone.

Alan muted the TV with the remote when the doorbell rang Wednesday afternoon.

Kate poked her head around the kitchen door. "Are we expecting anyone?"

Alan shook his head and prepared to stand.

His wife motioned him down, protective of him after mild episodes of dizziness and palpations last night and again this morning. Not bad enough, thank God, for a trip to the ER. More unnerving than anything else.

"Sit still." Kate crossed between him and the TV, drying her hands on a dishtowel. She draped the towel over her shoulder and pulled open the door. He watched as she stepped back to allow Mitch and Benton to enter.

Alan smiled. His old friends remained faithful despite the years and the distance. Gratitude changed to wariness when he read their grim expressions. "Guys, come in and have a seat."

Mitch and Benton took the two chairs across from the sofa. Kate settled on the sofa, next to Alan, feet tucked up beneath her. She wrapped an arm through his in what he understood as a silent show of support.

Mitch leaned forward and clasped his hands between his knees. "How are you feeling?"

Alan shrugged. "Fine—"

"He had a difficult night," Kate interrupted. "I hope you'll keep that in mind and not tire him further."

"Kate." Alan's tone was one of rare annoyance.

Kate shoved away from him and sat up. Her green eyes snapped with emerald fire. "Don't use that tone with me, Alan Archer. I can see trouble on their faces as well as you can. They'll temper what they've come to say with the truth of your condition, or they can keep it to themselves."

Alan pulled her back to his side and brushed a kiss across her brow. He studied the two men seated across from him. "I can still read you two like a book. What's happened? Please tell me you didn't tell Callie and Karla about my reasons for coming home."

The noise that escaped Benton's throat was half snort, half laugh. He lifted his hand and wagged a finger between Mitch and him. "Nope, we're still breathing. And because we want to keep it that way, your piece of intel is locked securely away." His laughter died away, and his serious expression returned. "Have you made any progress in your efforts to clear things with Pam?"

Alan shook his head. "Not in the last week. Why?"

"Harrison called me last night. Apparently Pam had a full-blown meltdown after dinner."

"This news did not sit well with our wives," Mitch added. "I don't know about Callie, but Karla is already suspicious about my silence on the subject of your sudden return." The tone of a cell phone interrupted Mitch. He pulled it out of his pocket. "Speaking of." He held a finger to his lips and pressed the receive button. "Good morning, my love. What's up?" Mitch listened for a few seconds. "I don't think I can come home for lunch, hon. We're pretty tied up." A wince followed. "I'll see what I can do. I love…" Mitch lowered the phone and stared at it. "She just hung up on me. This is bad. I think they know something. At least I think Karla may have guessed."

Alan stared at his friend. "All of the deep, dark secrets in the world, and you think Karla just happened to *guess* that you know I'm dying from a disease you can't even pronounce?"

"Hypertrophic cardiomyopathy," Mitch supplied absently. "Well something's up." He waved his cell phone. "Karla just called me by my full name and demanded I come home for lunch. She had that *look* in her voice."

"She had a look in her voice?" Alan would have laughed if the situation weren't so desperate.

"You know." Mitch explained. "That look they give you just before they peel the hide off the back of your neck. Karla has it verbally perfected. I don't even need to be in the same room to know I'm dog food."

Benton shook his head. "Mitch, there's just no way—"

"Maybe not." Mitch stood and pulled Benton to his feet. "But we're in this together, and you're having lunch with me today. I'll be safer with a witness present."

Plans made, Pam hurried around her kitchen in order to get the special meal she'd spent the afternoon preparing on the table before church time. Her decision had been hard but necessary, but she hoped to soften the announcement with something special for everyone. There were broiled salmon steaks for all, one of Harrison's favorites, homemade french fries for Jeremy, and Megan's much loved double chocolate cake for dessert. The meal wasn't just for them. Staying busy this afternoon kept her from second-guessing what she knew she had to do.

Pam surveyed the table a final time. They would eat in the dining room tonight, complete with the good china and her grandma's seldom-used silver. Her step was lighter than it had been in days when she went upstairs to fetch her family. Music poured from Megan's room, loud and pounding, competing with the explosions and whistles of whatever video game Jeremy played behind his closed door. She knocked on both doors, pitching her voice to be heard above the noise. "Kids, dinner."

She found Harrison seated at the small desk in the corner of their room, headphones his only defense against the noise in the hall. A tap on the shoulder drew his attention from the paperwork spread before him. "Foods on the table."

Pam pulled her chair from under the table just as Jeremy entered the dining room, Megan on his heels.

"Wow," he exclaimed, his nose lifted to the air. "What's the occasion? It smells like we're celebrating everyone's birthday at once tonight."

Harrison joined them, and Pam waited until everyone's plate was filled before helping herself. Appetite nonexistent, she kept her eyes focused on her meal, poking at her food, allowing her family's conversation to roll around her. *Get on with it.*

She looked up with what she hoped was a reassuring smile. "I have something I want to discuss with everyone." Her gaze moved from face to face until she was sure she had everyone's attention. "First of all, I want to apologize to each of you for my bad moods over the last few days." She paused long enough to link her fingers with Harrison's, drawing support from the strength of his steady presence. "I know you guys don't understand what's going on. Sometimes I don't understand it myself. I'm going to try and change that." Pam picked up her glass of tea with her free hand and took a deep drink before she continued.

"There's a place I know called Brookside Retreat. They help people work through hard problems. I spent some time there several years ago, and they helped me a lot. I've decided I need to go back for a few days."

Megan tilted her head and studied her mom's face. "The name sounds pretty. Is it a spa?"

Pam smiled in spite of herself. "No, it's my heart that needs treatment, baby, not my body. Brookside is a quiet place where I can do some serious thinking and praying. They don't have televisions or computers..."

"Count me out," Jeremy muttered.

"...just small cabins by a lake and Christian counselors."

Harrison rubbed a thumb across her knuckles. "I was going to suggest a return visit."

"I think God beat you to it." Pam leaned her head on his shoulder. "I got a lot accomplished when I was there before, but my doctor warned me that I was leaving things undone. I need to go and see if I can finish what I started." She looked at her kids. "Do you remember reading in your Bibles about how Jesus went away to pray sometimes? Apart from everyone who loved him and all the distractions that were around him?"

"You going to be gone forty days?" Megan asked.

"Not see your faces for forty days?" Pam shook her head in genuine dismay. "I'd never make it that long. No, I'll leave tomorrow afternoon and come home on Sunday night. A long weekend to try to put some things into perspective. Some quiet time to study my Bible and talk to God or a counselor, if I need to." She searched their faces. "Are you guys good with that?"

Jeremy pushed away from the table and crossed his arms. "This is just great. Dad comes home, so you're just gonna take off?" He faced his sister. "This is all your fault. If you'd kept your Thanksgiving wish list to yourself... I wish he'd never moved back here."

"Jeremy." Harrison's voice was even but firm. "It's three days, not forty." He raised Pam's hand and brushed her knuckles with a kiss. "I think I speak for all of us when I say you need to do whatever you need to do to get your smile back." He leaned forward and winked at the kids. "We'll eat out every night while Mom's gone, your choice of restaurants."

Jeremy rolled his eyes. "Whatever."

Megan countered by ticking off a list of her favorite

restaurants. "Barbeque tomorrow night, Mexican—"

Jeremy leaned forward. "Who said you got to choose first?"

The sibling bickering started immediately about who got first choice and why. A weight lifted off Pam's shoulders, and her appetite returned in a rush. She picked up her fork, relieved that some things were already getting back to normal.

CHAPTER FIFTEEN

Pam pulled open the door to the small cabin that would be her weekend home. She was weary from the six-hour drive. Her stomach had begun to growl a hundred miles ago. She'd resisted the urge to stop for food, both from the desire to get here before dark and the knowledge that the small kitchenette would be stocked with essentials. Brookside offered several meal plans for their guests. She'd requested the basic food package for her three-day stay.

She dropped her small suitcase inside the door, made a visit to the facilities, and headed to the kitchen. Inside the small refrigerator she found a supply of canned soda and bottled water along with a half-gallon of milk and several prepackaged sandwiches. A check of the shelves above the stove revealed an assortment of canned soups, single-serving boxes of cereals, small bags of chips, and a selection of microwavable entrees. There were even several packages of snack crackers, cookies, and a handful of candy bars. She smiled and selected a package of cheese and peanut butter crackers.

Part of Brookside's appeal came from the fact that you could stay here for days and not see anyone if that's what you wanted. She could supplement the groceries provided for her at the general store a couple of miles up the road, but she thought these things would do just fine for a couple of days. Her soul was far hungrier than her body.

She carried the crackers through the small cabin, picked up her bag, and walked back to the sleeping alcove. There was a note on her pillow.

Pam, welcome back to Brookside. As a return guest, you are already aware of many of the services we provide. Please settle in and make yourself at home. The chapel is open 24/7 for your convenience, and our staff of counselors and pastors are here to help if you need them. Per our conversation yesterday regarding the reason for your visit, here are some Scripture references to get you started on your journey to spiritual peace:

Ephesians 4:32. "And be ye kind one to another, tenderhearted, forgiving one another, even as God for Christ's sake hath forgiven you."

Colossians 3:13. "Forbearing one another, and forgiving one another, if any man have a quarrel against any: even as Christ forgave you. So also do ye."

Mark 11:26. "But if ye do not forgive, neither will your Father which is in heaven forgive your trespasses."

The front desk is always staffed. Please dial 0 if you need anything during your stay. The counseling session you requested with Dr. Sylvester has been scheduled for 10 AM Saturday.

Pam folded the note and laid it aside. She sat on the edge of the bed, releasing the stress of the drive and the tension of the past two weeks in a deep breath.

"Father, thank You for this place. It's just You and me for the next couple of days. Please help me find Your peace and restore balance to my life. I get it that You want me to forgive Alan, not just for his good but for mine. I need You to show me how to do that."

Pam lay back on the pillows and closed her eyes. "Father, I'm so tired." She only intended to rest for a few minutes before she unpacked her bag and found some dinner, but even though it was only six thirty, she drifted off to sleep. Somewhere in the night, she was sure she felt strong secure arms wrap around her, and she was positive she heard a whispered, *I've got you.* Comforted, she snuggled down in the darkness with a smile and slept until dawn.

Patrick juggled shopping bags, a cheese-covered pretzel, and a soda, trying to get to his phone before the call rolled to voice mail. The phone quit ringing just as he pulled it from his pocket. The cup, braced between his arm and his chest, lost its lid, rewarding his efforts with a soggy shirt. *Perfect.* He looked around the packed mall and spotted a wrought-iron bench. Dodging shoppers, he set down his cup, dumped the bags in the corner of the seat, and mopped at his shirt with the tattered remains of the soggy napkin that had been wrapped around the sweating cup.

The napkin disintegrated, leaving a trail of white across the damp, black shirt. Patrick rolled his eyes, tossed the drink and the napkin in the nearby trash, and retrieved the missed call. The small screen lit up with Samantha's number. A self-satisfied whistle slipped from Patrick's lips. He redialed the number while his gaze roamed the crowded aisles of the mall. *Where'd*

Mom go?

"That was fast." Sam's voice contained a giggle.

Patrick pulled the damp, sticky fabric away from his chest with his free hand. "Not when you consider that I've been waiting all day to hear your voice."

"That's so sweet. Are you trying to spoil me?"

"If you'll let me. Hang on just a second." He turned a complete circle, distracted, looking for his mother in the sea of shoppers. *Where did she get off to?* The landscape was a sea of blondes. He finally caught a glimpse of his mother's ponytail down by the entrance to Sears.

"Patrick?"

His attention snapped back to the phone. "What? Sorry, I was looking for Mom."

"Where are you?"

"I brought her out to the mall. Her box of Thanksgiving decorations got damaged in the move. We're shopping for replacements."

"Oh, that sounds like fun."

"We'll be here for a while longer if you can head this way. That's actually part of the reason I was trying to find you." He paused again, this time to make sure his mother was still out of earshot. "She's in manic shopping mode, something she only does when she's stressed out. I think the situation with my dad is beginning to get to her."

"I wish I'd seen your messages earlier, but my phone was in the car all afternoon." Samantha's sigh echoed though the phone. "But I can't tonight. I've got a big exam in the morning. I even paid Iris to sit with Bobbie so I could have some time away—"

"You have to pay your sister to babysit?"

Sam laughed. "Not as bad as it sounds. Her currency of choice is homemade chocolate chip cookies. Anyway, rain check?"

"Of course. I'd like to take you to dinner tomorrow night, just the two of us. The invitation for tonight was sort of a last minute thing. I thought Mom needed a break. Meeting you would help take her mind off...things."

"Is your dad worse?"

"Not that I can tell. It's just a little tense at the house right now."

"I'm praying for you, and him, every day. In fact, I've got a lot of people praying about the situation."

Yeah, that'll help. Patrick swallowed around the sudden lump in his throat "Thanks. Tomorrow night?"

"Tomorrow night is perfect. We can celebrate putting this exam behind me. What time?"

Time and restaurant agreed upon, Patrick brushed the screen with a fingertip to disconnect the call, wished for his discarded soda as he swallowed his last bite of pretzel, and searched for his mother. He found her standing in front of the pet store window, watching a trio of black cocker spaniel puppies wrestle over a tennis ball.

"Here you are." He motioned to the door of the store. "I was about to see if I could borrow a blood hound."

His mom's lips twitched up in a smile. "I saw you talking on the phone. Samantha call you back?"

"Yeah, we're going out tomorrow night. She's studying tonight, so she won't be joining us."

Kate nodded and laughed as one of the puppies won the battle and scurried to a private corner to guard his prize. It was a short-lived victory. The other two puppies pounced, sent the ball flying, and the battle began anew. "They're so innocent and carefree. I wish..." She leaned her head against the glass when her voice cracked. "Sorry, let's get back to it. I want some silk ivy to arrange between the pumpkins and gourds."

Patrick shook his head, took his mother's arm, and led her to a deserted corner. "We've always been a team, you and me. You need to tell me what's got you so messed up."

Kate tilted her head back to look into her son's eyes. Patrick saw her blink against tears a second before she buried her head in his chest. The shopping bags slipped to the floor as he wrapped her in his arms. "What...?"

He felt the breath shudder through her body. "He's lying to us, Patrick."

"Who? Dad?"

His mother nodded and took a step back. She pulled a tissue from her bag and dabbed at her eyes.

"Lying about what?"

Kate pinched the bridge of her nose, her answer a whisper. "The severity of his illness."

It was Patrick's turn to take a step back. "How...?"

"I don't know how. I just know." Kate laid a hand over her heart. "I know it here." She touched a finger to her temple. "And I know it here."

Patrick had enough experience with his mother's intuition not to argue. "Have you talked to him?"

She shook her head. "He's just trying to protect us...me. I know, but I don't want him to know that I know. Oh, I'm not making any sense."

Patrick gathered her back into his arms and let her cry it out. As far as he knew, this was his mom's first meltdown since learning of Dad's condition. She was too busy trying to be strong for the men in her life. The cry would do her good. There was a small part of him that longed to cry with her.

CHAPTER SIXTEEN

Pam assembled her morning dose of caffeine and then stepped onto the little porch of her cabin to wait for it to brew. The sun had not yet made it over the tree tops, but the sky grew lighter every second. She chafed her bare arms. Brookside was far enough south for the mid-November weather to still be mild, but the morning was chilly. Patchy fog dotted the grassy areas between the trees and the river. Pam watched a family of deer pause for a morning drink before settling down from their evening wanderings.

She went inside, put on her shoes, and grabbed her Bible and a light sweater. Returning to the porch, she settled down to begin her journey of self- examination. Before she opened her Bible, she closed her eyes in a few words of silent prayer. *Father, I need You. I need You every day, but especially today. I thought I had the issues and the hurts that Alan caused buried too deeply to ever resurface. I've spent the last two weeks learning how pathetic, and dangerous, it was to lie to myself. Please help me find some answers. Help me see things through Your eyes, and then give me the strength to act on what You show me. Thank You for rest last night and peace this morning. I love You.*

Pam put her coffee cup on a little table that flanked an old wooden rocking chair, pulled her sweater a little tighter, and opened her Bible. She unfolded the note from her pillow and looked at the Scriptures written for her. They all had the same theme. Forgiveness of others because Christ has forgiven us. The last one of the three seemed especially familiar. Pam turned to the reference to read the verse from Mark in context.

The margins of her Bible contained her own scribbled notes. A folded piece of notepaper nestled between the pages. Pam opened the paper and sucked in a surprised breath. No wonder that Scripture was so recognizable to her. Pastor Gordon had preached on it just two weeks ago. *The morning Alan had shown up in church.* She'd taken notes, but with her emotions in such turmoil, she'd given it no further thought.

Pam raised her gaze to the tops of the trees and watched absently as a hawk glided in lazy circles on an updraft. She grinned when the hawk descended in a sharp dive. *Breakfast was served.* She glanced back to her notes. *You gave me part of the answer two weeks ago, and I didn't even take the time to see it. Forgive me.* Pam smoothed the notes out on her open Bible and began to read what she'd written while Pastor Gordon delivered his sermon. *Un-forgiveness in our hearts will stop the flow of God's blessing in our lives. God wants to set us free to enjoy an uninhibited relationship with Him. The choice is ours.*

She contemplated what she'd written. If part of God's blessing in her life was happiness in her home and peace of mind, those things had certainly been in

SHARON SROCK

short supply the last couple of weeks. Her relationship with God had certainly suffered some serious hits as well—ignoring sermons, missing service, and not teaching her class.

Pam looked at the final line of her notes. *The choice is ours. Is it that simple God? A choice? A conscious decision to give the problem to You and walk away. What about the hurt and the disgrace Alan caused me? What about the edge he pushed me to? Don't those things count for anything? How can I just pretend that none of it ever happened? They're as much a part of my life as breathing.*

She finished reading through the book of Mark and paused when she came to the account of the crucifixion. "There's something missing from Mark's account." She flipped over to Luke's gospel. "Here it is..."

"Then Jesus said, Father, forgive them, for they know not what they do..."

Jesus, they beat You and mocked You. Dragged You out of the city and nailed You to a cross. I guess my hurt can't compare to what You suffered. She put her head in her hands. *But You're God and I'm not...*

Patrick rang Samantha's doorbell. He concealed the small bouquet of hot house daisies behind his back. Flowers were a bit old fashioned, but sometimes the old fashioned things were the best things. Besides, they'd caught his eye this afternoon while running an errand for his mom. They reminded him of Samantha.

His hand came up to smooth his hair and connected with his ball cap. Patrick whipped it off, shoved it behind his back with the flowers, and ran his fingers through his flattened hair. He couldn't make up his mind if today counted as their third date or their second.

In addition to their pizza date last week, they'd shared lunch at the university on Tuesday afternoon. Tonight they were going into the city for a real dinner followed by a movie. Since he planned to kiss Samantha good night later, he decided to count this as date number three.

The very pregnant woman who opened the door was definitely not Samantha.

She held out her hand. "You must be Patrick."

Patrick grasped the extended hand. "The one and only, if God continues to listen to my mother."

She laughed and gently pulled him inside. "I'm Terri. Sam's running just a little late. Come in and have a seat."

Patrick followed Terri into the living room and took a seat in the chair she indicated. He brought the flowers from behind his back and hesitated, looking for a place to lay them. He finally turned his hat up in his lap and placed the bouquet inside.

Terri's eyes settled on the white and yellow blooms. "Oh, I like you already. How did you know to get daisies? They're Sam's favorite."

Patrick smiled at his good fortune. "Intuition?"

Terri raised her brows and stared at him silently for a couple of heartbeats.

He tried again. "I got really lucky?"

"Humor and honesty. What a nice combination." She glanced at the clock over the entertainment center. "Let me run up and see what's keeping Samantha."

Patrick raised a hand to stop her. "Don't do that. I'm sure she'll be down as soon as she can." His eyes rested briefly on the mound of her pregnant belly. "The stairs can't be good for you right now."

"Honey, I appreciate your concern, but I've got a one-year-old and a husband whose office is on the second floor. I'm up and down these stairs a couple of dozen times a day. But trust me, I've learned the value of a good yell if that will get the job done."

She turned back to the stairs just as Samantha started down with a dark-headed man following close behind. Patrick stood to meet their approach. He grinned when Samantha caught his eye and hurried the rest of the way down.

"Sorry, we were bedding Bobbie down with my little brother for the night. I wanted her to sleep upstairs since I wasn't sure how late we'd be." She held out a hand to the man behind her and pulled him forward. "Patrick Wheeler, this is my dad, Steve Evans. Looks like you've already met my mom."

Patrick held his hand out to Steve. "Nice to meet you, sir."

"Nice to meet you, Patrick. I've heard a lot of good things about you."

Patrick smiled as he released Steve's hand and brought the flowers into view. He studied them carefully for a few seconds and chose a bright yellow blossom. He separated it from the bouquet and handed the single flower to Terri. The rest of the bouquet went to Sam.

"I didn't realize I'd be meeting a second beautiful woman tonight. You'll have to share."

The women accepted his gift with shared laughter. Terri held her hand out to Samantha. "Let me have those, Sam, I'll put them in some water for you. If you guys don't scoot, you'll miss your reservation."

Sam buried her face in the fragrant blooms and took a deep breath. She handed the flowers to Terri and smiled at Patrick. "They're beautiful, thanks."

Patrick took the jacket Sam had slung across her arm and helped her into it. "Several mushy comparisons come to mind, but I'll save them for later. Your mom is right. We need to be going."

Patrick held the door open on their way out of the theater. "Did you enjoy the movie?"

Sam laughed. "Of course. He's one of my favorite actors. That scar on his chin is so sexy."

"Sexy?" Patrick repeated. "The man is old enough to be your grandfather."

She sighed. "Some things never grow old, Patrick. That daredevil attitude, the *did I really do that* grin. Sexy, pure and simple." She glanced up at him from under her lashes. "Jealous?"

He snorted. "Of a sixty-year-old man? Not likely."

They passed under a streetlight on the way to his truck. Sam's grin was mischievous when she paused and looked up at him in the dim light. She tapped Patrick on the chin. "I wonder how he got that scar. I hope he had someone to kiss it better."

Patrick grabbed her hand and kissed her fingers before letting go to open the truck door for her. "You really like all that macho, rugged, he-man stuff?"

Samantha shrugged. "It has its place."

Patrick thought about that as he rounded the hood of his truck and climbed into the seat next to her. "I have a whip and a battered old fedora someplace. I could bring them over tomorrow morning and give you a demonstration..."

Patrick's truck returned to the curb in front of Samantha's house. He hurried around to open the door and held out his hand to help her with the steep step down. She allowed him to pull her hand through the bend of his arm before walking her towards the brightly-lit porch.

"I had a really good time tonight," he said.

"So did I."

Patrick detoured Sam to the porch swing. "Will you be cold if we sit here for a few minutes?"

Sam settled into the creaky swing, snuggling a little deeper into her jacket. "It's a wonderful night, and this swing is one of my favorite places."

"Why's that?"

Sam shrugged. "I don't know. I guess because it's old-fashioned. It just sort of says home and family to me. It's welcoming. When Dad first showed us the house, it was the only thing I liked. I want one just like it when I have a place of my own. Do you like old-fashioned things?"

He thought of the daisies and scored a mental point for himself. Patrick took the spot beside her and draped his arm along the back of the old wooden swing. "I like comfortable things," he answered. "I like you."

"Patrick..."

He touched a finger to her lips. "Shhh." He tilted his head and pulled her close. The kiss they shared was tender and just a little shy. Patrick straightened with a sigh. "I really liked that."

He felt her shoulders slump beneath his arm. *Way to*

rush things, Wheeler. "Sam, I'm sorry, I shouldn't have—"

This time it was Sam's turn to silence Patrick with a finger to his lips. "Patrick, it's not you, it's me...Well, I guess it's really both of us. I like you a lot, and I liked that kiss more than I probably should have." She squared her shoulders and met his eyes. "I've been thinking about you...and me...a lot since our pizza date." She rose from the swing, crossed the porch, turned, and leaned against the railing. Patrick couldn't see her eyes for the shadows, but he didn't like the direction the conversation had taken.

Sam used her fingers to comb her hair away from her face. "But I can't have a relationship with you, or anyone, who doesn't have a relationship with Jesus. I'm sorry if you're upset by that, but I need to be honest with you."

Patrick leaned forwards and folded his hands in his lap. *Not just a church girl, a committed church girl.* "Not upset but a little confused."

"And that's probably my fault. I enjoyed tonight so much, I probably flirted a little more than I should have. Bobbie comes by that trait legitimately." Samantha returned to the swing, sat beside him, and pried his hands apart, holding one of his in both of hers. "I've hurt your feelings and that was the last thing on my mind." She studied him in the soft porch light. "I know you think the whole religion thing doesn't matter, but it will at some point, and if it comes down to a choice, you'd lose." She bit her lip as she studied his expression." I want to be your..."

He flinched. *She's gonna say it...*

"...friend."

His breath whooshed out at that dreaded word.

171

"Define *friend*."

Sam's lips ticked up in a smile. "Getting to know you, spending time with you, but with the understanding that a physical involvement is out of bounds for now. That includes kisses like the one you just gave me." She squeezed his hand. "Trust me. That's gonna be as hard for me as it is for you."

Patrick shifted his hand so that he held hers instead of the other way around. They swung in lazy silence for a few minutes. She was obviously at rest with her choices. Him? Not so much. He studied her profile, considering the pros and cons of her comments. He liked this girl, but kissing was off limits? Sam had a child, and he still wasn't completely sure how he felt about that. Taking it slow would give him a chance to see if he fit into their world. Yes, it would be hard to rein in the physical, but he needed a friend just now, probably more than anything else. He opened his mouth to agree to her terms and felt a small shiver from Sam. "I'm sorry. I've kept you out here too long." He pulled her to her feet. "I have a radical idea."

"What's that?"

"Tomorrow's weather is supposed to be warmer than today. Let's take Bobbie to Party Palace tomorrow afternoon. She'll have a blast in the play area, and then she can bathe in pizza sauce again when she's all played out. I missed not getting to see her tonight." *Where did that come from?* He rolled it around in his head a bit and found it to be true.

"That's the sweetest thing..." Sam turned at the door to face Patrick. "I'll make a deal with you. We'll go play with you tomorrow if you'll come to church with me on Sunday."

"Sam..."

"It's not a regular church service," she wheedled. "Our youth pastors are launching an outreach to the college students in the area. I think they're calling it *College and Career*...or something like that. Anyway the young adults are meeting in the gym this week. We have a special speaker in the morning service followed by lunch and activities before a second service in the early afternoon. You don't even have to dress up. There's going to be some volleyball and basketball. It'll be fun. You might learn something new. At the very least, you'll meet some more people our age."

Patrick rested his forehead against hers. "You drive a hard bargain." When she didn't answer, he agreed. "Deal," he said softly. "I'll pick you and Bobbie up tomorrow at eleven."

Sam reached for the door, but Patrick gathered her into his arms before it opened. Man, this was going to be a long friendship. He hugged her tight, pecked her cheek with his lips, and sprinted for the curb. He really didn't know if kissing her cheek violated her *friendship* guidelines. He didn't stay around to find out.

CHAPTER SEVENTEEN

Pam paced Tina Sylvester's small office on Saturday morning, restless and just a little wary of the session to come. Dr. Sylvester was the same Brookside counselor Pam had talked with during her month-long stay four years earlier. Talking with someone already familiar with the deep, dark secrets of her past would make the process easier. Pam felt a twinge of conscience. She had a perfectly good pastor at home. Brother Gordon never failed to be a wise and thoughtful advisor. But there were things she'd never shared with him. Sharing them now that Alan had come back would feel like asking him to take her side. As justified as Pam thought her feelings were, it wasn't a position she'd put her pastor in.

She laid her Bible, stuffed with sticky notes, on the corner of Tina's desk and tried to make herself comfortable in the homey wing chair on the visitor's side of the office. She crossed her legs and chewed on a hangnail. Just as she was ready to resume her pacing, the door opened and Tina stepped inside.

Dr. Tina Sylvester, one hundred pounds and barely five feet tall. Bright purple reading glasses nested in a halo of brilliant red hair. Her brown eyes sparkled with an inner fire age had not dimmed. She came around the chair and took Pam's hand in a firm grip, pulling her forward into an even stronger hug. Pam returned the embrace with a slight hesitation, fearful of crushing fragile, aged bones. Tina tightened the hug in response to Pam's caution.

"You can do better than that, Pam. That's a major part of what's wrong with the world these days. Not enough sincere affection."

Pam knew, from her visit four years ago, that Dr. Sylvester, a semi-retired psychologist and one of the co-founders of Brookside, remained strong in her Christian faith, affirming that the Bible held the answers to all of life's problems if you looked and *listened* hard enough. At seventy-one, her mind was as sharp as the forged steel of a sword. Pam hoped nothing had changed that.

Tina released Pam and stepped back. "You look good. A vast improvement over the skinny, lost waif who spent so much time in my office four years ago." She circled behind her desk, sat down, and tapped the brown manila folder resting in its center. "I pulled this out on Wednesday morning after you called. I wanted to look over our session notes from your previous visit." She repositioned the reading glasses and motioned to Pam's Bible. "I see you've been reading."

Pam reached for the Bible and smoothed the burgundy leather absently. She looked at Tina. "A lot."

"Finding anything useful?"

Her reply came without thought or hesitation. "God loves Alan more than He loves me."

Tina sat back and slipped the glasses from her face. "Excuse me?"

Pam put her head in her hands. "I'm sorry. I can't believe I actually said that out loud." She paused and took a deep breath. "No matter how hard I try, when I think about Alan and this whole situation, something in me just snaps." Pam met Tina's gaze. "I've been reading a lot about God's forgiveness and how He expects us to forgive others. There's more than I realized in there about loving each other, and our Christian brothers and sisters, especially those who have wronged us."

"Your ex-husband fits nicely into the last category."

"Actually, if you enjoy popular fiction, he fits into both categories. He's managed to convince everyone that he's had some miraculous change of heart." Pam placed a hand over her own heart and deepened her voice. "God's forgiven him, so everyone else should just follow suit."

Tina put her chin on her fist and stared across the desk at Pam. "You don't believe that?"

"Please. I've known the man for more than two decades." She shrugged. "No one knows better than I do how low he'll stoop to get what he wants."

Tina raised a pencil-thin brow. "You're scheduled to leave tomorrow. What do you plan to do?"

Pam smirked. "Well, I'm going to forgive him, of course." She shoved to her feet and prowled Tina's office. "What choice do I have? It doesn't seem to matter that he destroyed me, destroyed our family. Six months of depression, weeks of counseling. I'm just supposed to smile and pretend it never happened while he goes about his life footloose and fancy-free." She shrugged. "So I will."

The counselor leaned back in her chair. "Pam, that's not forgiveness. That's lip service. Do you honestly think that's what God wants from you? For you to bury your feelings under a layer of insincerity? Is that really all you've received from what you've been reading?"

Pam turned to face the smaller woman and finally gave voice to reality. "I. Hate. Him." She waved to the open folder on the desk. "You said you reread our session notes from four years ago. You know what he did to me, what I almost..."

Tina held up a hand. "I was here, remember?" She paused for a few seconds. "Let's forget about Alan for a while and focus on you. Are you going to be helped by going back home with your hatred repackaged in a thin layer of acceptance?"

"Best I can do," Pam muttered.

"And when you see him at church, or your children come to you with another plea for some family time?"

"I'll have to grin and bear it."

"And when you stand before God and he strips away your cloak of indifference?"

"I'll..." Pam stopped in her tracks, her eyes filling with the tears she'd promised herself were a thing of the past. Her voice was barely a whisper. "What do you want from me?"

Tina shook her head. "It's not about what *I* want from you."

Pam threw up her hands in frustration. "I'm only human, Tina. God may be able to forgive and forget, but my insides are mortal and my memory is long. I still hurt."

"Pam, did you ever think this might be the reason God chose to bring Alan back into your life?"

When Pam only stared at her wordlessly, Tina motioned to the Bible lying on the desk. "Look up a Scripture for me, will you? I John 2:9-11."

Pam sat and picked up the Bible. She found the verses and read them silently. When she looked up with a shrug, Tina's mouth twitched in a grin. "Read it out loud for me, please."

Pam huffed out a breath but read the passage aloud. *"He that saith he is in the light, and hateth his brother, is in darkness even until now. He that loveth his brother abideth in the light, and there is none occasion of stumbling in him...."* She finished the rest of the passage and sat with her head bowed.

"Pam, despite everything you've said, I don't think Alan's return to Garfield is a plot to destroy your life. On the contrary, I think God is trying to restore your life to a fullness you've done without the last four years. When you called the other day, you told me you needed help to find your way." Tina stopped, circled the desk, and pulled Pam over to the sofa along the wall.

"Tell me, did one of your kids ever get a splinter and not tell you?"

Pam nodded.

"What happened?"

"It got infected."

The doctor nodded. "Exactly. Making the removal so much more painful than it needed to be."

Pam smiled in spite of herself. "Jeremy had a splinter on the side of his foot when he was just a little guy. It was a nasty thing when he finally showed it to me. Hot and swollen. I almost had to sit on him to remove it."

Tina squeezed Pam's hands. "Put yourself in Jeremy's place and imagine God in the role of loving parent. All of the anger and bitterness is a darkness in your heart that's been festering for four years. So much pressure, causing you so much pain. I think God's trying to lance that boil. I know the process hurts like the dickens, but if you'll let Him finish, I promise you'll feel better."

Pam lowered her head into her hands and wept. Tina wrapped her up in a strong hug. "Empty it out, Pam, and once that space is empty, we'll ask God to fill it with love." Pam continued to weep while Tina rubbed her back and prayed.

"Jesus, we need Your healing in this place..."

Patrick held his hand through the black netting screening the ball pit. Samantha laced her fingers with his and stumbled as she stepped from the explosion of slippery plastic spheres.

"Thanks. I'd forgotten how much fun this can be."

He watched as her eyes searched the enclosure. "Don't bother," Patrick said, guessing she was looking for her daughter. "I think she's part mountain goat. She scrambled out ahead of you, and she's already in line on the other side of the slide getting ready to go again."

"She's going to have to go without me for a while. I didn't remember how much work *serious* play could be. My legs are killing me. You might have to carry me back to the table."

When he reached out his arms to do just that, Sam

shoved him back with a laugh. "I was kidding." She retrieved her shoes from the jumbled pile next to the play area, emptying a green ball out of one of them. She held the shoes in one hand and stood on her tiptoes to brush a kiss across Patrick's cheek. "This was a wonderful idea. Thanks for suggesting it."

"You ain't seen nothing yet. While we've been playing on the inside, the temperature outside has been climbing steadily. The afternoon high is going to be low seventies. After we have our pizza, we're going to race the go carts."

Sam poked him in the chest. "Well, that explains the T-shirt."

Patrick ran a hand down the front of his shirt, smoothing a wrinkle out of a silkscreened stock car with a 24 emblazoned on the side. "Hey, fast cars and beautiful women cannot be overrated. Today my life is complete."

"I—" Sam's response was interrupted by a shrill voice from the play area.

"Mama!"

Sam waved at the toddler seated at the top of the steep plastic slide. "I'm watching, baby."

Bobbie lay back, threw her arms out wide, and disappeared down the slide into the multi colored balls below. When she surfaced moments later, she was laughing and clapping and scrambling out to do it again.

"We'll see how complete your life is when you're forced to bring her back here on a regular basis," Sam warned him.

Patrick dropped his arm around Sam's shoulders and steered her to a table with a clear line of sight to the play area. "Seriously, that isn't much of a threat. The only thing I can think of that makes me happier than spending time with you and Bobbie is spending time alone with you."

Sam sat across from him in the booth. She poured them both a soda from a pitcher. "That's a pretty serious statement for a two-week acquaintance."

"I've always been decisive."

"I'll just bet you have."

He smiled as her gaze left his face and darted back to the slide. He was beginning to understand that parenting was a job Sam took very seriously. It only made him like her more. Patrick accepted the glass she offered. "Just ask my mom. I knew at the first taste that I hated green beans. I knew at the age of six I preferred dogs over cats. By the time I was twelve, I knew I was going to be a lawyer." He stopped to stretch across the table and lace his fingers with hers. "And I knew when I climbed out of my mangled truck that you were going to be someone important in my life."

Samantha's eyes rested on their linked hands. "We like you too, Patrick. I hope we can be friends for a very long time."

He nodded. "Friends for now, but I'm hoping for a little more than friendship down the road, but we can work on that." He waited for her to look up. "Can I ask you a question? You can tell me to mind my own business if it's too personal."

He continued when Sam shrugged. "What's the story with Bobbie's father? Is he a part of your lives?"

Samantha's gaze shifted back to the play area, love visible in her smile as she watched her daughter play. "No, he left when I told him I was pregnant. I haven't seen him since, and hope I never do again." Her smile shifted to Patrick. "I know how amazingly selfish that sounds, but he's not the kind of person I ever want in her life."

"I get the feeling there's a long, involved story behind that statement."

Samantha laughed. "One filled with tears and tragedy. But it's had a happy ending so far. She's my whole world."

They both straightened as Bobbie left the play area and headed in their direction. She stopped next to Patrick and held out a small hand. "Patty come play."

Patrick looked from the toddler to the slide and back to Sam. "Uh...."

Sam shook her head in amusement. "Don't look at me, bud. This was your idea, and I'm all played out."

"I'm too big." He winced as male laughter echoed through the room. Several grown men were scattered through the play area. Climbing, sliding, chasing. Size did not seem to be a factor.

"Wrong answer." Sam laughed when Bobbie continued to tug at his arm.

Patrick allowed himself to be pulled up by the excited toddler. He picked up Bobbie and tossed her over his shoulder in a fireman carry. "Come on, short stuff. I'll let you show me how this is done."

Sam waved as they walked away. Patrick held tight to the squirming three-year-old. He'd never considered fatherhood. *I mean, yeah, I guess I want kids someday.* He stood Bobbie on her feet and followed her up the slide. Maybe sooner than someday.

Pam finally sat straight on the sofa, accepting

PAM: THE WOMEN OF VALLEY VIEW

another tissue. She pushed damp hair out of her face.

"How do you feel?" Tina asked.

"Emptied out. Exhausted." Pam blew her nose. "But in a good way."

Tina patted her hand. "I pushed you pretty hard, but if you've found some release, it was worth it."

"I think I have." Pam gave her a watery smile. "I know I can't forget the past, but I think I can move beyond it. I need to do that, not just for me, but for my family." She dabbed at her streaming eyes. "I promised myself a long time ago that Alan wasn't going to steal another moment of my life. I realize now that carrying around all of that emotional baggage meant I was *giving* him those moments, whether he wanted them or not."

"Good girl. You've made a promising start. You need to remember that God isn't asking you to be best friends with the man. I think you have to accept the fact that, as the father of your children, you have to find some level of comfort with him. You're going to have to talk to him, see what's driving his attempts to see you. Think about how you feel right now. Maybe your ex is looking for the same thing. Do you think you can listen to what he has to say?"

"Facing him is going to be one of the hardest things I've ever done." Pam straightened. "But I think God and I can handle it together."

"Pam, I know you can. Here's my prescription for the next few days. Get a good night's sleep tonight before you drive home tomorrow. Give your kids and husband a huge hug when you get there, and don't put off that meeting with Alan. I know we're coming up on Thanksgiving with Christmas close behind. The days are going to be very busy. Don't let Satan talk you out

183

of what you know you need to do."

Pam shook her head. "I won't."

"What sort of support system do you have at home?"

"Support system?"

"Girlfriends, sisters...not Harrison or the kids. Someone you trust enough to vent to."

"My three best friends. They've been praying and trying so hard to help me over the last couple of weeks," Pam said. "I wouldn't let them in."

"Good gracious, why not?"

"They don't know about—"

"Do you trust them?" Tina interrupted.

"With my life."

"Then you need to tell them everything, even about the abuse and the suicide attempt. If they're going to give you the support you need, you need to be open and honest with them. They can pray all day, but they can't help you fight this kind of battle without knowing what you're up against."

Pam laughed ruefully. "I have a lot to do over the next few days."

Tina nodded. "Yes, you do. It's all part of the process of healing. It's like taking a bottle of antibiotics. You might feel pretty good after taking half of the bottle, but if you stop there, it won't do you any long-term good. You'll be sick again in a month if you don't finish the whole prescription. Same goes here."

Pam swallowed and took a deep breath. "Tina, how can I thank you?"

"Thank God instead," Tina insisted. "All I did was remind your head of the things your heart already knew."

Patrick shifted Bobbie's sleeping form into Samantha's arms, surprised at how empty his arms felt without her sturdy little presence. It wasn't only Samantha he was feeling a growing attachment for. He'd given up trying to explain it to himself. Something about these two girls just clicked inside his heart.

He bent down and kissed Bobbie's forehead before Sam carried her away. "I think we wore her smooth out. She's a little speed demon."

Sam laughed in agreement. "Something neither of us knew until today." She inclined her head towards the sofa. "Have a seat while I put her down. I'll fix us a soda when I come back up. We can watch a movie if you'd like."

"I'd like," he said. "Point the way to the kitchen. I'll fix the sodas while you put the kid to bed."

"That works. Follow me." She paused at the door to her basement apartment and nodded to the refrigerator. "Sodas there, glasses in the cabinet to the left. I'll be right back."

When Sam came back upstairs a few minutes later she found Patrick on the sofa and icy glasses of soda on coasters on the coffee table. She handed him a slip of paper. "Here you go."

"What's this?"

"Directions."

"Directions?"

"To the church and a note about what time the service starts tomorrow."

"Sam..."

Sam crossed her arms. "We had a deal."

He took in her narrowed eyes and determined

expression with a sigh. "I know. I'll be there. Just don't get your hopes up, OK?"

"About what?"

"About me getting *saved.*" He rolled his eyes as he said the word. "I don't want to offend you, and I certainly don't want to end our evening on a sour note. But, I'm just not seeing much of a point these days."

"What are you talking about?"

His lips compressed into a thin line. "The whole religious, do-unto-others thing. It's such a crock."

Sam looked up at him, a frown of confusion on her pretty face.

"We moved back here when Dad got saved because he wanted to do the *Christian thing* and make some old mistakes right. The people he needs to talk to are supposed to be Christians, too, and they won't even listen to him." Patrick shook his head. "I'm sorry, it's frustrating. I really don't want to talk about it. Where's that movie you mentioned?"

Sam rubbed his arm. "It makes me sad that another Christian is setting such a poor example for you. I know it's discouraging, but please don't judge us all by one poor example." She motioned him to a shelf of DVDs next to the television. "Take your pick."

Patrick studied the selection. "Action, comedy, or chick flick?"

Sam settled back with her soda. "I had so much fun today, I'm willing to let you choose."

He skimmed a finger over the titles and plucked one off the shelf. "Ladyhawke"

Sam smiled her approval. "One of my favorites." She arranged couch cushions for maximum comfort while he cued up the movie. Patrick came back to the sofa, placed the remote within easy reach on the side table, and sat back shoulder to shoulder with Sam.

The movie played out while they sat in companionable silence. Somewhere along the way he found himself holding Samantha's hand. He studied her from beneath his lashes as swords clanked noisily on the screen. The soft lighting in the room, the shadows cast on her face by the flickering TV, the way she sighed as the hero and his lady shared a final kiss at the movie's end twisted his insides and put every ounce of his restraint to the test. His eyes traveled to Sam's mouth and lingered there as she leaned the tiniest bit forward to watch the final scene. *I'm gonna die.*

The cathedral rang with the hoof beats of the horse as Navarre battled the evil bishop. Swords clanged amid showering sparks and he saw Sam hold her breath as the final seconds played out, ending with the long awaited embrace between Navarre and the lady Isabeau.

Sam aimed the remote at the television as credits scrolled across the screen. "Oh, I love how this movie ends." She muted the volume and turned towards him. "This has been the most perfect day."

Patrick squeezed the hand he held before releasing it to brush long brown hair away from her face. He leaned in to kiss her forehead. Their eyes met and held for several long seconds. The battle in her eyes matched his. *Dead dog dead!* "You are so beautiful." He bolted from his seat, fished his truck keys from his pocket, and made a beeline for the front door.

CHAPTER EIGHTEEN

Pam sat on the top of a cement picnic table, her feet resting on the bench. She poured a cup of coffee from the thermos, allowing its warmth to seep through her gloves while the chill from the table penetrated the seat of her jeans. She took a cautious sip before setting the cup aside and clutching her jacket a little tighter around her neck. The sky was just beginning to lighten over the lake. Sunlight bounced off the wispy clouds in steaks of orange so brilliant, the sky seemed to be on fire.

She watched in silence as God brought light to a new day. This was how her heart felt this morning: new, bright, and full of possibilities. Probing her feelings gently she found a dull ache instead of the all-consuming pain of the past. Her heart accepted that there were more tears in her future—that's just who she was—but they would be healing tears. *I can deal with that.* Pam lifted her face to the cloud-feathered sky and allowed the warmth of the rising sun to bathe her face and her heart.

Thank You, Father. Thank You for not giving up on me. I don't know what's going to happen once I get home, but I know I need Your strength and resolve to bring an end to this over the next few days. You've given me peace this morning, and I'm beyond grateful.

I know I asked Your forgiveness yesterday, but I'm going to ask again. Forgive me for being stubborn and afraid, for allowing those things to control me. I'm going to leave this in Your hands now. Feel free to remind me later if I forget.

Tina said You were probably speaking to Alan about this as well. I don't need to tell You how unbelievable that is for me. But if You are, give us both the wisdom we need to deal with each other fairly, as Christian brothers and sisters.

Pam smiled and took another sip of her rapidly cooling coffee. The sun was fully up, and six hours of interstate stretched between her and her family. She took a last deep breath of the pine-scented air, scooped up the thermos, and headed back to the cabin to prepare for the trip home.

Patrick looked at his watch for the fourth time in five minutes, then glanced at the building. From where he was parked, he could see Samantha through the double glass doors. She paced back and forth, sort of like his feelings this morning. Why had he let himself get roped into attending another pointless service? *It's what you get for chasing a skirt, dude. She was honest with you about this Christian thing from the get go. You made a deal with the girl, and you've got two choices. Get in there and hold up your end of the bargain, or decide she's not for you and drive away.* His breath echoed in the cab of his truck. Driving away was not an option, especially once he saw Sam step outside and wave in his direction.

He tried to force some enthusiasm into his expression as he climbed from his truck. Sam rushed across the parking lot and grabbed his hand.

"I thought you'd bailed on me. We need to hurry. They're about to start." She pulled him forward and opened the thick double glass doors.

"Hey, I told you I'd be here, and here I am." He peered over her head into a gym filled with young people of every description. Clean cut and shaggy mingled with preppies and saggers. Kids with body piercings and tats stood side by side with Bible toters. Up on the stage, musicians tuned their instruments. The noise from half a dozen instruments, combined with the conversations of fifty or sixty young adults, produced quite a racket.

This is church?

"Interesting group you've got here."

Sam followed his gaze. "It's great, isn't it? We hung flyers and advertised for weeks. Sisko wanted to reach out to the college group. I think we succeeded. I can't wait to introduce you around, but we'll have to wait 'til lunch." Sam took Patrick's hand and tugged him into the noise. "Come on. I've got seats saved for us down front."

Oh, goody. Patrick allowed himself to be pulled up an aisle flanked with folding chairs. Sam led them to seats four rows from the platform. Her bag was in one, her jacket in a second. They took their places just as a sandy-haired stranger stepped to the podium.

The morning portion of the service surprised him. The crowd was friendly, the music loud, and the message unexpectedly thought-provoking. By the time lunch rolled around, he could admit his preconceived ideas had been off base. He might not be ready to embrace Sam's beliefs, but his thinking had certainly changed from this morning when he'd dreaded *church as usual,* his attendance a necessary evil if he wanted to continue seeing Samantha.

Now, as he and Samantha stood in the slowly progressing food line, he wasn't dreading the afternoon session at all. Platters, slow cookers, and bowls of food lined a row of tables in a makeshift buffet. Seating was open, and with the dismissal of the morning service, the noise level escalated back to a mild roar.

Patrick lifted his nose to the air and took a deep breath of the mingling scents. He shrugged when Sam laughed.

"Hungry?" she asked.

"Not so much until I got a look at the spread. Someone went to a lot of trouble."

"Everyone pitched in, even parents." Sam craned her neck to view the dessert table. She pointed. "You see that chocolate layer cake?"

"Yeah."

"Mine." Her smile beamed with pride. "That and the big pot of spaghetti."

"You cook?"

"I'm learning. There's not much you can do to mess up spaghetti, but the cake, that's a new recipe. Mom helped me put it together yesterday morning."

Patrick stared down at Sam. "Let me rephrase my question. You cook with actual recipes, not just cans, bags, and boxes."

Sam frowned over her answer. "I'd say more of a combination of the two. I like the quick and easy in a pinch, but I enjoy experimenting with new things when time permits. I love having my own little kitchen to play in. I'm building quite a collection of cookbooks." Her smile turned playful. "If you're nice, I'll fix you dinner sometime. I'm always looking for a new recipe and a fresh guinea pig to try it on."

Patrick grabbed her hand and made a show of trying to pull Samantha out of the line.

"What are you doing?"

"Kidnapping you now before someone else finds you. I'm taking you to Vegas tonight. We'll have a quickie wedding tomorrow. You can be my kitchen slave, and I'll be your lifetime guinea pig. Fair trade."

Sam gave him another smile and a small backwards shove. "Goofball. I could be a lousy cook for all you know."

The sandy-haired stranger from earlier darted past them, and Samantha snagged his arm. "Dave, slow down, I want you to meet someone."

The young man swung around and draped his free arm around Samantha's shoulder. His other hand held a pitcher of iced tea. "Sam, what's up?"

"I want to introduce you to my friend, Patrick Wheeler. Patrick, this is Dave Sisko, our youth pastor."

Dave handed the pitcher to Sam, wiped his damp hand on his jeans, and held it out to Patrick. "Call me Sisko. Welcome to the asylum."

Patrick grasped the proffered hand. "Thanks. Quite a party you're throwing here."

"Glad you're enjoying it. You are enjoying it, aren't you?"

He nodded. "So far."

"Patrick just moved to town," Sam said. "He's enrolled for next semester at the university. Prelaw."

Sisko snapped his fingers in recognition. "You're the guy Sam ran over at the Sonic."

Sam groaned. "Why do people keep saying that?"

"Sorry, kiddo. Iris ratted you out. I have to say, it's an interesting technique."

Sam rolled her eyes while the guys shared a quick laugh at her expense.

Sisko retrieved the pitcher and gave Sam another quick hug, "Hey, whatever it takes to get them in the building." He waved the pitcher. "Gotta move." His attention turned back to Patrick before he hurried away. "Have fun, and come back anytime."

Patrick watched Sisko fill cups at the end of the table, carry a loaded tray for a young lady with a broken arm, and come back to clear away a couple of empty bowls. "Does he ever stop?"

Samantha shook her head. "I don't think so. If you look up perpetual motion in the dictionary, Sisko's picture is the only definition you'll find. I've never seen anyone with such a heart for service."

"It's his job."

"Yes and no." Sam inched ahead in the line. "I think he'd find a way to do what he does, even if it didn't involve a paycheck. It's what Jesus tried to teach us."

"You see Jesus as a servant?"

"Absolutely," Sam answered. "Look at His life. He healed, He taught, He loved, and He died. He never asked anyone for a single thing He wasn't willing to give first." Sam handed him a plate and a plastic fork as they finally reached the food. "At last!"

Pam took a break four hours into her trip. She wanted to time her arrival home for after six this evening. Harrison and the kids would be at church by then. She'd have a couple of quiet hours to unpack and decide on a game plan for the next few days.

Armed with a fresh tank of gas, a candy bar, and a soda, Pam climbed back into her car and noticed the message light blinking on her cell phone. Harrison, checking on her progress and expected arrival time. She knew she'd given him plenty of reason to be concerned about her recently. She hoped to be able to alleviate those worries before the night was over.

She scrolled to her voice mail without looking at the number and pushed the button to replay the message.

Pam, it's Alan. Please hear me out. You weren't at church again this morning, and I really need to talk with you. Please give me a call—and a chance. I don't want to hurt you again. I don't want to make you feel stalked. I just need an hour of your time. Please call me back.

Pam sat behind the wheel of her SUV, thoughtful. She and her ex-husband operated with very little personal interaction, conversation limited to a rare adjustment of their visitation schedule. The kids spoke to him, regularly, on their own cell phones, but Pam established the ground rules of their current relationship early on. *I don't need anything from you. I don't want to talk to you. Stay off my turf.* Alan had never called her outside of those parameters. Until now. It had been four years since Pam had talked with him face-to-face.

She replayed the message, waiting for the sound of his voice to trigger the familiar panic, expelling a sigh of relief when the dread failed to materialize. "Thank you, Jesus." She saved the message.

She would call him, she decided as she continued her journey home, but she owed explanations to her family and friends first. She needed their support layered on top of what God was providing. She'd get back to Alan before the week ended. No reason to rush. It didn't look like he was going anywhere any time soon.

The last two hours of the drive flew by. Pam turned into the driveway and sat in her car for a few moments before pulling into the garage. She studied the home she'd made with Harrison. The family was at church, but lights had been left on. Even empty, the house spoke to her of safety, love, and comfort. Her haven. Just one of the things she'd forgotten recently.

Pam opened the door that led from the garage into the kitchen. She stepped inside and lifted her nose to sniff the air. The aroma led her straight to the microwave and the note taped to its door.

Pam, welcome home. We had lunch out today. We brought you your favorite potato soup and garlic bread. Can't wait to see you. We missed you. I love you, Harrison.

Pam hurried up the stairs to the bedroom she shared with Harrison. She washed the six hour trip from her hands and pressed a cold cloth to her face. Her travel clothes were exchanged for her favorite flannel pajamas before she headed back to the kitchen to enjoy the dinner her family had provided for her. Getting away had done her a world of good, but she was so happy to be home.

She punched numbers into the microwave timer. Tomorrow, there would be another special dinner for her family. Not one of apology this time, but one of love and celebration. A time to remind Harrison and the kids how much she loved them and to let them know about the change God had made in her life this weekend.

It was Karla's turn to host their Bible study tomorrow night. Enjoying dinner with her family would mean missing the main study, but that was OK. After dinner, she'd join her friends for coffee and cheesecake. She needed to give them the answers she owed them. By this time tomorrow, Pam planned to be two steps closer to filling Tina's prescription for recovery. Two steps closer with, hopefully, a plan for the last and final step towards healing.

Pam took her soup out of the microwave and the bread out of the oven. She poured the soup into one of her favorite bowls and relished the first taste. Oh, it was good to be home.

Patrick hunched in his seat Sunday afternoon as Dave Sisko wrapped up his sermon. This would be the point Patrick dreaded in any church service. The moment the minister offered an invitation for the *sinners* in the audience to come forward for salvation. The moment his heart always went to war with his head.

Sisko moved out from behind the podium, his voice low and confident when he spoke. "Today has been a good day. A chance to mingle with old friends and be introduced to new ones. It's my sincere hope everyone here will take at least one new friendship home with them tonight. You can never have too many friends."

Sisko took the two steps down to the gym floor. The youth pastor's eyes swept the crowded seats. Patrick winced when the steady blue gaze seemed to linger on him before moving on. "Before we dismiss though, I'd like the opportunity to introduce some of you to one more friend. Someone who will never let you down, someone who will never leave you on your own, someone who loved you so much He died for you." Sisko paced in front of the platform. "I want all of you to take a few minutes and look deep inside yourselves." Sisko spoke quietly, walking up and down the aisle, hands clasped behind his back. "We all grew up pretending. Cowboys and Indians, cops and robbers, doctor, nurse, hairdresser, mommy...

"Now you're all grown up. Some of you are away from home for the first time, looking at futures where the decisions are all yours and all too real. Some of you are still pretending. Pretending you don't need anyone, pretending that you have everything under control, pretending your life is all you thought it would be. Have you figured out yet how much you're lying to yourself?"

Sisko paused, the silence in the gym was complete as dozens of young adults waited to hear the youth pastor's next words. "None of us stands alone. None of us lives or dies alone. None of us is good enough to make our single lives, much less the world we live in, what God intended it to be, alone.

"Jesus can fix that for you. I'd like to introduce you to Him tonight." Sisko turned and went back to the platform. "I'd like everyone to stand. If you need prayer, would you please raise your hand?"

Patrick stood next to Sam, watching under lowered lashes as hands went up all around him. He kept his fingers clenched on the back of the chair in front of him. Why was the urge so strong to lift his hand for prayer? His thoughts slowed to a crawl. *No way am I getting sucked into this religious mumbo jumbo.* He tried to hold firm to the belief that he hadn't done anything to repent over. But there was no way to deny the crack Sisko's words had opened in his heart. Sam stood beside him, head bowed, eyes closed, lips moving in silent prayer. For him? *Oh, that helps.* His hand crept up to rub his chest. Maybe he didn't need salvation, but he did need answers to a lifetime of questions. Patrick slipped his hand into the air and yanked it back down.

Sisko continued his altar call. "I saw your hands, and I appreciate the courage it took to raise them. Can you take the next step now and come forward for prayer?"

Patrick held his ground as young people flocked to the front of the gym. *Not me.* That's not a cliff I'm jumping off.

Once service was dismissed, Patrick and Sam waited in the milling throng of young people for their chance to tell Sisko good-bye and thank him for the day. Their turn finally came. Samantha dropped Patrick's hand and threw her arms around Sisko in an enthusiastic hug. "It was a great day!"

Sisko met Sam's enthusiasm with laughter. "I think so, too."

He offered Patrick his hand. "It was good to have you with us today, Patrick."

Patrick took his hand. "I had a good time." He was surprised to hear the sincerity in his own voice.

"Wonderful." Sisko slapped Patrick's shoulder. "We can expect to see you back then?"

"I wouldn't be surprised." Patrick and Sam continued out the door. They stopped and turned when Sisko called Patrick's name.

"Hey Patrick, I'm praying for you, my friend."

Is he making fun of me? Patrick searched the other

man's face. All he found was a genuine smile. He nodded his thanks and allowed Sam to lead him out into the crisp night air.

CHAPTER NINETEEN

Pam slipped on her jacket and stood at the front door, hand on the knob, poised to leave. Harrison and the kids were cleaning the dinner mess, the clank of dishes, pots, and pans punctuated by their laughter. Her family had tossed her out, urging her on her way, sensing, she guessed, that this next step was just as important to the process as the discussion they'd shared over dinner.

The knowledge that something needed to be done didn't always make the doing easy. Worry over tonight's explanations had dampened the joy Pam normally experienced when she cooked for her family. There were things she could never share with her children. She left those alone without a backward glance and simply dealt with what they needed to hear. She'd promised that things would be better from here on out, paying special attention to Jeremy's attitude. His face had brightened with her assurance that she would be speaking to Alan in an effort to put some of the old hurts to rest. She hadn't given Megan permission to invite her father and his new family for Thanksgiving dinner. She couldn't see that happening under any set of circumstances, but the assertion that the anger and the bitterness of the last four years were things of the past returned a smile to Megan's face and erased some of the stress from Jeremy's. Laughter flowed through her home once again.

Pam's heart stung with a sad revelation. Her own attitude had rubbed off on her children, especially Jeremy. They'd been walking around on eggshells for a couple of weeks, and she'd been too wrapped up in her own feelings to see it. She could beat herself up over that or place it in the same hands that had so recently taken years of animosity from her heart. Closing her eyes, she imagined her small hands holding out one more bag of garbage. The hands reaching out to take it from her were so much larger and more capable than hers. She stepped out onto the porch and looked up at a sky dusted with stars. *Thank You, Father.*

She allowed herself a speculative smile on the way to her car. "I wonder what kind of cheesecake Karla came up with for tonight's dessert?" That sense of anticipation bolstered Pam's resolve during the short drive to Karla's house.

Her courage fled as she parked the car. Secrets were rare between the four friends and these went deep. Pam chewed her lip. Wouldn't a partial truth serve the same purpose? Sharing Alan's abuse would be hard, but it would answer most of their questions about her recent behavior and left over feelings. There was no need to...

The weight of deception settled back on Pam's shoulders. *The whole prescription, just like Tina said.* She took a deep breath, struggling to reach beyond her fears. Part of a memory verse she'd learned in her childhood flooded her heart and brought her peace. *I can do all things through Christ which strengtheneth me.* Pam pushed out of the car, her steps brisk and ringing with determination as she crossed the concrete walk to Karla's front door. There was no need to ring the bell. They were expecting her.

Pam followed the voices of her friends into the kitchen, shrugging out of her jacket as she walked. She stopped in the doorway, her attention drawn to the chocolate dessert sitting regally in the middle of the table. The conversation of her friends ceased as she tossed her jacket negligently across the back of a chair and smiled at Karla. "I knew I could count on you. What is that?"

Karla picked up a knife, prepared to slice through the cake. "Chocolate tuxedo cream."

Pam leaned over the back of the chair and stared as the first piece was lifted free, revealing three layers of chocolate. "Oh Karla. It's almost too pretty to eat. You have no idea how much I need this right now."

"Sure I do," Karla said. "Chocolate is God's ultimate comfort food. The way I look at it, loving chocolate is a requirement for every woman, especially Christian women."

"This I have to hear." Pam encouraged her, accepting a plate.

"Well, chocolate is the only food God made especially for women. He didn't make anything comparable for the guys." Karla shrugged, justifying her logic. "I figure that means He really does love us best."

Pam allowed her first bite to melt in her mouth. "This has to be sinful."

Terri forked up a big bite. "Explanations like that and dessert like this only reinforce the opinion that you have *way* too much time on your hands since you retired." The bite disappeared into her mouth with a sigh. "I'd say that's a good thing."

Callie accepted her plate. Never one to beat around any bush, she focused her gaze on Pam. "Did you have a good trip? Harrison said you'd gone away for the weekend, but he didn't say where."

Pam smiled at her friend's question. "It was...productive."

Karla settled at the table. "You look rested."

Pam smiled down at her plate. "That, too." She put her fork aside and looked up to find three pair of eyes watching her intently. She drew courage from the love she saw reflected there. "You guys are the best friends I've ever had," she told them simply. "I know you haven't understood my behavior over the last two weeks." *Only two weeks?* "I owe you all an apology and an explanation—"

Callie interrupted. "You don't owe us an apology. And the explanation...only if you're sure you're ready."

"I'm sure," Pam assured them. "But I think it would be easier if I let you guys start. Then I can fill in the blanks." She sat back in her chair. "Tell me what you remember about my last year with Alan."

The women picked at their desserts. The silence stretched out. It was obvious no one knew exactly where to start.

Pam broke the quiet with a promise to her friends. "Guys, you're not going to hurt my feelings. Just tell me what you remember. I'll fill in the blanks when you're done."

With an audible sigh and a shrug, Terri took the plunge. "I remember your mood swings. Tearful one minute, forced cheerfulness the next."

Karla agreed with Terri. "Your behavior was more than a little erratic. We worried about you then, same as now."

"It seemed like you were uncomfortable in your own skin back then." Callie offered up her point of view. "You changed your hair color and style, lost weight..."

"Weight you didn't need to lose," Karla inserted.

"...experimented with different styles of clothing." Callie shrugged. "Everything from daring to subdued."

Pam nibbled her dessert as her friends warmed to the subject.

"Long hair to short hair. Contacts to glasses and back." Terri shook her head. "It was sad watching you struggle, not knowing how to help."

"Then the whole thing blew up, "Callie said. "You caught Alan with his secretary. He left, you filed for divorce. You spent some time in Wyoming with your parents, and when you came home, you were better. You still had some bouts with depression, but Harrison had become such a part of your life by then, we worried about you a little less every day."

"Until now," Karla added.

Pam listened to her friends, nodding her agreement, eyes staring into the distance, filmed with the tears of remembered pain. "I was so wounded." Her voice caught, but she pressed forward. "One day you have everything you ever wanted in the whole world. The next day the world you loved ceases to exist."

Terri reached out to touch her hand. "You don't need to do this."

"Yes, I really do, for so many reasons." She squeezed Terri's hand before she continued. "You guys need to know the whole story, and I finally think I have the courage to tell it."

"Then tell us," Callie encouraged. "Get it off your chest once and for all. We're here for you, whatever you need."

Pam took a deep breath and wiped her eyes. "I know you've heard me say that I'm happier with Harrison on a bad day than I ever was with Alan on a good day. When I say those things, it's a defense mechanism against the hurt of failure. I think it gives you the wrong picture of our years together."

Pam prepared to walk down memory lane. "It really was love at first sight for Alan and me. High school sweethearts, a young couple just starting out. There was so much potential in our marriage. Those first few years, when the kids were small, those were good years. Memories and experiences I wouldn't trade for anything. As much as I love my life with Harrison, those years with Alan will always have a special place in my heart.

"My marriage and my husband were my whole life, so much so that I was willing to do anything to keep it and him." Pam drew restless pictures on her napkin with her fork, her body agitated, her mind struggling for calm. "If I had to pick two words to describe myself during that last year they'd be *desperate* and *inadequate*." Pam abandoned the napkin and got up to pace.

"You mentioned the physical changes I went through. They were all a desperate attempt to hold on to what I'd already lost. Alan wanted out of our marriage, and I wouldn't let him go. Couldn't let him go.

"We had horrible fights. He'd come home from work, and dinner or the house wouldn't be just what he thought it should be. The kids were too noisy. My job was taking too much of my time." She waved an impatient hand. "Something as simple as the blinds being up or down, when he wanted them down or up. I never knew what was going to set him off from night to night."

Karla narrowed her eyes. "What a jerk."

Pam turned a grateful smile on her friend before she continued. "I lost track of the times I dragged him to counseling. We spent so many evenings in Pastor's office we should have rented a space there. One time Alan would mention that my hair was boring, or I'd gained a little weight. I'd change styles or go on a diet. The next time it was my clothes. I was dressing like a grandmother, so I tried to perk things up. Then the next time, I was dressing like a slut, and who was I trying to attract? I was grasping at any straw I could find to keep from sinking."

"Oh, Pam," Callie whispered. "Why didn't you tell us?"

Pam's answered promptly. "Shame. I didn't want anyone to know how bad things had become. That I was such a failure. I convinced myself that if I could just stumble onto the right combination of changes, I could save my home." She stopped at the table and took a drink to clear her throat. "I knew you guys were praying. So was I, but it didn't seem to be doing any good. Things were going downhill at an uncontrollable speed. I was just along for the ride."

Karla sat back. "You hinted at emotional abuse a couple of weeks ago. I knew you were in trouble four years ago. I never dreamed it was so bad."

Pam stopped and prepared to enter the most painful memories. "It was worse. Everything I just mentioned is petty compared to what went on behind the closed doors of our bedroom." She paused again, stared at the far wall, and swallowed against words she'd never spoken aloud. *Stupid, fat, worthless, frigid slob.* "Despite everything, I still loved him. Still thought I could fix things between us. But every time the subject of intimacy came up, Alan would laugh at me." Despite her best effort, her voice broke. "I was 'stupid' if I thought he wanted to make love to a fat, worthless, frigid slob."

Callie's fork clattered to her plate. "He said that to you?"

Pam nodded. "I heard it every day for months in one form or another. I heard it so often I began to believe it. That's when you guys began to notice the changes. I was trying to be less of a stupid-fat-worthless-frigid slob.

"Then one day, that final day...We'd had another fight the night before about my job taking too much time away from my family. The house was a mess. The kids were running wild. I didn't appreciate anything he worked so hard to provide." She raised her hands in surrender. "I talked to my boss, and we agreed to reduce my schedule from five half-days a week, to three. I left work early and called Alan to tell him I was coming by the office with a surprise and, well, you know what I found."

"Alan and his secretary," Karla answered. "He planned the whole thing."

"Yeah," Pam admitted through her tears. "There's no way I can explain to you how it felt to be so demoralized. To jump through every hoop and land flat on my face. To finally understand that my best was never going to be good enough."

"That's enough, sweetheart," Callie began.

"No, Callie, I need to finish. I need you guys to know all of it." Pam sniffed and continued with her story. "I kicked him out, retained Harrison as my lawyer, and fought with myself every day while I waited for the divorce to be final.

"What was I doing to my kids? Could I make it on my own? What was wrong with me that he didn't love me the same way I loved him?" Pam's voice broke at the old memory.

"I had pills for depression. I was taking pills so I could sleep. I couldn't eat, and when I did eat, my stomach would clench up and double me over, so I had pills for that, too. I couldn't function. I was falling apart right along with my marriage. I finally quit my job altogether."

"That's when you flew out to Wyoming to spend the rest of the summer with your parents," Terri remembered.

Pam studied Terri for a few seconds before nervous energy forced her back to her pacing. Silence settled over the room, everyone waiting to hear the end of the story. Pam finally turned her back on her friends, unable to face them with this last confession.

"I took pills."

"You were depressed, honey," Terri told her. "Getting help is nothing to be ashamed of."

Pam turned to face her young friend.

Terri started to say something else, but Callie laid a hand on Terri's arm. Terri let out a small gasp as Pam's meaning became clear. "You took pills?"

Pam nodded. She turned back to the wall and wept. Karla went to her and held her for a few seconds before leading her back to her chair. "Finish it," she told her. "Get it out of your system for good."

"I didn't know what else to do," Pam admitted. "I felt like I'd failed in the most important thing in my life. My marriage was over. My children would spend most of their time without a father. Money had never been an issue, but it would be now. Would I be able to keep the house? Could I afford the things the kids needed? I can't even list the worries Satan put in my mind.

"School was out. Jeremy and Megan had gone to spend the summer with my parents. The day the divorce was final, I decided to pack away some things. I remember sitting on the bed sorting through some old pictures. I realize now what a bad idea that was. Each picture I picked up, each memory I relived, became a new dagger in my heart. All I could think of was the pitiful failure I'd become."

"Pam, you were never a failure," Karla assured her.

Pam waved her objection away. "In my eyes, that day, I was. I couldn't face it.

"I called the kids that afternoon, spoke to them for what I thought would be the final time." She stopped and looked at her friends. "Do you have any idea what it's like to tell your babies good-bye and mean it the way I meant it that day?

"I only have patchy memories of the rest of the afternoon. I remember cleaning the house. Being discovered in a house in need of attention would only validate Alan's claims. I read my Bible. I'm still not sure if I was looking for justification or comfort, or just something to make what I was about to do less of a sin. I did my hair and makeup and swallowed a half bottle of sleeping pills.

"Ten minutes later, there was someone at my door. I'd forgotten Harrison was bringing by a corrected custody document for me to sign. When I didn't answer the door, he called my cell phone. He says I answered the call, but my speech was so slurred by then he couldn't understand me. He broke through two doors to get to me and rushed me to the hospital."

"Thank God!" Callie exclaimed.

"Yeah, they pumped out my stomach and put me on three days of suicide watch. I begged Harrison not to tell anyone what I'd done. He agreed on the condition that I would get some counseling. He's never broken that promise."

"Oh, Pam," Terri said, tears running down her own face.

"Harrison knew about a place that offers Biblical-based counseling. He made some calls and drove me down there himself. I told everyone I would be at my parents' house for a few weeks. You know the rest. I was better when I came back home. I'd asked God to forgive me, and I know He did, but my heart was still broken. Harrison saved my life in more ways than one during those months." Pam dried her eyes and took a deep breath. "Can you guys ever forgive me?"

Callie's expression was puzzled. "Forgive you for what?"

"For not trusting you enough. I should have confided in you years ago, but I was so ashamed. Afraid you guys would think less of me."

"Pam, we love you," Terri said.

She gave her friends a watery smile. "I'm so glad."

"Is that where you went this weekend?" Callie asked.

Pam nodded. "This time, I think I've got it right. I'll be talking to Alan before the week is out."

"The nerve of that man," Karla grumbled. "I thought he was brash for coming back, but now—"

"He doesn't know." Pam picked up her napkin, blew her nose, and wiped her eyes.

"He doesn't?"

"Nope. Why should he? What would telling him accomplish?"

Karla was indignant. "He almost killed you."

"No," Pam corrected her. "I almost killed myself."

"But he..."

Callie scooped up a bite of cake and handed the fork to Karla. "Eat this and hush."

Karla sputtered to a stop and looked at Callie. "But he—"

"Yes," Callie agreed. "Alan has a lot to answer for, but we've been trying to help Pam get past this. Now that she's on her way, don't stir her back up."

Karla pursed her lips and looked back to Pam. "Are you on your way?"

Pam nodded. "I think so. I had serious discussions with a wonderful Christian counselor and with God this weekend. I've finally realized that the indifference

I've been living with is not forgiveness. I know I have to forgive Alan...for everything. That won't be an easy conversation to have, but for my family and myself, I know I have to let this go.

"Tina, my counselor, told me to draw strength from you guys. She reminded me that you are my support system. Will you pray with me?"

"Honey, you don't even need to ask." They bowed their heads over empty plates and linked hands. Callie led the way, four faces wet with shared tears and gratitude.

"Jesus, thank You for preserving us. Our circle of friendship remains unbroken tonight because You love us, and we are grateful."

"Amen," Terri whispered.

"Lord, Pam has suffered on her own for too long, and now she's looking for healing. You're the only one able to grant that request. Let there be healing in her heart and Alan's. Let there be wisdom, direction, and peace. Satan destroyed their home, but their family remains. Help them rebuild what can be rebuilt. Let there be complete forgiveness. In Your gracious name, we ask these things. Amen."

Pam looked up with a smile, fresh resolve in her soul clashed with the tears in her eyes. "Thank you," she whispered. "For the first time in years I think things are finally going to be all right."

CHAPTER TWENTY

Patrick searched for an empty parking spot in the crowded sub shop parking lot. Looking for a quick lunch in a small town with limited fast food choices, when every high school kid in town with a driver's license had the same idea, probably wasn't the smartest plan. But he was here, and he was hungry. If worse came to worse, he'd get his sandwich to go.

When he pulled open the door, the noise of the place assaulted his ears even as the heavy scents of garlic and fresh bread assaulted his nostrils. His mouth watered, his stomach growled, and his shoulders slumped. The dining area was as packed as the parking lot.

A misaimed paper missile sailed past his left ear. The corners of his mouth quirked up in a nostalgic smile. Straw wrappers flew through the air, wadded- up napkins and empty chip bags bounced off heads here and there while the culprits pretended interest in an object across the room. At least the individual salt packets eliminated someone getting a saltshaker dumped on his food. There were days he longed to be sixteen again with nothing more important on his mind than timeless pranks.

Resolved to carry out, he wove his way to the counter.

"Patrick!"

Surprised, Patrick did a full 360 turn before he located the source. The youth pastor from Sam's church stood and waved him to a small table.

Patrick crossed the room and shook Sisko's hand. "How's it goin'?"

"Great! Eating in or out today?"

Patrick turned to the wall-to-wall kids. "Out, I guess. Doesn't look like my timing's the best."

"Not a problem." Sisko jerked his head towards the counter. "Grab your food and join me. I'm flying solo today."

"You sure?"

"Absolutely. I'd enjoy the company."

Patrick tossed his jacket into the empty seat. "Thanks. I'll be back in a few." He joined the throng at the counter, making slow but steady progress to the head of the line. When it was his turn at the sandwich assembly line, he ordered a foot long meatball sub, chips, three cookies, and a large soda.

He came back to the table and scooted in across from his new friend. He caught the stare Sisko leveled at the loaded tray. "What?"

"Can you eat all of that?"

"Mom says I have hollow legs. I live to prove her right." Patrick unwrapped his sandwich and emptied his chips onto a napkin as a young girl approached the table, dragging a second girl in her wake.

She tapped Sisko's shoulder. "You got a second?"

Sisko wiped his mouth on a napkin and turned in the booth to face the youngsters. "Hi, Mandy." He held up a hand, and the teen slapped him a high-five. "What can I do for you?"

"I wanted to introduce you to Allison." Mandy paused and pulled the second girl forward. "She just transferred into my homeroom last week. I've been trying to talk her into coming to youth service with me."

Sisko held out his hand. "Nice to meet you, Allison. I'll second Mandy's suggestion. If you don't have a home church, we'd love to have you join us."

Allison ducked her head with a shy smile. "We don't go to church much."

Patrick chewed while Sisko took a few minutes to visit with the girls. It was hard to concentrate on his sandwich and not eavesdrop on the conversation across the table. Patrick's desire for lunch faded as every word Sisko spoke about the benefits of church attendance reminded him of his own lack in that area.

He had to give a point to the youth pastor though. The guy was good. Sisko's words sounded sincere instead of preachy. The girls finally waved in farewell, but kids continued to flow around their table in a living tide. He counted at least five more that stopped by their table before the youth pastor was left to enjoy his lunch in peace.

"You're a popular guy," Patrick said.

Sisko looked around the room. "I like to be a visible presence. It's important the kids, mine or not, know I'm available. I make it a point to eat lunch in town a couple of days a week." He took a bite and grabbed a napkin as dressing ran down his chin. "We've solved a lot of problems and exchanged countless prayer requests over a sub or a hamburger. It's less threatening for them than coming to my office at the church."

Patrick nodded. "They're all so young. They make me feel old."

Sisko grunted. "What are you? All of twenty-two?"

Patrick munched on a handful of chips. "Something like that."

"Wait 'til you're my age, with a young family. I feel a little older each time one of them has a birthday."

"Sam didn't mention that you were married. You have kids?"

"Now you've done it." Sisko smiled and fished in his pocket, withdrawing his cell phone. "You've pushed the daddy button." The small screen flared to life to display a picture of a little girl and two small boys. "Meet my family." He pointed to his daughter. "That's Alex. She's three and a half, and the boys are Jared and Jordan. They turned two in August."

Patrick admired the picture. "Great-looking kids. They must keep you pretty busy."

Sisko nodded. "It's a circus most days, and I'm the second string juggler." He flipped to a new picture. "That's my wife, Lisa. I'm sorry you didn't meet her Sunday, but she was pretty tied up in the kitchen. She's the pro in our little family."

"I've been spending lots of time with Sam and her daughter. I never really appreciated the sheer energy that goes into taking care of kids that age." Patrick grinned in sheepish acknowledgement. "I'm kind of enjoying it."

Sisko laughed and gave Patrick a warning that echoed Sam's words. "Bobbie is a little flirt. She'll break your heart if you're not careful."

Patrick shrugged. "I guess I'll have to risk it."

The men sat in silence for a few minutes. Sisko ate his lunch. Patrick merely picked at his.

"Eyes too big for your stomach?"

Patrick shrugged in response. "Nah, its fine. Just not what I was really hungry for I guess."

Sisko studied him for a few seconds while he gathered up his trash. "Funny how that happens, isn't it?" the older man asked. "Something looks so good, laid out right in front of us. Seems like everything we need, but it just doesn't satisfy. It fills up the empty spot in our stomach, but we're still hungry."

"Why do I get the feeling we aren't talking about sandwiches anymore?"

Sisko grinned and stood to leave. "I'm a minister, son. It's what I do. But I'm not going to preach to you today." He took a card out of his pocket and scribbled a few words on the back before handing it to Patrick. "Will you do me a favor?"

Patrick nodded as he accepted the card.

"Take a few minutes and read this. Then call me, day or night, and we'll talk." He clapped Patrick on the back. "Glad we ran into each other, but I have to split."

He raised a hand in a final farewell, ignored a shouted *Sisko* from across the room, dodged the wadded up sandwich wrapper that followed it, and allowed the door to close on the lunchtime mayhem.

Pam held her breath and waited for the phone to be

picked up on the other end. She wasn't normally one to procrastinate once her mind was made up about something, but even with God's help, it had taken her four days to work up the courage to dial Alan's number. Pam had no idea what she was going to say to him when he answered. When it rang the fifth time she almost sighed in relief. One more ring and it would probably roll over to voice mail.

"Hello."

Pam hesitated briefly, surprised when Kate answered instead of Alan. "Um, Kate? It's Pam. Could I please speak to Alan?"

"Sure, let me get him. Sorry it took so long to pick up. He's dozing, and it took me a few seconds to find his phone."

"Kate, if he's taking a nap or something, don't bother him. He can call me back." Maybe God was giving her a reprieve.

"Nonsense. He just fell asleep in front of the television. He'd never forgive me if I let you go without giving him a chance to talk to you."

Pam heard a muffled exchange.

"Pam?" Alan paused to clear his throat. "Sorry, I dozed off in front of the TV. My throat's a little raspy. I must be getting a cold."

"Hmmm." Pam's response was noncommittal. "I told Kate not to bother you."

"No bother," Alan assured her. "Thanks for returning my call. We need to talk."

"That's what I hear," she answered cautiously. "I'm listening."

"In person."

"I'd rather—"

"Please, Pam. This is a conversation that needs to happen in person. One meeting, that's all I'm asking for."

Is that all, really. Just one meeting. Pam swallowed. Not entirely certain she could work up the courage for Alan's "one thing."

"Let me buy your lunch on Saturday."

Father, I'm going to need Your help.

"Pam, are you still there?"

Old wounds throbbed and threatened to overwhelm her, but God's soft voice whispered in her heart. *Hear him out.* She glanced up at the ceiling and rolled her eyes at the invisible voice. "Where?"

"Do they still have that gazebo at the city park? I'll bring lunch."

"I don't think a picnic—"

"It's not a picnic, Pam. We just need a quiet place to talk, and the food will give us something to focus on while we do that. Do you still like chocolate-banana shakes?"

A shaky sigh escaped Pam's lips. A hint of impatience colored her voice when she answered. "Fine, whatever. I'll be there at one on Saturday."

"Thanks, Pam. One more thing?" Alan continued when Pam didn't answer. "I was going to call Jeremy after school to see if I could talk him into coming over here for dinner, maybe even spend the night. I think we need a little Dad time. Can I tell him I've cleared that with you?"

"He has ball practice, and it's a school night."

"We'll wash his clothes, we'll make sure he does his homework, and we'll get him to school tomorrow."

Her sigh echoed in the microphone of her phone.

"Fine, I'll see you Saturday." Pam disconnected the call and stared at the phone, feeling resentful. Four days to get this far, and now she had to fret over it for another two. She'd wanted it over with today. What could possibly be so important that it required a face-to-face meeting?

Pam caught her breath when she realized what she was doing. "Jesus, forgive me. Old habits die hard. Please give me strength and wisdom for Saturday. Help me be fair and open to whatever Alan has to say."

Alan bounced the phone in his palm.

"Well?" Kate asked.

He looked up from his place on the couch "We're having lunch on Saturday."

"Are you going to tell her?"

He considered. "I don't know. I guess I'll need to make that call when the time comes. I need to be sure of her forgiveness before I take it any further." Alan pushed himself upright. "In the meantime, how would you feel about Jeremy spending the night?"

Kate frowned at him, and he read the concern on her face. His energy had ebbed low today. He was still in his sleep pants at two in the afternoon. He saw her shake it off and silently blessed her resolve. "If he agrees, how does pizza sound for dinner?"

"Works for me." Her voice was tight, but she held out her hand.

Alan took it in his, eyebrows raised in silent question.

Kate simply closed her eyes. "Father, thank You for opening this door. Please continue to give Alan the physical strength he needs to do what You're leading him to do. Bring Your peace to this situation."

Alan squeezed her hand as he stood. He swayed, a wave of unexpected vertigo stealing his balance.

Kate grabbed his shoulders. "Alan..."

He pulled her close, changing her rescue into a hug. "I'm fine. For the first time since we moved back, I think it's going to be all right. I think I'll go to the school a little early and watch Jeremy's football practice."

Three hours later Alan stood next to his truck in the school's nearly deserted parking lot. He popped a peppermint into his mouth and waited for his son. Today's practice had included a scrimmage, and he'd been in the bleachers to see Jeremy score a touchdown. Pride and gratitude filled his heart. God was already storing up good memories for his kids. Memories they could hold onto after he was gone.

Jeremy ran from the locker rooms juggling a backpack full of books and a football. He yelled at his father, letting the ball fly in a perfect pass. "Dad, go long."

Alan saw the ball sailing towards him. His next moves were instinctive but ill-timed. He stretched out into a run, his head turned, eyes tracking the ball. He reached up to snag it from the air and dropped to his knees. A fit of coughing overtook him, the gasping sucked the half dissolved peppermint in to his throat and cut off his air supply. His chest felt as if it were wrapped in steel bands. He struggled for breath. *Not now, Jesus. Please, not now.*

Jeremy raced to his father's side. "Dad!" He knelt as Alan fought to catch his breath and relieve the pain in his chest.

"Dad?" Jeremy repeated, grabbing his cell phone to call for help.

Eyes streaming, unable to speak through the coughing, the world faded to black and back again. Alan reached out for his son's hand, speaking in a strangled whisper. "Wait."

Jesus, please. Finally the candy dislodged itself and his lungs expanded around a deep breath.

Father and son continued to kneel in the grass beside the parking lot. Alan's breathing slowly returned to normal.

"Wow, son. That pass took my breath away."

"Dad, this isn't funny."

Alan patted his son's back and accepted Jeremy's help to get back to his feet.

They walked back to the blacktop and leaned against the truck. "What just happened?" Jeremy demanded.

Alan spit the candy into his palm. "I had a piece of candy in my mouth. When I ran to catch your pass, I guess I swallowed wrong. All that coughing must have dislodged it. I'm fine now." *A half-truth wasn't the same as a lie, was it?* What else could he tell him?

Jeremy looked at his father, eyebrows drawn together in a worried frown. "You sure you're all right?"

Alan squeezed his son's shoulders while searching his pocket for his keys. "I'm sure. Do me a favor?"

Jeremy shrugged, obviously still shaken despite his father's reassurances.

"Let's keep this our little secret. Kate'll just fuss, and it's sort of embarrassing for a former quarterback not to be able to run and eat candy at the same time."

Jeremy stared into Alan's face. The worry slowly left

his expression. He nodded and ran to retrieve the ball and then climbed into the passenger seat of his father's truck. "I'll keep quiet, but it'll cost you."

"Blackmail?"

"Call it what you want," Jeremy quipped.

"Terms for your silence?"

"Pizza for dinner. Supreme, extra cheese."

Alan laughed. "Son, you drive a hard bargain."

Patrick propped pillows against the headboard and settled back against them. He planned to find a late night movie to watch, but he delayed switching on the television. After the noise of the evening, he found the quiet of his room relaxing. His stepbrother was spending the night, and once they'd worked through his homework and finished their pizza, the evening had progressed into some rowdy family time, including a cutthroat game of Monopoly and homemade banana splits.

Patrick had always been the only child and he enjoyed this newfound role of big brother. It was cool to have someone who looked up to him, asked him for advice, and considered his counsel sage. Jeremy had a crush on a girl named April, and he'd needed some suggestions on how to proceed, both with his pursuit of the young lady and Megan's constant torment. Patrick thought about Sam's beautiful face and grinned over the *crush* discussion. He could definitely identify.

Patrick didn't even mind having his name shortened to Rick. Since he'd begun referring to Jeremy as *the germ,* he figured they were even—in a comfortable, sibling sort of way.

A busy evening, but he had one more thing to do

before he looked for a movie. He picked up his Bible and the card Sisko had given him at lunch. He looked up the reference and read Mark 10:17-21.

The story was of a rich man asking Jesus how to inherit eternal life. ...*Thou knowest the commandments, Do not commit adultery, Do not kill, Do not steal, Do not bear false witness, Defraud not, Honour thy father and mother....*

And he answered and said unto him, Master, all these have I observed from my youth. Then Jesus beholding him loved him, and said unto him, One thing thou lackest: go thy way, sell whatsoever thou hast, and give to the poor, and thou shalt have treasure in heaven: and come, take up the cross, and follow me.

Patrick closed his Bible and stared into his heart for a few seconds. Even he could read between the lines on this one. *"I've obeyed all these commandments since I was young."* Sounded a lot like his story to Samantha. Maybe good wasn't always good enough. Maybe it wasn't about changing his life, but about adding the one thing he didn't have.

He turned off the lamp, picked up the remote, and settled in for the night.

Follow Me, a voice whispered in his ear.

Patrick groaned and thumbed on the television. His voice was a mutter in the darkness. "Heal my father. Then we'll talk."

CHAPTER TWENTY-ONE

Pam arrived at the park early and alone on Saturday. She preferred Alan come to her rather than her going to him. Harrison had volunteered to accompany her for moral support. Pam declined. He'd offered to drive her to the park and wait for her in the car. She refused that offer as well. She needed to do this on her own.

She'd fussed a little extra this morning with clothing, hair, and makeup. Female vanity demanded she look her best for this meeting with the man who'd tossed her aside. *Stupid, fat, worthless, frigid slob.* Pam shuddered and remembered Harrison's appreciative whistle, offered as she'd descended the stairs thirty minutes earlier, pulling it around her like an invisible force field. A lesser man might have been jealous of her efforts, but Harrison knew what this meeting would cost her, and he knew the importance of every second of preparation. Purple sweater topped her favorite black jeans, the ones Megan always said made her butt look good. She'd swept her hair up from her face and secured it behind her ears with silver combs. Her eyes were alert and free from tears. Pam had made up her mind to keep it that way.

She sat in the gazebo in sight of the parking lot and waited. Alan's truck pulled to a stop in the lot, and she prayed. She watched his approach and tried to sort out her feelings. He looked older, slimmer, face more finely chiseled, sandy hair a little thinner and longer than she remembered him ever wearing it when they were married. Their eyes met and held for the first time in four years. Her heart thumped hard against her breastbone.

Alan entered the gazebo quietly, placed the fast food bags on the bench next to her, and sat down.

I won't cry. I won't run. I won't be a victim ever again. Silence stretched. Pam searched for words and assumed Alan was doing the same.

Alan opened a bag and handed Pam a cup. "I had them add extra chocolate."

The sound of his voice startled her. Despite her best efforts, Pam's hand shook as she accepted the cup. She clasped it with both hands and lowered it to her lap, staring down at it, throat too constricted to even pretend to try it. "Thanks," she whispered.

Alan spread napkins on the bench and continued to dole out their lunch. "Would you like me to bless it?"

Pam's response was a jerky nod.

Alan held out his hand.

Pam looked at him from under her lashes, indecision gathered between her brows.

"I'm not here to hurt you, Pam."

She took a deep breath and slowly placed her hand

in his.

Alan held it for several seconds before he spoke. "Jesus, thank You for today." He paused, sniffed, and continued. "Just...thanks. Amen."

He raised his head and continued to hold her hand. When he finally spoke, his voice was gruff with emotion. "You look good."

Pam tugged her hand free. "Thanks. You've lost weight."

He shrugged. "All those years of eating my own cooking, I guess. Kate's trying to fatten me back up, but it's not working so far."

"She seems nice." Pam laid the burger aside, unopened. "I've only talked to her a couple of times, but the kids like her."

Alan unwrapped his lunch. "And she loves them, but I think she's partial to Megan. Kate has a son. This is her first chance to spoil a daughter. You OK with that?"

Pam shrugged. "I have Harrison. You're entitled to someone as well. It's good that Harrison and Kate both love our kids."

The gazebo filled with silence once more. Pam placed the milkshake aside, laced her fingers together, and rested her hands in her lap. Her attention focused on the squirrels chasing each other outside the gazebo. She'd agreed to lunch, hoping food would serve as a diversion, something to keep their hands busy while they talked. It wasn't working. The food lay there between them, ignored, while Pam waited for Alan to say what he wanted to say.

Alan covered his uneaten sandwich with a napkin.

He reached out with a hesitant hand and turned her face to meet his. "I have so many things I need to say to you."

Pam levered her chin out of his grasp, but she forced her eyes to remain on his face, determined he wouldn't see her cower. "I'm listening."

"I don't know where to start."

"Then why are we here?" Pam's question bordered on impatience. "You're the one looking for this meeting."

"I guess...I just..." Alan fumbled. "I wanted the chance to tell you that I was sorry."

The simple apology robbed her of speech. Pam found it impossible to sit still. She rose to her feet and circled the confines of the gazebo twice before turning to look at her ex-husband.

"You're sorry? You drove me to the brink of insanity. You stripped my self-esteem to the bone, ripped our home apart, and cut the heart out of my chest. And you're sorry?" She was bewildered and frustrated. "For this we needed a face-to-face meeting, complete with lunch?" Pam faced him, her hands on her hips. "That's what you've been chasing me all over town to tell me? You're sorry?"

Alan ran a hand through his hair. "Please sit down. We need to talk. I want to apologize for those things."

"Let me save you some time, Alan. I forgive you. It's taken me four long years, but I refuse to drag your baggage around for one more day. I'm not doing it for you. I have our children to think about, and Harrison. I can't continue to make them pay for your mistakes. It's finally been brought home to me that that's what I've been doing." Pam stopped and a silent sob racked her body. "So, I forgive you," she repeated. "Sincerely forgive."

She swiped at her eyes with the sleeve of her sweater. "Live in Garfield. Attend church at Valley View. Renew your old friendships. Spend as much time with the kids as you want. Be as happy with Kate as I am with Harrison. You have my blessing." She headed to the gazebo's entrance and dug her keys out of her pocket. "Is that what you needed to hear me say?"

Alan let her run down. He patted the bench. "Please?"

Pam crossed her arms, returned to the bench, and sat with a thud, refusing to meet his gaze. When Alan reached for her hand, she tried to pull it away, but he held fast.

"Please look at me." His request was barely a whisper.

When she complied, he continued. "Pam. I'm sorry. I know how insignificant that seems, but I don't know how else to say it." His voice broke but he pushed forward. "It wasn't your fault. Not one single ounce of blame is yours. It was all me." Alan stopped and closed his free hand over hers. "I humiliated you, I hurt you, and I was so wrong. There's no way I can make up for any of it. There are no words I can say to fix it. All I can do is finally take the blame squarely on my shoulders where it belongs. I rededicated my life to Christ, but He won't let me rest. I had to come and apologize to you."

Pam searched his face, trying to find the monster that had haunted her for so long. "Why?" She struggled to keep the tears at bay. "Alan, we had so much. I just need to know why. What did I do to make you stop loving me?"

Pam recognized sincere pain on Alan's face before he bowed his head over their clasped hands. "I don't know why. I've asked myself that question so many times over the years. When I look back at what we had and what I turned it into..." His eyes were sad when they met hers. "I have no answers for either of us. No excuses that would begin to justify the things I did and said."

He stopped and shifted to kneel at her knees. "The only thing I have is God's forgiveness and a prayer for yours. I know you have no reason to trust me, but I'm praying God will show us how to put the past behind us. Pam, I'm begging you for a chance to show you that I'm a changed man. Please tell me what I have to do to make things better."

Pam looked down at his bowed head and heard the words that mirrored their daughter's request a week earlier. The last remnants of bitterness melted away. Her heart soared out from under the ashes of that burden, and she breathed a prayer of thanks. She lifted a hand and touched the back of Alan's head.

"I forgive you, Alan." Her words held a sincerity lacking in her earlier pronouncements. "I accept your apology." *Don't just say the words, show him,* a voice inside her heart urged. She didn't argue, just took a deep breath before she could think it through.

"Alan, we've gone our separate ways, but we need to be a united family for our children. Would you and your new family like to join us for Thanksgiving dinner? I think it would be a wonderful day for celebrating new beginnings."

Alan nodded and continued to weep at her knee.

Pam bent down, laid her head on his back, and allowed their mutual tears to heal what had been broken for too long.

At the convenience store directly across the highway from the park, Kate stood at the large plate glass window and watched the scene unfolding in the gazebo. Unable to hear their conversation, she studied their body language, mildly surprised when the opening tenseness between Pam and Alan morphed into what appeared to be tears and prayers. Her presence wasn't about spying, and their physical contact didn't bother her. Concern for her husband's health, should Pam refuse his apology, was her only motivation. She wanted to be close in case Alan needed her. Satisfied things were going to be fine, she took a step back and stumbled on the person standing slightly behind her. Kate reached out to steady herself and came face to face with Harrison Lake.

Harrison raised his eyebrows. Kate shrugged her shoulders.

"We're pretty pathetic, aren't we?" he asked.

Kate's eyes cut back to the park. "Just keeping watch from a distance."

"Afraid Pam might throttle him?"

"The thought crossed my mind, but no. I knew he'd need me if she refused to listen."

Harrison glanced back out the window. "He looks more than capable of taking care of himself."

Kate followed his gaze. Seconds passed, their ticking morphed into the beeping of heart monitors, counting off the moments of Alan's life. Her response was a whisper. "Looks can be deceiving."

"It seems like things are headed in the right direction," Harrison observed. "I don't think either of them would appreciate our presence here, regardless of our good intentions."

Kate agreed. "Probably not. I was about to leave. Let's just keep this between us."

Harrison stole a final glace out the window. "Absolutely."

Silence settled over the gazebo once more, but it was a silence washed clean of bitterness. Pam finally made a move to gather up their cold and abandoned lunch for disposal. Alan looked on as she stood to toss cold, greasy french fries out onto the grass for the birds and squirrels.

"Pam, there's something else I need to tell you. I wasn't sure I'd be able to go into it today, but I think the time is right."

She registered the gravity in his voice and put the trash aside. "OK," she answered cautiously, reclaiming her seat next to him.

Alan took her hand again. "Do you mind?" He raised their joined hands. "This is hard for me. I need something to hang onto."

Pam studied his face, the internal debate was obvious in his shifting expression. "Whatever it is, Alan, just say it and get it over with. It can't be any worse than what we've already dealt with this afternoon."

"I wish that were true." Alan's voice was a soft murmur. "I'm dying, Pam."

Pam jerked her hand from his. She sat back in disbelief. "Dying?"

It was Alan's turn to pace. Pam watched him prowl the small area, waiting for him to deliver the punch line of this tasteless joke. When it didn't come, she studied him closer. "You're serious," she whispered. "What...?"

Alan stopped her questions with a gesture. "Give me a second, OK?"

For the second time in an hour, Pam was robbed of speech. She nodded while he continued to pace. When he finally turned to face her, she would have sworn that his countenance was grayer and his shirt a little looser across his shoulders. She shook the image from her mind. *This has to be a mistake*, she told herself. *He's always been a bit of a hypochondriac.* She opened her mouth to question him further, but Alan spoke first.

"I found out four months ago that I have an advanced heart condition, hypertrophic cardiomyopathy. After some extensive testing, it's been diagnosed to be in the final stages. It's terminal. I don't know how much longer I have, but the cardiac episodes are accelerating. I've been to the emergency room twice in the last two weeks, and there was a milder episode two days ago when I was with Jeremy."

Pam tried to deny what she was hearing. "He didn't say anything."

"I told him I choked on a piece of candy," Alan admitted. "What reason would he have to believe otherwise?"

"Alan. You're serious about this."

"Deadly," he said, "if you'll forgive the pun."

"That's why you came back?"

He nodded. "Partly. The last year of my life reads like the outline for a bad movie. Salvation, wedding, conviction, terminal diagnosis, a return to the scene of my crimes, and the hunt for absolution. All that's missing is the funeral at the end, and its coming, sooner rather than later."

"Alan..."

He waved away her protests. "I need your help."

Pam covered her mouth as Alan's words hit home. "Jeremy and Megan."

Alan sat back down. "When I came back, I wasn't sure if, or how, I'd tell them. Maybe I was still in a little bit of denial. I certainly didn't want them wasting what little time I had left worrying about something they can't change. In any case, I couldn't tell them until we'd had a chance to talk."

"They need to know. They need time to prepare."

"I agree, but finding the time and the place...actually saying the words. Pam, I don't know if I can do it."

Pam held out her hand and waited until he took it. She held it silently until he met her eyes. She studied the face of the man that had been her best friend, first lover, and worst enemy. "We'll do it together."

Pam sat in her car for a long time after Alan left. The mixed emotions he left behind threatened to overwhelm her. Relief at finally putting years of hurt behind her, guilt over certain comments she'd made recently regarding Alan's life, dread at the thought of what this news would do to her babies, and gratitude that Jesus had given her a chance to make some of her own mistakes right. She rested her head on the steering wheel.

Jesus, I'm so sorry for some of the things I've said. I keep seeing Kate's face in the store that day when I told her I'd gladly dance at Alan's funeral. How my words must have hurt her.

What a lesson you've taught me today about keeping my mouth closed. Please forgive me.

Jesus, this is going to destroy Megan and Jeremy. Give us all wisdom. They're going to need all of us before this is over.

Pam straightened and turned the key in the ignition. She needed to talk to Harrison and then she *really* needed to rally her friends around her. Dr. Sylvester called them her support system. That was so true. She needed them tonight.

She pecked out a text message while the car idled. Three responses popped up on the little screen before she even had the chance to start the drive home. How could she have ever doubted that her friends would stand beside her? They arranged to meet at Terri's house after dinner.

Harrison was in the garage when she got home, practicing his golf putts with an automatic ball return. The ball shot out of the hole and sailed past him as he opened his arms to take her in. "You OK?"

Pam melted into his embrace. "I'm fine."

Harrison must have heard the unspoken addition to her simple comment. "But...?"

She took a deep breath as his arms tightened around her. "Harrison, Alan's dying. That's part of what he's been trying to tell me."

"What?"

Pam rested her forehead on his chest, her words barely a whisper. "I don't remember what he called it, and I didn't ask for the details. Once he convinced me that he was telling the truth, all I could think of was the kids. How are we going to prepare them for this?"

Harrison rested his chin on the top of her head. "Babe." His hands rubbed her back, the simple contact offering more comfort than any words could have.

"I invited them to come for Thanksgiving dinner." Pam bit her lip. "I know you're probably not comfortable with that. I should have talked it over with you first, but there was this little voice urging me on. Then he told me he was dying..."

"Shhh. You don't have to explain. It was the right thing to do. The kids are going to need all of us right now."

Pam shifted under Terri's stare.

"Are you sure you don't want a soda or something?" Terri asked.

"Maybe when the others get here. I'm sorry to barge in on you at the last minute."

Terri frowned. "Don't you dare apologize. You'd do the same for me."

Pam nodded. When she heard the doorbell chime and the noise of Karla and Callie's arrival, she expelled a sigh of relief.

They joined Terri and Pam at the table, expectation on their faces.

"Thanks for coming, guys," Pam told them.

Callie's answer was simple. "You needed us. We're here."

"We don't need to be thanked." Karla was quick to agree. "Assurance that you're OK after your meeting with Alan is what we need."

Karla's candor made Pam smile. "It was fine."

Three sighs of relief echoed around the table. Callie expressed what they were all feeling. "Thank You, God."

Karla's scrutiny was intense. "If it was *fine*, why are

you still so anxious?"

Pam followed Karla's gaze to her white-knuckled hands fisted tightly on the table top. She forced her fingers apart and shook them at her sides. The words were as difficult to speak the second time as they were the first. "Alan came back to Garfield because he's dying."

"Dying?" Terri asked in confusion. "*Dying*, dying?"

Pam nodded. "I was in such a state of shock when he told me, I didn't get a lot of details. I don't remember what he called it..."

Karla pursed her lips. "Mitchell David Black, you are dog food when I get home. Hypertrophic Cardiomyopathy."

"That's it," Pam verified, her expression bewildered. "How...you knew?"

Karla shook her head. "Oh no, honey, I'd have told you." She shared a look with Callie. "But I'm thinking our husbands knew."

Callie cocked her head, confusion obvious. "Why?"

"Do you remember asking me a few days ago if Mitch was acting *weird*?"

Callie nodded. "I blew it off. Those two are always up to something. Two men, one brain."

Pam smiled. *I used to say that about Alan and them.*

Karla sat back and crossed her arms. "*Weird* morphed straight into *panic* when I booted up the computer the other day to search for a stuffing recipe. Instead of my lost recipe, I found a whole list of searches for a heart disease I'd never heard of. Mitch just had a physical a couple of weeks ago. He told me that Dr. Banks had given him a clean bill of health. But when I saw all that stuff on the computer, I jumped straight to the wrong conclusion."

Callie's blue eyes were round with concern. "Karla..."

Karla brushed Callie's concern away. "I called him home for lunch and confronted him about it. He assured me that it was a friend who was sick, not him. I should have known. Those three always were thick as thieves." She frowned at Callie. "Benton was with him that afternoon. He didn't mention it?"

"When I get home..." Callie began.

Pam stopped her. "It's not important now. What matters now is preparing Jeremy and Megan for this news, giving them the support they're going to need to get through this." Pam put her head in her hands. "That, and begging Kate's forgiveness."

Terri leaned back in her seat. "Kate's forgiveness?"

"The day of your shower," Pam explained, "I saw Kate in the grocery store. She offered to buy me a cup of coffee so we could get better acquainted. When I refused, rudely, I might add, she tried to convince me to speak to Alan." Pam closed her eyes against the memory. "I offered to dance on his grave first."

Callie groaned. "Oh, Pam."

"Yeah," Pam's voice dropped to a whisper. "I didn't understand the look on her face that morning, but I do now. What am I going to do?"

"*We.*" Karla stressed the word. "We are going to make it a point to invite Kate for Bible study Monday night. We'll make sure you get a few private moments to offer your apology, but there's more to it than that."

Terri nodded her understanding. "A support system."

"That's right," Karla agreed. "Megan and Jeremy

aren't the only ones who are going to need people to lean on. We need to try and be there for her as well."

CHAPTER TWENTY-TWO

Kate nibbled cheesecake, comfortable for the moment to listen and observe. Amusement replaced her earlier uncertainty about attending the Bible study at Pam's house this evening. *Why did it have to be Pam's house this week?* She'd vacillated most of the day between attending and staying home. Hunger for the fellowship of other Christian women finally decided the issue for her. She faced a new town, a new church, and an uncertain future. She instinctively knew she couldn't face them all alone.

She'd been prepared for some resistance, maybe even a little of the attitude Pam had served up in the market several days ago. But Pam and the others had been friendly and attentive without making her feel like the newbie in the group, and if Pam had shared Alan's illness with the others, they didn't let on. She found her most fortified defenses soundly defeated.

Jesus, I asked You for friends. Is this Your answer? Can these women possibly welcome me into their circle? Maybe some of them, but Pam?

She shook it off and turned her attention back to the subject at hand. These ladies were out of control— in a good way. This was Bible study elevated to the level of a competition sport. Their topic tonight was Miriam, the sister of Moses, and for every positive point that came up, someone in the room managed to shoot it down with two negatives. One of the ladies referred to Miriam as a *sulky, jealous brat.* The resulting laughter brought the discussion and the evening to a close.

The women trickled out over the next few minutes. By eight thirty, Kate decided it was time for her to leave as well. She stood and faced her four hosts. "I enjoyed the evening. It was...enlightening."

The woman with the beautiful silver hair laughed at Kate's choice of words. "That's one word for it. Feel free to join us anytime. We *enlighten* each other every Monday night."

"I'd like that." Kate picked up her plate, and prepared to carry it to the kitchen as the other guests had done.

Pam held out her hands. "I can get that for you." Kate shook her head. "I've got it."

Pam watched Kate disappear into the adjoining kitchen. Had there been a hint of snippiness in her voice? *Stop it*, she scolded herself. *If you heard snippiness, it was no less than you deserve.*

"Go after her," Callie whispered.

"But..."

"No buts." Terri jerked her head towards the door. "Get in there and get it over with."

Pam squared her shoulders and prepared herself for

a four course helping of crow.

Kate looked up from rinsing her plate when Pam joined her at the sink.

"I'm glad you decided to join us tonight." Pam leaned against the counter. "Did Alan tell you about my Thanksgiving invitation?"

Kate nodded, keeping her eyes trained on the dish. "We appreciate the invitation, but—"

"I owe you an apology, Kate. There's no justification for what I said to you that day in the store. I was hurting and wanted to take as many people with me as I could. You offered me friendship, and I responded in anger."

Kate turned to face Pam, her chin lifted in a small gesture of defiance. "Pam, I'm relieved that you and Alan have managed to work out some of your differences. The memory of how he treated you was a ghost that was going to haunt him to his grave." She shrugged, adding her plate to those already stacked in the sink. "You were right that day in the store. I don't have any part..."

"But you do." Pam threaded her fingers through her hair and hoped she looked as repentant as she felt. "Megan and Jeremy are so fond of you. Alan told me Saturday how much you've come to care for them. Please don't let my foolishness take away from that. They're going to need all of us to get through this. We're going to need each other."

Pam shrugged. "Don't forgive me out of obligation. Don't come on Thursday if you're sincerely uncomfortable, but if that offer of friendship is still open, I'm willing to give it a try."

Kate's chin lowered a notch. "I guess we're all going

to learn a lesson in forgiveness before this is over." Her expression softened. "I've got a really good recipe for pumpkin bread, if you need an extra dessert."

"One of my favorite things."

She returned to her dining room after escorting Kate to the front door and nodded in response to the question behind three pairs of eyes. "It was close for a few minutes, but she accepted my apology. I really hurt her feelings." Pam rubbed her face with both hands. "I have such a big mouth."

Callie jumped to her friend's defense. "You were in pain. It's just one more thing you can give to Jesus and be thankful that it's over."

"Yeah, I've loaded Him down pretty good over the last week or so. I'm glad He's got broad shoulders." She switched her attention to Terri. "The other good news is she accepted my invitation for Thanksgiving dinner. We'll have a house full."

"That's great," Terri told her. "It'll be nice to have a chance to get to know her better, unless..."

"Unless what?"

Terri chewed her bottom lip. "Well, it's just...Are you sure you still want us there?"

"Why would you ask that?" Pam asked.

"You've got a lot on your plate right now. Steve and I would understand if you wanted to make Thursday just a family thing." Terri rubbed her belly. "I'm not so pregnant that I can't manage dinner in my own kitchen."

Pam held up a hand. "Don't even go there. I'll admit the original motive for the invitation was to give you a bit of a break. But you've been promoted from pregnant and needy to necessary and please-don't-leave-me-alone-with-these-people." She laughed at Terri's expression. "I'm making strides in the right direction, but I think having you and Steve there will make conversation a little easier for everyone. Are you good with that?"

Terri nodded. "We're still set for four o'clock, right?"

When Kate opened the front door, she was assaulted by the roar of the Monday night football game blasting from the television's surround sound. She cast a look in Patrick's direction. "You can hear that all the way down to the curb."

Patrick grinned at his mother while juggling chips, salsa, and the remote. "Sorry." He lowered the volume. "How was your meeting?"

Kate searched for an appropriate word. "Interesting," she finally answered, "and only slightly less fierce than your game." She peered into the kitchen. "Where's Alan?"

"His team's losing. He conceded defeat and said he was taking his new book to bed. I think I heard him on the phone a little bit ago, but it's been pretty quiet otherwise."

She tossed her purse and jacket onto the sofa and leaned over to kiss her son good night. "Keep it down in here, OK?" She filched a handful of chips, stole a drink of his soda, and headed down the hall.

Alan looked up from his book with a smile of greeting when Kate entered the bedroom. He turned the corner of a page down to mark his place and lifted his face to receive her kiss. "Welcome home." He grabbed her around the waist and pulled her down on the bed beside him, rolling with her to the other side of the mattress.

Kate squealed, returning his kiss as they landed with a bounce. Kate batted playfully at his hands, squirming among the pillows when Alan transitioned from hugging to tickling. "I give. I give..."

Alan tucked her head onto his shoulder and snuggled his arms tightly around her. "Looks like you survived the evening."

"It wasn't as awkward as I expected. I actually had a pretty good time. I enjoyed the chance to visit with some of the ladies outside of a church setting. Pam's friends made me feel very welcome." Kate cuddled closer. "Pam made a point of pulling me aside to issue a personal invitation for Thursday."

"I told you on Saturday, it's up to you," Alan reminded her.

Kate chuckled softly. "I know, and I was inclined to say no...until tonight. Now, I'm making pumpkin bread."

Alan dropped another kiss on the top of her head. "I love you, Kate. I know this situation is difficult for you."

"Not difficult, Alan, just...odd. I certainly never expected to have more than a passing acquaintance with your ex-wife. Now, I'm celebrating the holidays with her. But, hey," she said with a small shrug, "we're all Christians. We might as well learn to live with each other now if we're planning to share Heaven with each other later." She changed the subject. "What did you do while I was gone?"

"Watched part of the game with Patrick, read a little, missed you a lot." His tone lost some of its playfulness.

"I talked to Harrison. We have an appointment in his office Wednesday afternoon."

Kate propped herself up on an elbow. "Whatever for?"

"Estate planning."

She pushed away and rolled to her feet. "Alan..."

"Kate, it's time. The house in the Kansas City is sold, my business holdings are pretty much in order, but I have a stock portfolio and the trust fund from my grandparents. It's going to be a mess. I don't want to leave it for you to deal with. If you're planning on staying here...You are planning on staying here?"

She nodded.

He continued, "Then it makes sense to have a local lawyer. Who better than Harrison? I hesitated to call him, but it's just one more link in the chain. He has a vested interest in seeing that things are kept in order for Jeremy and Megan."

Kate sat on the edge of the bed, her back to her husband, her shoulders hunched in a protective ball. She felt Alan's hand on her back and couldn't stop the silent tears or the shudder that racked her soul.

"Kate." Alan's voice was a whisper as he rubbed small circles on her back.

"I'm not ready."

"Babe..."

Kate twisted her hands into a knot at her waist as she stood up. His words had opened a hole in her heart she'd tried hard to ignore. "I'm not ready," she repeated. "I'm trying to be supportive and strong, but I'm falling apart inside." She faced Alan and smiled through the tears. "I look at you and I see everything I wanted my future to be." Her smile disappeared, her lips pressed tight in an effort to hold it together. "And I'm going to lose it...again. How is that fair?" Kate paced away, emotions falling free on the outside while she struggled to cap the well of personal bitterness spewing on the inside. "I raised my son for twenty years on my own. In all that time, I never once asked God to bring someone new into my life. I was content as long as I had Patrick. And then, out of the blue, there you were." She spread her hands as she faced her husband. "I had no defense against that smile."

Alan patted the mattress next to him. "Come here."

Kate climbed back onto the bed and surrendered to Alan's arms. "There you were."

CHAPTER TWENTY-THREE

Pam leaned back in her desk chair, put her hands over her head, and stretched. The kink between her shoulder blades let go with a gratifying and audible *pop*. She straightened and frowned at the time display in the bottom corner of her computer screen. She'd been sitting there too long. "I need a breath of fresh air and a cappuccino." Her snicker echoed in the room. "Well, what passes for cappuccino at the convenience store across the street." She stepped from her office and decided to check on Harrison. If he needed a break as well, they could walk across together.

Harrison's door was open. Stephanie sat across from him, her iPad in her lap. Even from this angle, Pam could see lines of concentration on both faces as Stephanie tapped the screen.

"I've juggled your appointments for next week and freed you up for Monday and Tuesday. I'll work on the rest and see what I can do. I know you don't normally work the Friday after Thanksgiving, but I might have to shift one or two things over there to make this work."

"Thanks, Steph..." Harrison looked up. His features softened with a smile as he saw Pam in the doorway. "I thought I heard your door open. Did you decide to come out of hiding?"

"For a few minutes. I came to see if you wanted to walk across the street with me. There's a pumpkin spice cappuccino calling my name."

Harrison shook his head. "Can't. Judge Lambert's office phoned thirty minutes ago. He wants to move our trial date up a week. Since that assures we're done by Christmas, I agreed. We start bright and early Monday morning." He motioned to Stephanie. "We're juggling. Bring me one?"

Pam nodded and caught sight of Stephanie's fingers in the air. "Me, too. Cookies and cream. I need caffeine—chocolate caffeine."

"Oh, that may have just screamed louder than the pumpkin." The front door to the office opened. Stephanie started to her feet. "Stay put," Pam said. "I'll deal with it and be right back with our afternoon dose of energy."

Pam stepped around the corner and stumbled to a stop, her involuntary gasp at seeing Alan and Kate standing in the reception area covered, she hoped, by a feigned cough. She pasted a smile of welcome on her face and hoped it didn't look as strained on the outside as it felt on the inside. *Breathe. We're all friends now.*

"Alan, Kate. What can I do for you?"

Alan glanced up from helping Kate with her jacket. "We have an appointment with Harrison this afternoon." He looked around the empty room. Pam read the puzzled frown between his brows. "I thought he said Wednesday afternoon."

Pam took a step back into the hallway, still uncomfortable in Alan's unexpected presence. *I guess it's gonna take some time to get used to seeing him as something besides the enemy.* "He probably did. It's been a strange day." She motioned to the sofa. "Have a seat. I'll tell him you're here."

"Pam." Alan halted her retreat with a word. She turned to look at him over her shoulder. "If you can spare the time, I'd like you to sit in on our meeting."

Pam nodded her response and escaped up the hall.

Alan sat across from Harrison's desk, here today as a client instead of the enemy in the camp. *What a difference a couple of weeks can make.* While Harrison glanced through the packet of paperwork, Alan tried not to fidget. Kate sat beside him, keeping his hand gripped tightly in hers. He sent a reassuring smile her way. She'd been a little clingy today. Monday night's conversation and tears reflected in her eyes every time he looked at her. His heart fluttered in his chest, reminding him of the borrowed time he was living on. *Jesus, please give me a little more time.*

Harrison cleared his throat, tapped the papers into a stack, and slid them back into the manila envelope. He looked at Alan over the top of his cheaters and rapped a knuckle on the thick envelope. "That's a pretty impressive piece of work. It all seems to be in order. I'm not sure what you want me to do for you."

Alan squeezed Kate's hand and then pulled away from her grasp. He leaned forward and rested his elbows on his knees. "It is in order. I've done my best to make sure of that. But there are loose ends, and there will be more later. I don't want Kate to have to mess with any of this when I'm gone." His peripheral vision caught the shift in Kate's posture as she turned away from his words. He addressed his next comments to Pam. "Do you remember the conditions of my trust fund?"

Pam nodded. "Twenty-five percent on your twenty-fifth birthday. We bought our house and started your business with that portion. Another twenty-five on your thirty-fifth birthday."

Her breath caught.

"And the balance when I turn forty-five. Said balance to go to my children in the case of my death."

Pam covered her mouth and looked at him over her fingertips. "We had a prenup where the trust fund was concerned. I'd forgotten..."

Alan nodded as he sat back. "Our children are going to be independently wealthy. That's one reason I wanted you in on this meeting. There are some things I wanted to discuss..."

Pam stopped him. "Alan, it's your money. I don't have a say."

"They're our children, and in my absence you do have a say." He glanced at Kate, who still refused to meet his eyes. Her face was calm, but the tapping of her foot revealed her agitation. "The majority of my grandparents' money remains untouched and accruing interest every day. I checked the balance yesterday. There's a little more than three million dollars in the account."

Pam gasped, Kate continued to stare at the wall, and Harrison studied Alan from across the desk. "I want to set up three funds, equally divided between our children and Kate's son, with the same timed payments that my grandparents originally designated." He looked at Pam. "Are you good with that?"

Pam repeated herself. "It's your money. You don't need my permission."

"Permission, no. Blessing, yes." Alan motioned to the papers resting under Harrison's clasped hands.

"I'm an accountant. I understand the importance of planning for the future, and I've tried to put the same wisdom I give to my clients into practice for myself. I've got some long-standing investments, money from selling my share of the partnership, and a significant life insurance policy." He stopped to reclaim Kate's hand, lifting it to his lips for a quick kiss. "The proceeds from those things, along with the house we just bought, will be Kate's."

He turned to Kate and waited until she met his eyes. "I've seen to it that you're well provided for."

"Alan..." Kate's voice was heavy with emotion.

Alan leaned forward to lay a finger across her lips. "Shh. We have to discuss this. I don't want to hurt you, but I won't leave you wondering about the future." His attention returned to Harrison. "I've got some instructions in that folder regarding potential investments. You'll need to have a conversation with my personal accountant once everything has been probated. I've crunched some numbers, and there's a note in there regarding the monthly annuity I want Kate to enjoy from the estate. Which brings us back to the kids."

He closed his eyes against the burn of tears and toughened his voice. If he gave in to despair now, the meeting was over. "I know we're spending the day together tomorrow, but if you guys are free on Saturday I'd like to take everyone to lunch, maybe an activity afterwards. We need to talk with them, prepare them." He popped a mint into his mouth. "I don't think we can wait much longer."

Pam returned to her office, shut down her computer, and left for the grocery store. The turkey for tomorrow's dinner was in an ice chest at the house, soaking in her secret brine of brown sugar, garlic, and Worcestershire sauce. She'd purchased the non-perishables for the feast weeks ago, but she needed an excuse to get away by herself, and shopping for the fresh groceries she needed worked as well as any.

She sat while the car idled in the crowded parking lot and the windows fogged over from the inside-out. Her energy seemed to have walked out the door with Kate and Alan. *This is really happening. Alan is dying.* Pam mulled the phrase around in her mind. Not was or would...*is.* And something she'd never really considered would change the lives she valued most in the world, forever. She searched her heart. There was still hesitancy. It still gave her pause to come upon Alan in unexpected places, like today at the office. And tomorrow, having him in her home. She could admit to nerves there, too, but dancing on graves or hiring hit men no longer appealed. God had taken those things out of her heart.

She rested her head against the steering wheel as tears fell. Tears for Alan, tears for the life they'd had and lost, and tears for her kids mingled on her cheeks.

Father, this is too hard.

CHAPTER TWENTY-FOUR

Pam frowned at the alarm clock on Thursday morning. She slapped at the snooze button impatiently. "Ten more minutes," she whispered to the room at large, burrowing down into the warm nest of blankets. When her ten minutes seemed more like ten seconds, she gave up, turned off the alarm, and crawled out of bed. She rubbed her face, searching for the enthusiasm generally present at the prospect of a day spent with family and friends. The thought gave her pause. Did Alan and his wife fall into the category of friend or family? Was there a place on the scale for something in the middle? Ex-husband and ex-wife-in-law? *This is all just too weird.* Eyes closed, she lifted her concerns in prayer.

Jesus, it's Thanksgiving. Help me focus my mind on the things I need to do today. You know how much I love the mess and the noise of a houseful of people. I'm thankful You've allowed me to have that this year more than ever.

I want to make this day special for everyone, especially Jeremy and Megan. Please let there be smiles and laughter in this house; those are the memories that will take the edge off their grief down the road.

Pam threw on her robe and went to the kitchen to start the bread and cookie dough. Terri was bringing stuffing and pumpkin pies. Kate had promised pumpkin bread, but Pam still had a chocolate cake and pecan pies to put together. The turkey would need to be in the oven by eight, bread dough rising by noon, potatoes peeled and cooking by three, and lots of little steps in between.

The house gradually came to life around Pam as she worked. Her kitchen filled with the aroma of coffee, cinnamon, and cocoa. Those soon became laced with the spicier scents of cloves, oranges, and onion from the roasting turkey. It wasn't long before she heard running water and footsteps in the rooms over her head. She drew comfort from those things, allowing the performance of familiar chores to melt the weight of tension lodged between her shoulder blades. With her hands buried to the wrists in enough bread dough to produce two dozen hot rolls, she sighed with contentment. God was going to give them a good day. Pam looked up as Jeremy and Megan wrestled each other through the door.

Jeremy managed three words around a huge yawn. "Here we are."

Megan simply waved as she crossed to the counter to assemble her favorite morning brew. The fourteen-year-old stirred hot water into an instant cocoa mix, added a splash of coffee, and topped it with a squirt of canned whipped cream and a drizzle of chocolate syrup. Pam grinned. *Coffee with training wheels and about two hundred calories.* Oh, to be young and weight *un-conscious.*

Her daughter licked away the white foam from her upper lip and smiled. "We promised we'd help with dinner. What do you need us to do?"

Pam gave the dough a final pat, covered the bowl with a clean towel, and rinsed her hands. She took the cup from Megan and indulged in a single sip of her daughter's concoction. She savored the chocolate and threw caution to the wind. "You can make me one of these. Use the fat free cocoa mix, a little more coffee, and skip the chocolate syrup."

She smiled at her son and delegated her least favorite chore. "You are on veggie duty."

Jeremy's eyebrows rose in question beneath his sleep tousled hair. "OK..."

Pam began to lay fresh vegetables on the counter next to the sink. Baby carrots, celery, yellow and red peppers, green onions, purple radishes, dark green broccoli, and white cauliflower. A vegetable rainbow. "When you're done with that, I'll introduce you to the complexities of the relish tray."

Jeremy washed his hands, tossed the towel across his shoulder, and accepted the knife she handed him. He picked up a pepper.

"Jeremy."

Her son turned and the snick of Megan's camera filled the room. "Just wait 'til your dumb jock Facebook friends get a load of you cooking."

"Mo-om."

Pam shook her head and held out her hand. She paged through the phone and deleted the incriminating picture. "I hereby declare the kitchen a photo-free zone for the remainder of the day." She passed the phone back to her daughter. "Now, are you helping or hindering?"

Megan passed a steaming cup to her mother and handed a unsolicited third to her brother.

"Thanks, prissy."

"Welcome, dork face." She flashed a disarming smile at her mother and batted her eyes. "Helping. What do you want me to do?"

"Want to make your dad's favorite dessert?"

Megan's smile widened. "Coconut cream pie? Yes."

"I thought you might enjoy that. First thing you need to do is bake the pie shell. I have one thawed. You'll need to poke some small holes in it so that it doesn't get air bubbles as it cooks."

"Ouch." Pam heard Jeremy's knife clatter into the sink. She turned to see her son holding his finger in one hand while he danced in place.

"I cut myself."

Pam rushed to the sink and grabbed his hand. "Show me."

Jeremy released his wounded finger. She stared in bewilderment. "Where?"

He pointed to a miniscule red dot on the pad of his right thumb. "Right there. Can't you see the blood?" He yanked it away and stuck it under the water. "It stings."

Pam pulled his hand out from under the rush of water. "You probably got some onion juice in it." She glanced at Megan. "Hold the fort. We need to go find a bandage."

Megan sneered at her brother. "Wuss."

"Mom!"

"Guys, enough!" But there was laughter in her voice. The bickering was so normal and, today, normal was a very good thing. "Finish the crust, put it in the oven, and then start on the filling. We'll be right back."

Pam led her son up the stairs to the bathroom. While he washed his hands she collected first aid supplies from the medicine cabinet. She sat on the edge of the tub and tried to hide a grin when Jeremy stuck his hand under the running water, and winced. *Guys are such wimps.*

He sat on the closed toilet, and she pulled his hand into her lap and dabbed at where she thought the cut should be, grateful for a few seconds alone. "Jeremy, you OK about today?"

Her son shrugged in response.

"I really want you to be OK."

Jeremy met her gaze and turned the tables on her. "Are you OK with today?"

Pam studied his earnest blue eyes. "That's a fair question. The only answer I can give you is that I'm trying. I thought I'd done such a good job of keeping my hurt feelings to myself. I never, ever wanted my bad attitude to affect the way you feel about your father."

Jeremy lowered his head, sniffing as Pam applied a bit more of the antiseptic.

"It stings a little."

Pam nodded and allowed his excuse to preserve his fifteen-year-old dignity. She lifted his hand and looked at his finger, sorely tempted to kiss it. Instead, she wrapped it in an adhesive bandage before threading her fingers through his. When she tugged his hand his gaze met hers a second time. The indecision in his eyes and the secret in her heart scraped at the thin layer resolve.

"I really want today to be a do-over. A fresh start for our family."

Jeremy ducked his head. "I don't want to be mad at either of you."

She pulled him to his feet. "Let's go down there and cook the best Thanksgiving meal your dad ever ate."

Jeremy nodded. "Let's."

Thumb amputation averted, Pam and Jeremy walked back into the kitchen as the oven timer sounded. She grabbed a pot holder. "I'll get it," she told Megan. "You keep stirring or the pudding will stick." Pam pulled the pie shell out of the oven, slid it onto the cooling rack, and studied the small half-moon piercings in the shell.

"What did you use on this crust?"

Megan looked at her hands and back to her mom.

"You used your fingernails?"

She shrugged. "My hands were clean. You said to poke holes. I poked holes."

"I meant with a fork."

Behind her, Jeremy began to make gagging noises. "Oh. That's just gross!"

Megan narrowed her eyes at her brother and took a step in his direction. Pam put a hand on each chest. Normal only went so far.

Pam and Harrison converged on the entry hall at the sound of the doorbell later that afternoon. Her stomach tensed and her mouth went dry when she reached for the knob. *Friends now. One big* happy *family.* Harrison took her outstretched hand and squeezed. She looked up and found courage and reassurance in the depths of his brown eyes. He continued to hold her hand as he opened the door to admit Alan, Kate, and a handsome young man with striking blue eyes. The men shook hands while Pam hurried forward to take a cake plate from Kate so that she could shed her jacket. The heavy silence was broken when Megan raced into the tiled entryway and skidded to a stop in her stocking feet.

She launched herself into her father's arms and managed to pull Kate into the embrace as well. "Daddy! Jeremy, they're here."

Jeremy rushed to the door. He nudged his sister aside, hugged his father, kissed Kate on the cheek, and punched the young man on the shoulder.

"Mom, Dad...H...Dad..." Jeremy waved a hand between them as the adults shared a laugh at his obvious confusion. "You all know who you are." He clasped his hand around the younger man's upper arm. "This is Rick, my only slightly nerdy stepbrother."

Rick held out his hand to Harrison and Pam, simultaneously hooking his other arm around Jeremy's neck in a mock chokehold. "Nice to meet both of you." He looked at Pam. "Do you have a private room available? I need to give the germ his daily beating. He needs to learn some manners."

The initial awkwardness melted away in the presence of the youthful banter. Pam marshaled her troops, handing out assignments to all. "Harrison, take Alan and Kate into the living room. Megan, please hang up their jackets." She smiled at her son. "Germ, you can show Rick out to the backyard. Please take your beating like a man."

Alan followed Harrison to the living room. Kate detoured to the kitchen behind Pam. "I'd like to help, if there's something I can do."

Pam placed the pumpkin bread on the small dessert table alongside the sweets she'd prepared earlier. "Never enough hands on a day like this. I..." She stopped as the doorbell rang a second time. "That'll be Terri and her family. Follow me. I'll introduce you to the ones you haven't met."

Confusion returned to the entry hall as more jackets were discarded, pies juggled, and introductions exchanged. Megan was reassigned to jacket detail and as soon as Pam introduced Iris to the rest of the visitors, the two teenage girls, heads together, mouths going at warp speed, disappeared up the stairs. Once they were gone, the decibel level in the hall dropped significantly.

"Wow, I almost remember having that much energy." Terri took over the introductions. "Kate, this is my husband Steve, our son Seth, and Samantha, our oldest..." The rest of the introductions were lost under Bobbie's excited squeal.

"Patty!" She jerked her hand free of her mother's grasp and ran through the door where male voices echoed.

Patrick turned from his examination of available snack foods and intercepted the three-year-old's charge. He swung her into the air. "Hey there, short stuff. Where'd you come from?"

Bobbie pointed down the hall. "Mama."

Patrick tossed the excited child across his shoulder and went back to the crowded entry hall.

Sam and Patrick's eyes grew round in mutual bewilderment. "What are you..?" They both stopped and waited for the other to continue.

Pam looked from one young person to the next. "Rick...Patrick..." She finally focused on Sam. "This is the friend we've been hearing so much about?"

Sam nodded.

I'll pray for your friend, and his father, *every day.* Pam's laughter filled the hall. She took Harrison's hand and ushered all of her guests into the living room. "If I ever have a reason to doubt God's sense of humor, remind me of this moment."

Thanksgiving dinner was T minus ten minutes and counting. Pam escaped the heat and noise of the kitchen to make a final check of the dining room. The polished oak table was extended to its full length and groaning under the abundance of holiday food. She dug a book of matches from a drawer of the china cabinet and struck one to light the candles in the Thanksgiving centerpiece. Her nose wrinkled as the acrid smell of sulfur overrode the more traditional scents of hot yeast rolls and pumpkin pie. Pam stared at the candle flames as they flickered and settled into a steady burn.

"Thank You, Father. I don't know what I expected from today, but so far it's been OK." Youthful laughter echoed from the living room and teased a smile from her lips. Jeremy and Megan were making the most of the day. "More than OK, Father. Thank You for filling this day with special moments for my babies." Pam dropped the cold, blackened match into the small trash can in the corner of the room and followed the laughter into the other room.

She stopped in the doorway, hands on her hips, a frown directed at her children. Megan sat next to Kate, the cat physically restrained on her lap. Reddy's muscles were visibly bunched to pounce, her yellow eyes locked on her target. Jeremy sat beside Alan, feet propped on the ottoman, a four-foot iguana stretched the length of his legs. Fully aware of the cat across the room, Spot's tail whipped nervously from side to side, his little lizard eyes darting, obviously looking for a place to hide.

"Guys, what have I told you about tormenting those animals?"

Jeremy looked up with a boyish grin. "I brought Spot down to show him to Dad. It's not my fault Megan's stupid cat followed us into the room." He shrugged and looked at his father. "Besides, the conflict is good for them. They don't get enough exercise. A little hatred gets their heart rate up."

Megan eyed the lizard and shuddered as her hand stroked the cat's fur. "That snake with legs gives us both the creeps." She stood with the cat in her arms and motioned for Iris to follow.

"Mom, where are all the picture albums from our vacations. Iris and I have a project for school and I wanted to show her the pictures of the luau in Hawaii."

Pam swallowed and the small hairs on the back of her neck prickled. Her panicked glance swept past Alan and landed on Harrison. She couldn't think of those pictures and the last time she'd seen them, not if she wanted this day to continue to go well.

Harrison cleared his throat. "I think they're wrapped up in a box in the attic. After dinner I'll help you and Iris find what you need on the computer."

"Cool, thanks! Come on, Iris. Let's take Reddy back to my room."

SHARON SROCK

A relieved breath flooded Pam's lungs. She stepped away from the door to allow the girls to pass. "Spot, too. Secure the animals, and wash up. Dinner is served."

Pam watched the youngsters troop up the stairs with their menagerie. Despite her best efforts, her mind went back to the pictures stored in the attic. The beginnings of an idea took root in her heart.

Wonderful food, noisy conversations, and a muted sense of urgency he could have cut with a knife. Patrick clenched his jaw as Sam parked the Mustang in front of his house. He'd accepted her offer to bring him home even though he knew his mood was less than sociable.

Sam put the car in park, checked on her sleeping daughter in the backseat, and boosted the heat up a notch before she took his hand.

"Patrick, why didn't you tell me? I mean, Mom told me that Pam's ex-husband was terminally ill, but I didn't connect you with him."

Patrick scrubbed his free hand over his face. "I told you my dad was sick."

"Sick, but not..."

He squeezed her hand to stop her. "Hi, my name is Patrick. We moved to Garfield because my father is dying." His chuckle lacked any hint of humor. "Not the best get-acquainted line."

"I'm praying for him every day." She tilted her head. "You've got to be relieved that at least one hurdle is out of the way. Who knows what other prayers God might answer before it's over."

Patrick's head came up in the shadows, his eyebrows raised in question.

"You told me the other day that you were worried because your dad was trying to make some things right, and the people he needed to talk to wouldn't listen." She squeezed his hand. "God worked that out, Patrick. Don't you see it?"

Patrick stared out the window for a few seconds. "I guess. I mean, yeah, that part of the problem is resolving itself. I just didn't see it from the *answered prayer* perspective." He changed the subject. "Go out with me Saturday afternoon. You and Bobbie. I need something to keep me busy."

"What's happening on Saturday?"

"They're going to take the kids out for lunch to break the news about Dad's condition. They invited me, but I've lived through that discussion once; I can't do it again. I need a diversion."

Sam agreed quickly. "Of course." She studied him for a few seconds. "May I pray for you...and them?"

Patrick found an odd comfort in her offer. He nodded and bowed his head as Sam closed her eyes.

"Jesus, thank You for the prayers You've already answered. Lord, please bring some comfort to this situation. None of us knows Your will, but I know You love us. Be a shield for Jeremy, Megan, and Patrick. Help them know they can lean on You. Bring them some peace in the knowledge that Alan is Yours and he's only going home." She paused when Patrick released a muffled sob from the passenger seat. "Jesus, give Patrick strength. He needs You now more than ever. Help Alan and Pam find the words their kids need to hear. Let there be unity and peace and Your will in everything. Amen."

"Amen," Patrick whispered.

"Patrick," Sam whispered. "Come to church with me on Sunday. Take it from someone who's been there. That's the only place you're going to find what you need."

Patrick didn't trust himself to speak for several seconds. *I won't fall apart in front of Sam.* He patted her hand and nodded his agreement in the darkness. Raising her hand to his lips, he brushed a kiss across Sam's knuckles. "I'll call you Saturday morning." He bolted from the car before his resolve crumbled.

Pam settled herself in bed next to Harrison. He was already asleep, but she needed some time to unwind after the busy day. She adjusted the lamp light away from her husband's face and found the place marker in her Bible. A soft knock on the door interrupted her reading. "Come in."

The door swung inward, and Jeremy and Megan stood framed in the doorway.

"What's up, guys?"

Jeremy spoke for both of them. "We wanted to tell you thanks. We had a really good time today."

Megan smiled. "We know it took a big effort for you to give us the day. It went OK, didn't it?"

"More than OK," Pam assured them. "I told you, God cleaned all the ugly stuff out of my heart. I'm just glad you both had a good time."

Megan looked at the floor. "We wanted to ask...I mean...I know it's a year away and all, but could we maybe do it again next year?"

Pam struggled to keep a smile on her face and felt Harrison stir beside her, maybe not asleep after all. "We'll see. You guys go on to bed. Close the door on your way out." Pam sat where she was until she heard the door latch. Her Bible discarded, she turned into Harrison's arms and wept. This time the tears were for her children.

CHAPTER TWENTY-FIVE

Alan wrapped his arm around Megan's shoulder while they waited for the restaurant staff to prepare a table for six. When offered the opportunity to pick a restaurant for lunch, the verdict had been unanimous. His children might bicker about many things, but Mexican food wasn't on the list.

Alan slipped into prayer for the hundredth time that day. *Father, I'm not ready for today. How could anyone be? I've imagined scenarios, replayed what I need to say so many times. I can't get past their faces, God. I can't get past the fact that the reality of telling them is going to be so much worse than anything I've imagined.*

I need Your help. I don't want to offer them any false hope. Just show me how to offer them the hope You promised. If I ever needed wisdom, I'm going to need it today. We all are.

I'm so grateful to You. For Pam and Harrison...and Kate. I know they'll take good care of them once I'm gone. I know Jeremy and Megan have been taught to lean on You, but they're just kids. Please be with all of us today.

Megan leaned against him. "I can't believe you've never eaten here. They have the most awesome cheese dip." She smiled in obvious anticipation. "We'll probably need to order two or three bowls."

Alan bumped her hip to hip and looked into the face that reminded him of Pam at that age. His daughter's hair was a little longer, and freckles sprinkled across her nose—a trait from his side of the family, but she resembled Pam nonetheless. "Whatever you guys want. This is my treat."

Pam overheard his comment. "Alan..."

"My treat," he said firmly. "Consider it a thank you for all your work on Thursday."

Pam shrugged and held up four fingers. Megan's eyebrows rose in question. "Hey, if he's buying, I get my own cup of queso."

The hostess finally led them through the crowded dining room to a large table and handed out menus all around. Alan soaked up the laughter of his kids as lunch items were discussed, discarded, and finally agreed upon. *Can I take that laughter with me when I go? Just that one thing.*

Conversation flowed around the table as they enjoyed their meal. Countless tacos, a taco salad—his concession to Kate after breaking his diet on Thursday—six sopapillas, and one hundred dollars later Alan sat back to stare at the carnage remaining on the table. Unable to finish the large portions, white foam boxes sat in front of Pam, Kate, and Megan. The plates in front of the *men* were cleaned spotless.

Pam cocked her head. "Did you guys lick those clean while I was in the ladies' room?"

Kate chuckled and eyed her husband. "I have a

more pressing question. Can you still move?"

Alan jerked a thumb toward Harrison and Jeremy. "I can if they can."

Kate sat back and crossed her arms. "Why do men feel the need to turn everything, even lunch, into a competition? I think you're all three pathetic."

Jeremy sat up in his seat and muffled a belch behind his fist. "Eight tacos. I am the winner!"

"I just think you're all gross." Megan shuddered. "Who eats that much?"

Jeremy shrugged and looked at Alan and Harrison. "There's a reason I call her prissy pants."

Megan tossed a stray tortilla chip across the table, hitting Jeremy squarely in the forehead.

Alan called for a truce before it got out of hand. "I think we need to take some of this pent up energy to the parking lot."

Outside, the late afternoon sunshine was tinged with just a touch of chill. The prolonged Indian summer was finally giving way to fall. Alan took a deep breath, determined to ignore the invisible bands that squeezed his chest a little tighter every day. "We've still got a couple of hours before dark. Who's ready for some miniature golf?"

Harrison groaned.

Jeremy whooped. "Bring it on."

Pam looked at their son with raised brows. "You and your male cohorts can barely stand upright after all that food."

Jeremy pointed at the females in turn. "You're. Still. Goin'."—he turned his thumb to the ground—"Down."

Pam shook her head as the women walked to the

cars. The men lagged behind, their progress more of a crawl.

By the time the group reached Party Palace, lunch had settled. Megan and Jeremy raced ahead to check in and argue over ball color.

Pam put a hand on Alan's arm, stopping him. "How do you want to do this?" she asked.

"I don't want to do this at all." He stopped with a deep breath. "Sorry. Let's just play a game or two and see how it goes."

Jeremy and Kate tied in the first game. As the winners, they both agreed to a handicap for the second round. Kate played every hole with one hand behind her back. Jeremy played the odd numbered holes blindfolded with Megan coaching him on where and how to hit the ball. Laughter erupted when they tied a second time, this time for last place.

Despite the laughter that bubbled and flowed, a sense of foreboding hovered over Alan and made his head ache. It lodged there, heavier with each hole they played. The glances he stole in Pam's direction told him she shared his anxiety. The fall afternoon was fading away. They weren't going to be able to stall much longer.

After two games, the group trooped back into the center to return their clubs. Alan caught Pam's eye over the children's heads. Pam bit her lip and nodded.

"I don't know about anyone else, but I need a soda," Pam announced.

Alan indicated the deserted pavilion next to the batting cages. "Why don't you all go out and have a seat? I'll bring us something to drink."

Patrick heard his name, blinked, and pulled himself back to reality. "I'm sorry, Sam. What?"

"It's our turn."

"Sorry." he repeated. He hefted Bobbie a little higher in his arms, stepped around the gate, dodged a departing child, and carried Bobbie up steps decorated in tufts of white cotton sprinkled with silver glitter.

Today was Santa's first day at the mall, and this was Bobbie's first visit. Sam and Patrick both held their breath when Santa reached out to take the three-year-old on his lap.

Bobbie studied the red-clad, bearded stranger with serious blue eyes. She hung onto Patrick's sleeve with one hand while she reached out with the other to touch the curly white beard. Finally, she smiled and surrendered herself to Santa's arms.

Bobbie held tightly to a candy cane while Patrick and Sam took positions on either side for a group photo. Santa asked her if she'd been a good girl and "Ho-Ho-Ho'd" at her solemn nod. After promising her the moon wrapped in a shiny silver bow, he handed the child back to her mother.

Patrick led the way out of the enclosure, and they waited for their picture. "It's been a long time since my last picture with Santa." He looked at the elf manning the cash register. "How much and how long for a second copy?" Price and time settled, they continued their walk around the mall.

Patrick put his hand over Sam's on the handle of the rented stroller. "Sorry about that."

"About what?"

"Zoning out on you back there. I'm having a little trouble staying focused today. I wonder if they've told them yet?"

Sam rubbed his arm and nodded her understanding. "Maybe the mall wasn't the best choice."

"No, I'm having a good time. Standing in line just gave me too much time to think." He grinned. "I enjoy the mall."

Sam laughed at him. "You're such a girl. When I called you the other day, you were here with your mom."

"Yes, but that was PSC."

"PSC?"

"Pre-Santa Claus," Patrick clarified. "Besides, I'm not afraid of being in touch with my feminine side. It's part of my charm."

Sam rolled her eyes at him.

They passed the pet store, and Patrick backed up a few steps. "Let's look around in here for a minute."

Sam hesitated. "Fine, but don't get any cute ideas. We have a dog at home. Anything you fall in love with is yours, not ours."

"Killjoy," Patrick muttered. He lifted Bobbie out of the stroller once more. "Come on, short stuff, let's go look at the snakes."

"Ewww." Sam cringed and followed them into the store.

Puppies barked, kittens batted at small felt balls, and birds in all sizes and colors squawked at the patrons. Bobbie pointed in excitement to a small pen where a couple of cocker spaniel puppies, black coats as shiny as polished onyx, had their noses wedged between the mesh of the fencing. They looked out with eager brown eyes, their tails wagging at a hundred beats a minute.

Patrick allowed her to rub the silky snouts. Bobbie

howled with unrestrained laughter as the puppies jockeyed for her attention while their small pink tongues licked at her fingers, removing the last traces of her recent candy cane.

A harried clerk passed by on her way to the register. "You can take one out for a few minutes if you'd like."

Sam shook her head. "No, thanks."

Patrick vetoed her response. "Thanks. We'd like that."

"Patrick."

He grinned. "Hush, woman. Don't spoil our fun."

The clerk escorted them to a small room. She released the puppy into Patrick's waiting arms.

"Oh, you're a handsome little guy, aren't you?" He held the excited puppy nose-to-nose, dodging the little mouth that tried to give him puppy kisses. "Sam, I think I'm in love."

"I tried to warn you."

"Can I have him?"

Sam laughed at him. "Your house, your yard, your money." She rubbed her fingers through the silky fur. "He is pretty cute, though."

Patrick put the puppy on the floor so Bobbie could play with him for a few minutes. "Seriously, I think I want him. He'd make a great Christmas gift for Mom."

"She likes dogs?"

Patrick took a step back, watching while Bobbie trapped the puppy in a corner of the tiny room. "Yeah, and this is her favorite breed. She had one when I was small. We had to give him away when we moved into an apartment that didn't allow pets. Mom always wanted another one, but we never got around to it." He stooped down and rescued the puppy from the toddler. "When we were here the other day, these little guys were in the main display window. She stood and watched them play for the longest time. I could tell her fingers were just itching to get her hands on them." He turned the pup on his back for a belly rub, laughing when the little hind legs trembled with ecstasy. "You're a good boy, aren't you?" he asked in universal baby talk. "I wonder if they can kennel him until Christmas Eve?" Decision made, he went to find the clerk. A puppy would give his mother something positive to focus on through the long days ahead.

Alan carried drinks to the pavilion with lead feet and a heavy heart. Pam already had the kids seated at a circular table. Megan scooted over and patted the empty space between her and Kate.

"Sit here, Dad."

He nodded, climbed into the seat, and handed out the drinks. A moment later Kate laid a hand on his knee and squeezed. He stole a glance at Pam. Harrison held her hand. Exhibits of silent support and encouragement, but neither of their spouses spoke. There seemed to be an unspoken agreement between them to let Mom and Dad take the lead in the difficult discussion ahead.

Alan was grateful beyond words that his kids would have these two extra parents in their lives once he was gone. Silence stretched out, heavy and uncomfortable. He slid his drink aside, unable to take a single swallow because of the nausea rolling in his gut. "We need to talk to you guys."

Jeremy crossed his arms and nudged his sister. "Here it comes." His words were sarcastic. "I told you something was fishy about this whole deal."

Pam put her arm around Jeremy's shoulders. "What do you mean, son?"

Jeremy shook Pam's arm off and glared at his father. "I told Megan last night that this was all too good to be true." He motioned to his parents. "You guys don't speak for years and then, all of a sudden, we're having meals together. I mean, I know Sis asked you for Thanksgiving, but twice in a week? Something's up. You guys need to be straight with us for once."

Alan studied his son, taking in the narrowed eyes and the sullen expression. He breathed a prayer and searched for words. "I have an illness," he began. "I've probably had it for a long time, but I just found out about it a few months ago."

Megan frowned. "What kind of illness?"

"A heart disease." He looked at Jeremy. "You remember the other day when you threw me that pass?"

Jeremy nodded. "You weren't choking on candy."

Alan shook his head. "Not entirely."

"You lied to me?" Jeremy shook his head and rolled his eyes in obvious disgust.

"I had candy in my mouth, but—"

"How often does that happen?" Jeremy interrupted, his tone growing more confrontational with each word.

"A lot," Alan admitted slowly. "Sometimes, I can get over it on my own like I did the other day. Sometimes I have to go to the hospital for a few hours."

"Are you going to have surgery?" Megan asked.

"They can't do surgery for this condition, baby," her father whispered.

Megan and Jeremy glanced at each other. Jeremy

inched a little closer to his sister in a rare show of protection. He met his father's eyes with an unblinking stare, his words measured and cautious. "Then how do they fix it?"

Alan lowered his eyes, unable to say the words.

"They can't," Pam answered for him.

Megan patted Alan's arm. "Then you'll just have to be more careful." Her voice held a scolding, maternal tone. "I know how much you guys like to play ball and stuff, but if it's going to make you sick, you'll have to stop." Her voice turned soothing. "Don't be sad; we'll all help." Her gaze traveled around the table. "Won't we?" Her brows came together in a frown when silence met her question. "What?"

Alan put his arm around his daughter. "It's not that easy, sweetheart."

Megan pushed away, her eyes searching his face. "Daddy?"

"Slowing down won't help." Alan delivered the final blow with a swiftness he hoped would be merciful for everyone. "I'm dying." He gathered Megan into his arms as her tears broke free to soak his shirt. He closed his own eyes. He'd been right. Telling them was much worse than he'd imagined it would be. *Jesus, if You can't give me more time, give us all strength.*

"How long?" Jeremy asked.

Alan looked up and met his son's eyes. "I don't know. Maybe a year, but probably not that long."

Jeremy looked at his father over Megan's head. "This is why you came home?"

Alan nodded, rubbing Megan's back. "I wanted to spend as much time as I could with you two." He moved Megan back so that he could look into her face.

My baby girl, I love you so much. He cupped her chin in his hands, his gaze moving to include his son. "Guys, I need you to be strong for me because I'm going to ask you to do a hard thing. I don't want the time we have left to be filled with fear and tears. We need to spend that time making good memories for everyone like we've done this week."

"But—"

Alan stopped his daughter's whispered word with a finger across her lips. "I'm not trying to tell you not to be sad or scared. I get sad and scared some days. But I am going to ask you to be honest about those feelings when you have them. Come to one of us. Talk it out and move on to happier thoughts. We all love you, and we're going to do our best to help you through this." His nod took in the other three adults at the table. "We aren't going to hide anything from you." *Liar.* "But..." Alan's voice caught in his throat, "we aren't going to spend time worrying about things we can't fix either. Can we do that?"

Megan nodded and buried herself back into her father's chest.

Jeremy shoved away from the table and climbed to his feet. "This bites. You should have just stayed in Kansas City!" He turned and ran for the parking lot.

Pam shook her head when Alan started to stand. "Stay here with Megan. I'll go after him. I'm afraid most of his attitude is my fault."

She found Jeremy standing next to their car. The tears tracking down his cheeks contradicted the angry expression on his face. He turned away as she drew closer, but he didn't shrug her hand from his shoulder.

My poor baby.

"Jeremy, I thought we moved beyond this on Thanksgiving Day. I thought we both agreed to let the past be the past and move forward."

"Forward to where?" He jerked his shoulder away from her touch. "He just ruins everything."

"That's not true."

He turned to face her, hands on his hips. "Yes it is. He's the one that left. He's the one that broke up our family and hurt you." He paced away, his voice low and jagged when he continued. "And he's the one leaving again."

Pam studied her son and found herself in the unexpected position of defending Alan Archer. *Oh, Jesus, this is so much my fault. Help me get through to him.* "Jeremy, he has no control over this." Moving forward, she gathered him into her arms. "I'm so sorry," she whispered into his ear. "Your father has not always been a good husband, but he's always been a good dad." She held him tighter when he tried to push away. "You guys never had a problem with each other 'til he moved back and I let my attitude get out of hand. He's your father, he loves you, and he needs you. Despite what you're feeling right now, I know you love him, too."

Jeremy's only response was a shrug.

Pam heard gravel crunch and looked up. "They're coming back. You need to apologize."

Jeremy shook his head. "Just let me in the car."

CHAPTER TWENTY-SIX

Pam swung her legs over the side of the bed Sunday morning to find the sleeping forms of her children. When they were small and scared of something in the night, their habit had been to crawl into bed with their parents. As they outgrew the bed but not the need for comfort, they chose to make pallets on the floor instead, creeping in quietly to seek refuge from things that went bump in the night, turning their fright into an excuse for an overnight camping trip.

She studied them with a sad smile. Jeremy, hair tousled across his forehead. Megan, her arm wrapped around the same stuffed bear that had brought her comfort since she was a two-year-old. This morning her children held hands as they slept, drawing comfort from each other. Pam couldn't remember the last morning she'd been forced to pick her way through tangled limbs and blankets. Certainly not since she and Harrison had been married.

She felt motion beside her. Harrison leaned around

her and took in the landscape between the bed and the door. "What's this?" he whispered.

Pam shook her head. "Old habit from their toddler years. I guess they needed a little extra comfort last night."

"Yesterday was hard on them," Harrison said. "Looks like it caught up with them overnight." He rubbed Pam's back. "Let them sleep for as long as you can. They're going to need their reserves as things sink in over the next few days."

Pam leaned back into Harrison's warmth. She searched behind her for his hand, pulling his arm around her waist. "You've been a good father to them. They're...we're...lucky to have you."

He squeezed her hand. "I'm the lucky one. I couldn't have asked for better kids than these two." He ran his hand down her back and gave her a gentle shove. "Now, scoot. I need some coffee."

Pam nodded and gained her feet. She plucked her robe off the hook on her closet door and tiptoed around her sleeping children.

Kate sipped hot coffee while she studied her Sunday school lesson. A shadow fell across her page. She looked up and smiled into her son's sleepy eyes. "You're up early."

He grunted a response and crossed the kitchen to pour his own cup of morning caffeine. He rummaged in the drawer for a spoon and shoveled sugar into his mug.

Kate knew her son liked his coffee hot and sweet, combining sugar and caffeine to jump-start his morning.

Patrick turned, leaned against the sink, and blew steam away from the mouth of the cup before taking a cautious sip. "What time are we leaving this morning?"

"We?"

He made an unsuccessful effort to stifle a yawn. "Yeah. I promised Sam I'd come to church this morning."

Kate didn't bother to hide her smile. "I knew I liked that girl." She glanced at the clock on the microwave and pushed a second chair away from the table with her foot. "You've got about an hour and a half. Have a seat."

Patrick snagged a handful of oatmeal cookies from a jar on the counter before he sat.

"I can make you a proper breakfast."

"I'm good," he said around a second hearty yawn. "I just need to get some sugar pumping to wake me up." He dunked a cookie into his cup and almost managed to get it to his mouth without making a mess. "Where's Dad?"

Kate nudged the napkin holder closer to her son. "Still asleep. Yesterday took its toll. I'm not going to wake him until I have to."

"Bad, huh?"

"Patrick, it broke my heart. I knew there'd be some anger when he told them. Jeremy just left the table and refused to speak to him again. Megan's in shock. She hugged Alan good-bye, but I could tell she was afraid to let him out of her sight, even for the night." She reached across the table, broke one of his cookies in half, and took a small bite.

"Alan went straight to bed once we got home. He tossed and turned and mumbled in his sleep. I don't think he slept a full hour all night long."

Patrick glanced down the hall. "Maybe I should go..."

"No, sweetheart, there's nothing either of us can do for him right now. He's made his peace with Pam. The hurdle of telling the kids is behind him. We just need to keep praying that God will bring him through this according to His will."

Patrick snorted, so Kate changed the subject. "Tell me more about Samantha. That baby of hers is adorable."

"Bobbie? Yeah, she's pretty special." Patrick paused, finally looking his mother in the eye. "Sam's pretty special, too."

She sipped her coffee and considered. "You with a church girl. I'm a little surprised at that considering your current attitude about all things religious. How's that working out for you?"

He dunked a second cookie. "It's weird, actually. She won't even let me kiss her. Has our relationship locked into friendship mode. But..."

Kate studied her son as he searched for words.

"I like her. I might more than like her if I get the chance. I think she just might be the one."

Kate opened her mouth and forced it shut. If ever there was a time to choose her words carefully, it was now. She settled for a single word response. "Really?"

"What?" Patrick sat back. "I know that look. What were you going to say?"

Kate sipped her coffee. "Nothing."

"And I know that tone. You just got through saying that you liked her."

"I do like her."

He crossed his arms. "Then why get all...*motherly*...when I tell you she's the one?"

Kate sighed. So much for careful. "Patrick, you just met her."

"Yeah..."

"She has a baby." Kate stopped and tried to regroup her thoughts. "Sweetheart, you're an adult. I'm not trying to get in your business. I really do like Sam, and Bobbie is a delightful little girl, but..."

Patrick's brow wrinkled, his stare a mixture of wariness and confusion.

"But..."Kate leaned forward. "We're all going through a hard time right now. I just don't want you to allow what's happening with Alan to drive you into a relationship, a ready-made family, before you're ready. That's good advice for you and Samantha."

"Mom, I like her, but I'm not quite ready to get Grandma's engagement ring out of mothballs." He wadded up his napkin. "But I think our relationship has definite potential." A smirk marred his expression. "As much potential as two college students, a Christian and a not-so Christian, and a baby can have, that is."

Kate patted his hand. "You wanted to be a lawyer. You knew that meant eight years of school before you started." She paused, thinking about the inheritance that would likely come his way sooner rather than later. The money would open a lot of doors for his future, but he didn't need to know about that now. "When this year's over, you'll be halfway there. What does Samantha want to be when she grows up?"

"She's still deciding, leaning heavily towards social work. This is her sophomore year, so she'll need to make up her mind soon. Whatever her final choice, she still has two or three years to go."

"I'm sure you guys will figure it out. Just take it slow, OK?" Kate collected their empty cups. "Go get ready. Are you riding with us?"

"Probably," he answered. "I think we're going to lunch after church, and Bobbie's car seat is already in Sam's car. She can drop me off here when we're done."

Kate watched her son disappear down the hall, shaking her head. She was glad he'd found a Christian friend to lean on, but how could her son be talking about babies and car seats?

Pam hurried down the hall, fumbling with the back of her earring. She passed Megan's door, stopped, and turned back. Megan was sitting on the side of her bed, hair pulled back into a ponytail, face freshly scrubbed, but still wearing her pajamas. Reddy lay curled in her lap. Megan stroked the cat, but her eyes were unfocused and staring into space. Pam sighed. Her daughter looked so young and lost this morning.

She went in and sat on the bed beside her. "It's almost time to go."

"I know. I just can't seem to get going."

"Do you want to stay home? I'll let you if you need to. You're dealing with a lot this morning. I'll even stay home with you if you want me too. Karla would be happy to teach the class under the circumstances."

Megan shook her head and continued to stroke the cat. "No, I want to go. I'm just...It's going to be hard, seeing Daddy this morning. I don't want to cry all over him every time I see him, but when I think about what he told us, that's all I want to do." Her voice cracked.

"I'm trying to be brave, like he asked...but...it's really...hard."

"Sweetheart, there's nothing wrong with grieving over this. It's going to take some time to get over the initial shock. I can promise you that your father doesn't expect you to walk around like a little robot for the next few weeks."

Megan sniffled and rubbed an arm across her eyes. The cat, apparently bored by the conversation, jumped to the floor with a disparaging look at her master and a flick of her tail for Pam before she stalked from the room. Megan watched her go with a sad smile. "Can I ask you a question?"

"Anything."

"Do you really think he's scared? Dads aren't supposed to be scared. It's just..." she rolled her eyes, "scary."

Pam hugged Megan tighter and gave her daughter the honesty she deserved. "I guess he's probably a little scared. He's worried about what's going to happen to you guys once he's gone. That's natural, I think. We all need to do our best to let him know we're going to be all right." She tipped Megan's face up to meet hers. "He's a Christian. You and Jeremy are going to miss him, but you can be together again."

The tears she saw in her daughter's eyes stung her own. "I know when you're fourteen...or fifteen, the idea of Heaven can seem sort of far away." Pam smoothed a stray wisp of hair back from her daughter's face. "But it's what you need to hang onto right now. Daddy loves you, and Jesus loves you. Neither one of them is going to lie to you. You believe that, don't you?"

Megan nodded, fighting back more tears. "I do believe, Mom, but it's so hard."

"I know. This isn't the way I would have chosen to make Heaven real for you and your brother, but we don't always get to choose." She enfolded her in a full hug. "Are you going to be all right for now?"

Megan's breath was shaky, but she nodded. "Thanks, Mom. I need to finish getting ready. Can you give me fifteen minutes?"

"Absolutely." She pulled the door closed behind her and leaned against it. *Jesus, we need You.*

Patrick held Sam's hand while they shuffled slowly towards the exit of the church.

Despite his best efforts, his attitude had soured with each moment of the service. He understood the foolishness of feeling like Pastor Gordon's sermon on the Prodigal Son had been directed at him, but it still felt like he'd been hammered on nonetheless. On top of that, he'd watched Jeremy and Megan with a heavy heart. Megan's over-bright expression and unconscious clinging was almost too painful to watch. On the flip side, Jeremy had done his best to ignore Dad's presence. It was not shaping up to be a good day.

Samantha seemed to sense his mood. She was doing her best to comfort him. That just made him feel worse. He thought about making an excuse to Sam and going home to lick some of his wounds, but that didn't feel right either.

They finally broke through the throng and presented themselves to Pastor and Mrs. Gordon for farewell handshakes. Samantha hugged them both. Patrick shook hands stiffly and only nodded when Pastor

Gordon expressed his happiness at seeing him in service this morning.

They proceeded down the line to Lisa and Dave. Sisko grabbed Patrick's hand in a hearty grasp. "Made it back to service, I see."

Patrick nodded and shuffled his feet when Sisko continued to hold his hand.

"Sam, can I borrow Patrick for a few minutes?"

Sam shrugged. "Fine with me. I need to get Bobbie from the nursery." She rubbed Patrick's arm. "Take your time. I'll meet you out front in a bit."

Sisko tugged Patrick from the line and into a quiet corner. "What's up?"

"You got a week?" His joke fell flat.

Sisko dropped the pretense. "Patrick, Megan told me about your dad. I'd like to help if I can. Just tell me what you need."

Patrick lowered his eyes. "I don't know how you can. I appreciate the offer. It's just...there's just too much...Too much."

Sisko was quiet for a few seconds. "Do you have class tomorrow?"

"Not 'til Tuesday."

"Come have lunch with me tomorrow. Stop by the gym at noon. We'll shoot a few baskets. I'll open up the kitchen and whip up some of my famous nachos and hot dogs. We'll work up a good sweat and have a talk."

Patrick shrugged. "I don't want to interrupt your schedule."

"You're not an interruption."

Patrick lifted his eyes, cringing at the pity he read on the older man's face. "I'll be there."

"Outstanding!" Sisko pulled him into a full hug and

whispered. "I'm still praying for you, Patrick."

Prayer and pity. What a combination. Unable to respond over the lump clogging his throat, Patrick nodded and left to find Samantha.

CHAPTER TWENTY-SEVEN

Patrick zigged, Sisko zagged, and the ball sailed through the hoop, ending their third game of one-on-one basketball, twenty to sixteen, Sisko's favor. Both young men halted under the net, bent at the waist, harsh breaths wheezing in and out.

Sisko huffed with the effort it took to speak. "That's two out of three. You give?"

Patrick snagged the ball from the floor and dribbled it absently. "I've got four inches on you. Where'd a little guy like you learn to play like that?"

"Survival of the fittest, my friend. The kids in this youth group take their competition seriously." Sisko slapped the ball out of Patrick's hands and tossed it through the net. "I either keep in practice or get eaten alive at their next opportunity. You didn't answer my question. You give?"

Patrick used the sleeve of his shirt to wipe sweat from his forehead. "It pains me to say it, but yeah, I'm done."

Sisko led the way into the kitchen. "Good, I'm starving." He stirred the cheese sauce warming in the slow cooker and lit a fire under the half-dozen hot dogs he'd allowed to thaw while they played. He pointed to the fridge. "Grab us something to drink."

Patrick popped the tops on two root beers and slid one over to Sisko. "You shoot hoops and cook?"

"All tools of the trade," Sisko assured him. "Food is the great ice breaker. Puts people at ease while I contemplate how to move in for the kill." He drizzled melted cheese over two bowls of chips and passed one to Patrick. "So, what's up with you?"

Patrick snorted in response. "You play a decent game of ball, Bro, and your cooking is tolerable, but you could use a few lessons in subtlety."

Sisko turned and leaned against the counter. "Subtlety is overrated. We both know why I invited you here today. Why beat around the bush?" He went to get the buns for the hot dogs. "I really felt like you were ready to take a step towards Christ. Instead you're backing up. Want to tell me why?"

Patrick frowned into his bowl with a troubled sigh and made designs in the cheese with a chip. How could he make Sisko understand the tangled knot of feelings in his gut? He set the bowl aside. "It's hard to explain."

He shrugged and decided to make the effort. "I never had the chance to know my real dad. He died overseas when I was a baby. I think he saw me once before he shipped back out to the desert. Mom raised me by herself, and I think she did a pretty good job."

Sisko grinned and waffled his hand back and forth.

"Whatever." Patrick smirked. "If Mom was lonely, she never let it show, and I never really missed having a dad. We took care of each other." His stomach grumbled. He stopped his explanation, downed a few chips, and chased them with the frosty root beer.

"Then she met Alan. I saw her life change right in front of my eyes. He brought something into both of our lives that we'd never had before. We finally had the chance to be a complete family." He lowered his eyes and his voice. "Now God's taking that away."

"Patrick..."

He stopped Sisko's objection with an upraised hand. "No. You asked. Let me finish. I've known for a few months that Dad was dying. It's why we moved here. My head knew it. My heart didn't want to accept it. But when they told the kids this week, I couldn't lie to myself any longer."

He paced the small space. "I mean, they haven't even been married a year. He probably won't make it that long. Why would God do that?" Patrick faced the older man and ran a hand through his sweaty hair. "I figure Mom prayed for my dad's safe return from the war. I've watched her pray for Alan every day since we found out he was sick. He just gets worse."

He chugged root beer. "I told Sam that I didn't get the whole religion thing for a lot of reasons. If you add this to it, I'm just not sure I see the point."

"Patrick, the Bible says we all have to die."

"And it also says God answers prayers," Patrick countered. "From my experience, the answer is mostly no. So why does anyone bother?"

Sisko boosted himself up onto the broad countertop. He consumed a hot dog in silence, while Patrick did the same. He licked chili from his fingers. "Patrick, do you believe your dad is going to Heaven once he dies?"

Patrick shrugged. "Honestly? I don't know what I believe anymore."

Kate folded her book and frowned at the clock. It was almost two. Claiming exhaustion shortly after breakfast, Alan had opted for a nap. If he didn't wake up soon, he wouldn't sleep again tonight. Her stomach growled, reminding her that lunch time had come and gone while she read. She'd let him sleep a little longer. No sense in waking him up before lunch was on the table.

She hummed as she assembled salads and opened a can of chicken noodle soup. Nothing too heavy. They had a date night planned for this evening. Kate smiled. They were driving into the city to visit their favorite French restaurant. They might see a movie afterwards. Even if they split dessert and shared a small popcorn, all she intended to allow Alan to have, the calories would undermine her diet for a week.

Kate paused in the doorway of the bedroom and watched her husband sleep. Her heart stumbled. *I love him so much.* She was trying to abide by the advice they'd given Jeremy and Megan on Saturday. It was a waste of their time together to be sad over things they couldn't change. She shook off the melancholy mood. "Alan, you need to get up. Lunch is ready. "

She studied her husband's immobile form. "Alan?" Her breath caught as she approached the bed. "Alan?" She stopped and caught the rise and fall of his chest. Her noisy exhale of relief filled the room. Exhausted and sleeping too soundly to hear her. Kate shook his shoulder gently. "Sweetheart."

Alan rolled from his side to his back, and Kate's knees went to jelly. His skin was gray, his lips almost blue. He was breathing, but shallowly.

Kate snatched the phone from the bedside table. Her hands trembled so severely she couldn't find the right buttons on the small keypad. She clutched the phone in a fist and froze, forcing herself to take a single calming breath. *Jesus, please.*

She tried the phone again.

"9-1-1, please state the nature of your emergency."

Kate's voice came out in a hoarse croak. "It's my husband. I can't wake him up."

Patrick watched as Sisko digested that last statement.

Sisko opened his mouth in response but obviously decided against what he'd been about to say. Instead he hopped to the floor and busied himself with another hot dog. He continued after several seconds. "You've got a lot on your plate right now. I'm going to ask you to make me one promise."

Patrick hesitated, but finally nodded his agreement.

"Give me a year."

"A year how?"

"Just a year," Sisko repeated. "Come to church faithfully. Be a part of the new college group. Hang out with me when we're both free. Give me twelve months to show you a side of God you've overlooked. I'm not going to pressure you to make decisions you're not ready to make. I'm not going to tell you that life is better or worse because you haven't made those decisions. You've got some tough days ahead. Let me share them with you and help you when I can."

Patrick stared at the young minister. What was Sisko

asking him to agree to? The indecision in his heart must have reflected on his face.

The youth pastor shook his head and held out his hands, palms up. "No tricks or hidden conditions, Patrick. If you still have questions at Christmas time next year, we'll dig a little deeper."

"It's OK with you that I'm not saved?"

"You didn't hear me say that," Sisko clarified. "I'm going to be praying for you every day, but I'll let God do His own convincing." He held out his hand. "Do we have a deal?"

Patrick stared at his new friend. What would it hurt? He liked Dave Sisko. He didn't plan to stop seeing Sam. This could buy him some time in her eyes as well. He clasped Sisko's hand. "Deal." Patrick took a step back and raised his soda can in salute. "I have to admit, you have a unique approach."

"Tell me about it," Sisko muttered around the ringing of Patrick's cell phone.

Patrick looked at the display. "It's Mom."

CHAPTER TWENTY-EIGHT

Pam parked in front of the school. She'd called ahead. The kids would be waiting in the office. Would they know why she was here? *Of course they would.* She leaned her head against the cushioned rest and closed her eyes. "Father, it's too soon. Megan needs more time to adjust, and Jeremy...Please don't let my baby live the rest of his life with un-forgiveness and guilt over harsh words." Pam's heart slipped into a prayer for Alan, surprising her at the ease of transition. "Touch Alan. Hold him close during this time. Not just for the kids, but for him. He's Your child." Pam stopped and swallowed as a little nugget of truth blossomed in her heart. *I still love him.* She allowed herself to explore that realization. Not *in* love, but love nonetheless. The love of an old friend who knew more about her than just about anyone else on earth. Some of her happiest memories were wrapped around her life with Alan. They'd raised babies together, rejoicing over first steps and first teeth. They'd shared the frustration of sleepless nights, the pride of grade school achievements, and the simple joys of being a family. Since God had banished the pain of that last year, Pam could admit to herself that most of their marriage had been good. She wouldn't trade those years even if she could.

She shook herself out of her musing. The kids were waiting. Pam opened the door to the school office to find Jeremy and Megan seated on a worn wooden bench, holding hands, and staring straight ahead. They scrambled to their feet.

Jeremy put his free hand on his hip in a gesture so like Alan, it almost made Pam smile. "Is it Dad?"

Pam nodded, and Megan bit her lip as her eyes filmed over with tears. "Is he gone?"

She pulled her daughter into her arms. "Oh, baby, no. But he is in the hospital. Kate called the house to tell me that it was more serious than normal. They took him straight to the new heart center in the city."

Pam held one of her children's hands in each of hers as they rushed back to the car. She started the engine while they buckled in.

"Do we have time to say a prayer?" Jeremy asked. "I mean...I've been praying ever since they called me to the office, but...can we say a prayer...together?"

Pam slid the gearshift back into park and twisted around in her seat. "There's always time to pray."

Jeremy nodded and bowed his head. "Jesus, Megan and I are really scared right now, but it must be even scarier for Dad." He stopped and Pam saw her son swallow a couple of times before he continued. "Please don't let him be scared. Don't let him hurt..." He looked up. "Do you think going to Heaven hurts?"

Pam couldn't force any words past her constricted throat. She shook her head.

"Jesus, please don't let him die before I can tell him I love him."

The bubble of the oxygen pump, the beep of the heart monitor, the hiss of the blood pressure cuff as it inflated and deflated, and Alan's ragged, irregular breathing became the focus of Kate's world. She sat by the bed and held her husband's hand. She held her own breath in between each of Alan's, as if her need to inhale or exhale would encourage him to do so. When she wasn't holding her breath, she talked. When she wasn't talking, she prayed.

"Alan, can you open your eyes? Just for a minute sweetheart. The kids are on their way." *Jesus, please not now. If it's time for him to go, I know you'll help me deal with it, but please let him wake up for a bit. He needs to see the kids. The kids need a chance to tell him good-bye. I need a chance.*

"Are you thirsty? If you'll open your eyes, I'll bet I can get some apple juice in here. I know how dry all this medicine makes you." *Jesus, please let him open his eyes. I need...Oh, I just need more time.* She closed her eyes and laid her head on the mattress next to his hand. "I won't cry," she whispered. "I won't let the last sight he has of me be weepy and lost. I won't—"

"Mom."

Kate straightened and held out a hand to her son.

Patrick walked into the room and pulled her into his arms. "What are they saying?"

She took a step away and looked at the bed with a small shrug. "Not much. The doctor just left. He didn't seem very surprised to see us." Kate stepped back to the bed and smoothed a few stray locks of hair from Alan's forehead. She threaded her fingers through the sandy growth. Her husband needed a haircut. An odd thought at a time like this.

"Mom?"

Kate came back to the present. "I've known for a couple of weeks that things were worse than he was telling me."

"I'm sorry, Kate."

"Alan." Kate's knees buckled at her husband's whispered words. She sank back into the chair and took his hand in both of hers. "Shh. You don't owe me an apology. I know you had things to do." She searched his face.

His eyes remained closed, some of his color had returned, but the muscles around his mouth were tight.

"Are you in pain? Do you need me to call the nurse?"

"Your voice is all the medicine I need." His head moved on the pillow in a small shake. "It's not too bad. I don't want anything putting me to sleep right now. Did I hear Patrick?"

Patrick stepped to the other side of the bed and took Alan's other hand. "Right here, Dad."

Alan's lips twitched. "You're a good boy, Patrick. I've enjoyed being your dad."

His words came out in a whisper with just the slightest pause between each one. Kate touched his cheek. "Don't talk sweetheart. You need to save your strength."

He turned his head into her hand and brushed a dry kiss across her palm. "It's OK. There are things I need to say. Did you call the kids?"

Kate nodded. "They're on their way."

His answering nod was almost imperceptible. When he continued, Kate and Patrick had to lean close to hear his whispered words.

"Patrick, I'm giving your mom back to you."

Despite her best efforts, Alan's words ripped a sob from her throat. Alan searched for her hand, and Kate clasped it in both of hers.

"You guys took care of each other for a long time." He paused for a couple of seconds. "I need you to do that again."

"You can count on it."

The assurance seemed to satisfy him. He slipped back into a deep sleep.

The beeping, the bubbling, the whisper of machinery continued, accented by muffled tears.

The kids rushed into Alan's hospital room, but Pam hesitated at the door. Jeremy and Megan needed to be here, but did she? This should be family time, and she no longer qualified. *Do I?* She watched from the hall as Kate looked up, swiped her face free of tears, slipped an arm around Megan's shoulder, and provided whispered answers to a barrage of questions.

Kate glanced her way and disentangled herself from Megan. She started across the small room, motioning for Pam to join her. Pam took a deep breath and a few slow steps forward, meeting Kate in the middle of the impersonal room.

"How is he?" Pam asked.

Kate glanced at the bed. She pressed her lips into a thin line and the trembling of her chin ceased. "It's not good. He's been awake a time or two, but he seems weaker each time. He talks, but he doesn't open his eyes." She stopped and brushed a single tear from her cheek. "It's like he had some hidden reserve of strength that carried him through these last few weeks. Now that he's done what God sent him back here to do..." A single sob escaped her throat. "He told Patrick and me good-bye a few minutes ago. I think he's just waiting on the kids."

Pam studied Kate and tears welled in her own eyes. She didn't stop to think but pulled the other woman into her arms and ushered her out to the hall. "Let some of it out, Kate. You don't have to be strong for me." The taller woman crumpled into Pam's arms and wept.

"I just want some more time, just a few more days. That can't be too much to ask. Why do I have to go through this again?"

Pam tightened her arms around Kate. The woman who'd taken her place. The woman who would be alone when all was said and done. "Jesus, grant us Your presence in this place. Even when Your will seems unfair, You have a purpose." She fished a tissue out of her bag and pressed it into Kate's hand. "Is there someone I can call for you? I'm sure Pastor would come—"

"I didn't even think..."

Patrick spoke from the doorway. "Dad's awake again."

Kate sniffed, wiped the last traces of her crying jag from her face, and hurried back to Alan's side.

The room seemed muffled in cotton. Pam found herself drawn into the room despite her earlier hesitation. Alan's voice was low but easily heard. Kate and Patrick each took a step back to allow Jeremy and Megan access to their father.

Alan's eyes cracked open a bit. "There's my babies."

Megan took his hand. "Daddy..." She stopped and cleared her throat. Pam watched the emotions play across her daughter's face. The fourteen-year-old bit her lip and leaned down to place a kiss on Alan's cheek. "I love you, Daddy."

Pam wondered if she was the only one who noticed Alan's breathing growing shallower.

"I love you too, baby girl." Megan's face tightened at his words, the effort required to keep the tears at bay obvious to everyone in the room.

Jeremy shuffled forward, tears dripped unheeded from his chin. "Dad, I'm sorry..."

Alan's eyes closed and a few labored breaths passed before he answered. "None of that now. You're here. That's all that matters. I..."

Alan's voice trailed off. Jeremy looked at Pam, panic etched on his face. "Is he...?"

Pam shook her head and nodded his attention back to his father's face.

Alan's raspy voice filled the room again. "I want you guys to know that I've been the luckiest dad in the world to have you." His eyes opened, but they held no focus. "Is Patrick still here?"

"Right here, Dad."

Alan turned his head towards Patrick's voice. "I've been the luckiest man in the world to have you three for my children. You know this doesn't have to be good-bye."

Three "yes, sirs" layered in tears echoed through the room.

Alan nodded in satisfaction. "I'll be waiting." His eyes drifted closed for the final time.

Pam stood with her arms around her children as the beeping from the monitor slowed along with Alan's breathing. The tears of her children, the sight of Kate sitting by the bed, head bowed, forehead pressed to Alan's hand, the pacing of a young man she hardly knew, squeezed prayers from her heart.

Father, why does it have to be this way? Look at these faces, look at these broken hearts. The grip on her children tightened as alarms sounded from the monitor and the beeping stopped. Pam's tears mingled with those of her children as Alan slipped into the arms of his Heavenly Father.

Pam sat in the pew, a child on each side. The organist played soft music in the background. The air of the church was heavy with the scent of flowers. Neither child bothered to wipe away the tears streaming down their cheeks.

It happened too fast. Outside the streets were damp with the first December flurries, a precursor to a Christmas Alan wouldn't be here to enjoy. Pam had a feeling he wasn't going to miss it.

Kate sat one pew in front of them. Her head rested on Patrick's shoulder. Her tears flowed as freely as those of Jeremy and Megan.

Pam pulled her children close and whispered a suggestion. "You guys can go sit with Kate and Patrick if you want."

Jeremy looked at her. "Really?"

"Really," she repeated. "I think she could use the extra support right now."

"Thanks, Mom." Megan sniffed, grabbed a handful of tissues, and moved to the next pew.

Jeremy circled around and sat next to Patrick. The older boy put his arm around Jeremy and gave a supportive squeeze.

Kate welcomed her stepdaughter with open arms, their heads coming together in a shared moment. Pam looked on when Kate wiped tears from Megan's eyes with a tissue. Megan leaned forward to whisper something in her ear. Kate nodded in response.

Pam took a deep breath. There was no jealously in her heart. She could share her daughter with this other woman without hesitation. She scooted closer to Harrison, filling the spot vacated by Megan.

Harrison took her hand and raised it to his lips for a quick kiss. "That was nice," he whispered.

Pam dabbed at her eyes. "Those four hearts are so broken. I'm glad they have each other."

He studied his wife. "Are you OK?"

Pam thought about his question before she answered. "Yes. I've thanked God every day this week for allowing Alan and me to make our peace with each other. I don't know what I would have done if things had turned out differently." She wiped her eyes again, leaning her head on his shoulder. "My tears are for them. I'm good as long as I have you."

"Then you'll always be good," Harrison promised her as Pastor Gordon took his place behind the pulpit.

The preacher cleared his throat, his way of calling the congregation to attention. "We're here today to celebrate the life of Alan Wayne Archer. Shall we pray?"

Pam stopped in the doorway of the living room. Jeremy and Megan sat on either end of the couch, eyes red from weeping, expressions subdued. Pam's heart ached for her children—a pain she couldn't kiss and make better.

She hefted the two wrapped packages, offering a silent prayer that the gifts would ease their pain and begin the healing process for their hearts.

She sat down between them, handing each of them a box. "I have something for you."

Neither child rushed to rip through the paper. The boxes rested in their laps untouched. Megan was the first to crack. She rubbed a hand over the paper. "What is it?"

"Open them and find out," Pam encouraged.

Jeremy and Megan glanced at each other, shrugged, and slowly began to peel the wrappings away. The paper fell to the floor; the box lids followed. When the contents were exposed, they both looked up with the same question.

"Picture albums?" Jeremy asked.

Pam nodded. "Not just picture albums," she explained. "I remembered Megan asking me about the time I met your father. It occurred to me that some of these pictures could tell the story of our family better than I could.

"I sorted through some boxes, had some duplicates made, and arranged them in albums. I think they're happy memories. I knew you two would need some happy memories today."

Megan lifted the cover of her album and giggled at the first picture. "Braces, Mom?"

Pam allowed the laughter of her daughter to confirm

her instincts. "Yep."

Her children scooted closer on the couch, and she put an arm around each of them. "That's the first picture I have of me and your father together."

ABOUT THE AUTHOR

Sharon Srock went from science fiction to Christian fiction at slightly less than warp speed. Twenty five years ago, she cut her writer's teeth on Star Trek fiction. Today, she writes inspirational stories that focus on ordinary women and their extraordinary faith. Sharon lives in the middle of nowhere Oklahoma with her husband and three very large dogs. When she isn't writing you can find her cuddled up with a good book, baking something interesting in the kitchen, or exploring a beach on vacation. She hasn't quite figured out how to do all three at the same time.

Connect with her here:

Blog: http://www.sharonsrock.com

Facebook: http://www.facebook.com/SharonSrock#!/Sharon Srock

Goodreads: http://www.goodreads.com/author/show/64487 89.Sharon_Srock

Sign up for her quarterly newsletter from the blog or Facebook page.

Made in the USA
Las Vegas, NV
14 June 2023

73459259R00184